RAGE
OF THE
DRAGON
KING

J. KELLER FORD

Month9Books

RAGE OF THE DRAGON KING by J. Keller Ford
All rights reserved. Published in the United States of America by Month9Books, LLC. No part of this book may be used or reproduced in any manner whatsoever without written permission of the publisher, except in the case of brief quotations embodied in critical articles and reviews.

Trade Paperback ISBN: 978-1-946700-36-0
EPub ISBN: 978-1-946700-37-7
Mobipocket ISBN: 978-1-946700-38-4

Published by Month9Books, Raleigh, NC 27609
Cover Designed by Danielle Doolittle
Cover Copyright © 2017 Month9Books

Month9Books

For Month9Books: Thank you from the bottom of my heart for making my dreams come true.

For my husband, Tom, and my wonderful kids: there are not enough words to express how much I love you.

And for my brilliant editor, Cameron: thank you for believing in my story from page one and making it better than I ever imagined.

"You cannot throw a pebble in a pond and not expect a ripple." King
Gildore

RAGE
OF THE
DRAGON
KING

Chapter 1

Eric

Eric sat on the edge of Trog's bed, violent images of war and death lingering on his mind like maggots on a festering wound.

He'd been there since before dawn, incapable of sleep, nightmares zapping his eyes open whenever he closed them. He could only relive the horrors of the past month so many times without wanting to bash his head against a wall.

The sounds, the images, the smells. They never went away. He hung his head and fought against the sobs begging for freedom. What did he have to do to make it end? What did he have to do to not hear the castle walls exploding into oblivion, to unsee the vacant expressions of the dead, or worse yet, the ones who wished they were? How much longer would he have to endure the sudden stabs of pain in his back, a reminder of where Einar's talon plucked him from his horse like a fish from a lake?

By all rights, he should be dead. That should have been the punishment for failing in his duties as a squire. It didn't matter if he helped rescue the king from the dragon's clutches or that he fought valiantly to save his master in battle. The fact remained the dragon still lived, and David, the paladin and savior of Hirth, lay ill and unresponsive in his suite for the past two weeks because of him. Because he'd failed to protect. The sorceress, Slavandria, tried her best to console him, telling him David's comatose state was not his fault, that the sickness remained a mystery to every healer who visited. But Eric knew better. Trog was right. He was nothing more than an inept fledgling, and if he'd done what he was supposed to do, David wouldn't be wandering in his own darkness.

For the past fourteen days, Eric cursed his fate as he threw all his anger, frustration, and anguish into clearing the castle grounds. He rarely spoke to anyone, ate even less, and would often spend his nights in the forest beneath the stars, hoping something—someone would find him and remove him from his misery. But every day, he woke to birds chirping, the endless rattle of wagon convoys weighted with people and supplies, and a prevailing sense that all would be right with the world.

But not all *was* right with the world. Einar was out there, waiting, plotting, and the next attack would be far worse than the first. More would die, and once again, he would be called upon to defend his home and his people. Would he be able to do so? He didn't know.

Eric thought talking to Trog would help. Put some perspective on death and destruction. On war. After all, Trog had seen his share.

But as Eric watched him sleep, he couldn't bring himself to wake him. The man had been through hell and back, risking his life for king and country.

And his son.

Eric fought back the surge of emotions. Out of everything that had happened since Einar attacked, finding out Trog was his father was about the same as swallowing a piece of pie laced with glass—sweet, but cutting. Trog said they'd hidden the truth to protect him. Perhaps, but a betrayal was a betrayal, regardless of the reasons.

Still, the man almost died for him, would have died for him, without giving it a second thought. Eric was not sure he could do the same. Sure, he fought when necessary, when he needed to save his own skin or impress his master, but to purposefully sacrifice his life for the life of another? That was another story altogether, and one he hoped he would never have to write.

In the corridor, booted footsteps and raised voices drew closer. Eric jumped to his feet as Sir Farnsworth burst through the door, his clothes disheveled, as if slept in all night; his hair wild and unkempt. Behind him marched four, pointed-eared Duwan guards donned in green leather armor, their dark hair long and silky about their shoulders, their expressions stern and vacant.

"What's going on?" Eric asked. "Why are they here?"

"They're arresting him."

Farnsworth glowered at the guards as they attempted to rouse Trog from his sleep.

Eric rolled his fingers into fists. "What? Why?"

"Sedition. Treason. Whatever ludicrous charge the mages can come up with."

"And you're going to stand there and let them? Are you mad? You know what they'll do to him! He won't survive one night in a mage prison. Look at him!"

"It's all right, Eric," Trog said, wincing as he stood. "I've been through worse."

Eric's gaze fell to the sutured wound that pinched and puckered the man's skin. How he'd survived the shadowmorth attack boggled the mind and defied all magical and human comprehension. The wound, spanning Trog's chest from armpit to navel, remained vicious and angry, refusing to mend despite all of the healer's potions and sleeping elixirs to keep Trog relaxed and comfortable.

"But you've done nothing wrong!" Eric said.

"Since when did right and wrong ever exist among the political elite, Eric? They need a symbol exemplifying their power. I'm it."

Eric clenched his fists, his every nerve on fire as the guards shackled Trog's bare feet. How dare they not give him the decency of a shirt and shoes! He lunged forward, his fingers prying at the Elven hands restraining his father. A guard shoved him to the floor.

Eric scrambled to his feet and charged again, but Farnsworth's grip, like bands of iron, dug into his forearm. The knight spoke low, his breath warm on Eric's ear. "Stop acting an ass and alert the king. Tell him what has happened. He'll know what to do. Go."

Eric rubbed at his arm. *Of course. The king!*

He sprinted from the room to King Gildore's apartment where

two sentries he'd never seen before stood guard.

"Move!" Eric said, his chest rising and falling. He had no time for politeness. "I need to see the king! It's urgent."

The guards shouldered together. "His Majesty is not to be disturbed."

"He'll want to be disturbed for this, now get out of the way!"

He shoved at the guards, his muscles screaming as he struggled to push the men apart.

"Be gone with you!" The sentries tossed him by his armpits across the landing.

Eric smashed against the wall.

Hammers pounded in his brain.

Bam. Bam. Bam.

Through the pain, his gaze settled upon a porcelain vase studded in rare gems perched on the table beside him. Clambering on his hands and knees, he snatched it and hurled it at the apartment door.

The guards ducked. The vase shattered. Precious jewels scattered everywhere.

The door to the apartment flew open. King Gildore stood in the threshold, his face pinched. "What in blazing dragon's breath is going on out here!"

"It's this page, Your Majesty," said one of the guards. "He is unruly, refusing to listen."

Eric hastened to his feet. "I'm not a page, you imbecile!" His eyes met the king's. "Your Majesty, I apologize for the intrusion, but you've got to come. They're arresting Trog."

The king shoved his way through the two sentries. "Who is arresting Trog?"

"The Duwan. They're in his quarters as we speak."

Gildore's sky blue eyes turned deep as a storm. "The High Council? They're here? Damn those warlocks!" Gildore stormed into his suite. "I told them not to step foot in my castle." He tore his sleepshirt over his head and threw on black trousers, a plum shirt, and soft leather shoes. "How dare they think they can insert their authority anytime they want!" He stormed from the room, shouting for the guards to find Slavandria.

They were met by an advisor on the sixth-floor landing.

"Your Majesty," the man bowed, "the Chancellor of the High Council has requested your presence in the upper courtyard."

"Yes, I'm sure he has."

Gildore rounded the man and continued down the steps, his jaw tight, his eyes dark and focused.

It had been a long time since Eric had seen the king so angry. It was energizing in a way, seeing him so riled. It made the idea of mages being drawn and quartered all the sweeter.

Eric squinted as they stepped into the bright sun and made their way across the courtyard through the crowd gathered around a half-dozen men with lavender hair and sapphire-blue robes—mages of the High Council.

A deathly quiet stifled the air. Even the finches in the hedgerows were still, their morning song squashed into an eerie silence. Eric tilted back his head, his hand shielding his eyes from the sun. Onlookers appeared on the higher balconies as the turrets of the castle drifted in and out of the low, wispy clouds. On the ground around him, nobles, vassals, and townspeople stood together, shoulder to shoulder, their tongues still, their eyes wide.

"What is the meaning of this?" Gildore's voice boomed around the courtyard. "On whose authority do you enter my grounds and demand arrest?"

An inhumanly tall and broad-shouldered mage in the center of the group faced Gildore, his lips turned up at the corners.

Eric's breath caught in his throat. Master Pusrig, the pyromancer with eyes of swirling amethyst kissed by liquid moonfire. The lone surviving mage of the kingdom of Braemar.

"They are here under my authority," Master Pusrig said, his voice as thick and gagging as tar. "And might I add, Your Majesty, how splendid you look, considering your ordeal."

"I care less for your opinion of me. Where is my Grand Master Knight and General? What have you done with him?"

The mage jutted his finger toward the palace doors. "Why, he's coming now."

Eric clenched his jaw as the guards escorted Trog toward them down the aisle of stone warriors and potted topiaries. Blood dotted the wide bandage now wrapped around his bare torso.

"It's bleeding again," spoke a girl behind Eric. "Why is it bleeding again?"

Butterflies skittered through Eric's stomach. He knew that voice. He glanced over his shoulder and set his gaze upon Charlotte, the girl he met two weeks earlier, the day Einar and the shadowmorths attacked them on the Field of Valnor. She'd vibrated a chord within him then, a note no other girl had ever touched, much less played, and now that tune deepened, thrumming in his chest.

He wished he could say it was the way her brown hair melted over her shoulders, or the way her eyes sparkled as blue as the Prill Tides that captivated him, but he knew, deep within, the attraction went much deeper. Even now, seeing her dressed so unladylike in brown pantaloons, a matching vest, and an ivory shirt with puffy sleeves that ended just above her elbows, he remained drawn to her like an ocean to a shore.

Her eyes, however, were not for him, but for David, the dark-haired boy standing beside her—the lauded paladin, summoned to save the world. The savior who almost died.

When had he awakened?

The clash with Einar two weeks before left him a mangled mess. The dragon had broken almost every bone in the boy's body. It took hours for the sorceress Slavandria to fix the damage, and by that eve, David seemed well. But something happened to him mid-night. David turned ill, feverish. He lost consciousness. Both Eric and Charlotte rushed to his side, but the chalky pallor of David's skin resembled Sestian's before he died, and Eric fled, the pain of his best friend's death still too raw.

He would not return to David's side.

Charlotte, however, remained at David's side for the entire duration, and judging by the way she looked at him now, she'd be with him for as long as David would have her.

Eric swallowed his envy and turned his attention back on his father who stood as strong and formidable as a mountain, his jaw squared, his head held high. All thoughts of girls fled from Eric's mind as anger clawed at his throat. He approached the king, his fingers flicking at his side.

"Your Majesty, you've got to stop this. You can't let them take him. He isn't guilty. You know this."

"Shush, Eric," Gildore said. "We've been expecting something like this. We need to play along for now."

The king sidled around him and planted himself before the Duwan guards, blocking their path. His gaze locked with Trog's for a brief moment, before turning and addressing Master Pusrig. "On what grounds is he being arrested? I demand to know the charges."

The pyromancer withdrew a scroll from within a sleeve of his robe and presented it to the king. Gildore unrolled it and began to read as the mage addressed the assemblage. "Sir Trogsdill has been identified as a person of interest in your disappearance and the attack on Hirth. There are allegations he may have conspired with the Dragon King to dethrone and possibly murder your king."

A gasp circulated the courtyard.

"That's a lie!" Eric shouted, anger boiling his blood. How could these mages, these *protectors,* be so corrupt? Deceiving? Surely no one believed their words, did they? He glanced at the surrounding faces riddled with shock, confusion. Contemplation. His heart ripped in half. *No. They can't believe this!*

Gildore whipped around and shot him a look that could peel leather off a boot. Eric clamped his mouth shut and looked away as defeat chomped at his sanity. He couldn't let it win. He just couldn't. *Breathe. Just breathe.*

Master Pusrig smirked and continued. "As such, all suspicions of treason and sedition must be investigated and tried by the Senate and the Mage High Council."

King Gildore re-rolled the scroll. "These charges are preposterous. Provide proof immediately or release him."

"You will get your proof at trial, which will take place one hour past mid-day today in Avaleen." The mage beckoned the Duwan forward.

Gildore turned and snapped at the guards. "Stay where you are! Sir Trogsdill is not going anywhere with any of you." He faced Pusrig. An air of authority clung to him. "The laws of this land provide that anyone of the royal court accused of crimes against the kingdom shall be incarcerated in this castle until a trial with an impartial jury can take place."

"Your laws are worthless," Master Pusrig seethed, "as the crime in question involves collusion between a human and magical forces. Stand aside."

Gildore's brow furrowed. "No."

Eric swallowed. His jaw ached from gnashing his teeth.

The crowd murmured.

Master Pusrig poised his hands at chest level. Tiny balls of fire danced on his fingertips. "Do not challenge me, Your Majesty, for you will lose."

Eric's heart throbbed against his rib cage. It was coming. An attack, but against who? The king? The crowd? He had to stop it. His gaze fell to Pusrig's legs. *Lunge! Knock him to the ground!* Gildore's voice shattered his thoughts.

"And what do you plan to do with those? Set me on fire before my people?"

Master Pusrig laughed. "Oh, no. Not you. Them."

"Noooo!" Eric wailed.

With a flick of the mage's wrist, a fireball skipped across the ground. Screams ripped through the morning air as onlookers scattered, fleeing like rats through doorways and down the steps to the lower courtyard. A little girl's scream fragmented the chaos as the hem of her shift caught fire. A woman whipped her shawl from her shoulders and beat at the flames.

Eric froze, disbelief spreading like an illness through his body. Why? How?

A spindly boy, not much older than the girl, darted toward the fountain and returned within moments, water sloshing from a wooden bucket in his hands. He doused the girl, took one look at Master Pusrig, and ran, the dropped bucket skipping across the cobblestones before landing at Eric's feet. From the retreating crowd strode half a dozen men, their fists clenched, their eyes as dark and furious as an angry sea.

An undercurrent of fear rippled through Eric. He sucked in a monstrous breath. What to do? There was no way they could win, not with a cabal of mages at Pusrig's command. He had to stop them before they got hurt.

But his legs grew weighted, as if they were nailed down, and the warning on his lips froze in his mouth. Two mages stepped in the men's path, their arms tucked into their sleeves, their faces hidden in shadow by the hoods of their robes. They chanted and their words carried like rolling thunder on a whispering wind. In an instant, the men froze in their steps. Their eyes rolled in the backs of their heads. One by one, they crumpled to their knees, and then tipped face first into the unforgiving cobblestones, their bodies still.

Eric's nerves twitched. He drew a deep breath, his heart struggling like a bird trapped in a chimney. How dare the mages attack innocent people! He forced his legs to move and took a step.

Gildore jerked him aside and faced the pyromancer, his face red, his eyes fuming. "So this is how you get what you want, by assaulting the humble? The meek?"

Master Pusrig smirked. "That will depend on you. Are you willing to put them all in danger for one man?"

Gildore pursed his lips. "Get off my grounds. Now. That wasn't a request. And take your hounds with you."

Eric gulped as Sirs Farnsworth, Crohn, and Gowran closed in behind David and Charlotte, their hands poised on the hilts of their swords. He reached for his own, only to curse himself for leaving it lying on his bed.

Master Pusrig's face cracked into a smile. "I think not." Another flick and two large fireballs hurled from his hands.

The blazing globes encircled the courtyard, unfurling into wide ribbons of fire, shielding what few onlookers remained behind a wall of flames.

Gasps and cries of terror plunged into Eric's core. Who did this mage think he is?

Swords hissed from their scabbards. Gowran, Crohn, and Farnsworth lunged forward, but their battle cries turned to wails of pain. Their weapons clanged to the ground as fire licked at their flesh.

Eric's nerves snapped. Enough was enough. He bolted from his spot and stormed forward, drawing back his arm. He released his fist like he would a pebble from a slingshot.

Wham!

His knuckles connected with the mage's jaw. He may have well crammed his fist into a mountain wall. Bones cracked and sharp pain vibrated through Eric's hand and up his arms to his shoulders. He hunched over and cradled his wrist with his other hand, the words *it's broken* repeating in his mind.

The mage staggered, his eyes swirling an amethyst mist. "Imbecile! Insignificant mortal fool!" A massive fireball appeared on his palm. With a sideways flick, it soared toward Eric.

A separate blast of ice-blue energy hurled into Eric's chest, knocking him off his feet and onto the flat of his back. Above him surged a raging torrent of water, a river with no visible bed to hold it. It collided with the fire and drowned the flames. The deluge fell in a waterfall, drenching Eric.

He rolled to his hands and knees, and sputtered and coughed

as the puddle around him gathered into a spiral and spun around the courtyard, dousing the wall of fire. Out of the corner of his eye, Eric saw a woman approach, her lavender hair sweeping the ground behind her like a veil, her bare feet peeking out beneath the opalescent gown with each step she took.

Slavandria. Queen of the Southern Forest and daughter to the most powerful mage to ever live.

Eric swept an arm across his face, wiping away the moisture. He labored to his feet, his gaze pinned to the sparking threads spooling from the sorceress's fingertips and coiling around the Duwan guards, encasing them in singular, electrifying cocoons. What it must feel like to have that sort of power. That sort of control. To command such respect.

She faced the pyromancer.

"Hello, Pusrig. Fancy finding you here among the rabble."

Eric turned to the mage. There was something in his face that wasn't there before. Unease? Fear?

"Get away from me, witch."

There was a slight tremble in Pusrig's voice. Eric heard it. The unmistakable sound of cowardice.

Slavandria smiled. "Oh, I am not going anywhere. You, however, will remove yourself from these grounds while you still have the opportunity to do so."

Master Pusrig's lips twitched. Storms of purple fire brewed in his eyes. "How dare you usurp my authority! Stand aside or I shall take my prisoner by force!"

"Touch him in any way and I will terminate your existence where you stand."

Eric's heart pounded against his ribs. He wanted to move, to get out of the dueling zone, but he couldn't unglue his feet from the cobblestones.

Master Pusrig stepped toward Slavandria. "You wouldn't dare attack me."

Slavandria dipped her brow. "Are you willing to take that chance?" She circled the mage, her gown swishing as she walked. "You know," she said, her voice dropping so low Eric had to strain to hear, "I know of the Council's secret to undermine Sir Trogsdill. I know of the planted letters, the threats made against those that refused to cooperate with yours and Master Camden's plan."

Eric's throat tightened, anger spreading like a poison through his veins as the letters he'd found among Sestian's things crept up from the depths of his memory. How dare they play with lives in such a way! Bastards!

Master Pusrig's nostrils flared. "I have no idea what you're talking about."

Slavandria stopped circling and locked her gaze with Master Pusrig's. "Do not lie." She stepped a bit closer to the mage until their noses almost touched. "And if you know what is best for you, you will drop these allegations and release Sir Trogsdill right now. Otherwise, I fear you will find yourself in an exhausting conversation with my father, trying to explain your blatant interference with the affairs of men, and I think you and I both know how that scenario will play out, do we not?"

Eric gulped. Only a fool would be stupid enough to challenge her.

Master Pusrig's jaw tensed. The corners of his mouth twitched. "How dare you try to intimidate me! We all know you are equally guilty of fraternizing and interfering with these … humans."

"I am not the one attacking an assemblage of innocents, am I?" Her eyes remained locked on his.

Silence. Immeasurable silence.

"You're running out of negotiating time," she said.

"Ahh!" Master Pusrig scowled. "Release my guards and we will take our leave, but heed my warning. Do not become too complacent for someday you will find yourself in desperate need of your father, and he won't be there to save you. I, however, will be there to see you grovel for your last breath, and I will rejoice in your passing."

A smile touched Slavandria's lips and eyes. "I look forward to it. Now collect your henchmen and leave these castle grounds. And if I see or hear of you stepping foot within the confines of Gyllen again, I will personally see to it you never do so again. Have we an agreement?"

Master Pusrig growled in response. Slavandria snapped her fingers and the spiral of magic holding the Duwan guards faded. Master Pusrig barked a single word and vanished in a puff of purple smoke, taking the guards and the cabal of mages with him. The king and the knights swarmed around Trog.

Eric's lungs deflated, the sting of Slavandria's energy still tingling his skin. In no way did he want to be on the receiving end of her anger. Ever.

"Eric Rhain Hamden!" He looked into her eyes, her glare strong enough to shatter glass. "What were you thinking, punching a member of the High Council?"

Oops. Too late. His gaze flicked around the courtyard at the hundreds of eyes upon him, all ogling him as if he were the danger. His stomach churned. Eric took a tight breath and clenched his fingers against his thighs. All he had to do was bite his tongue. Say he was sorry. It would all be over. The humiliation. The desperate need to scurry beneath a rock and stay there.

"I am waiting for an answer."

There was something in Slavandria's demanding tone, in her arrogant stance that coiled his gut. It was one thing to berate him in private, but how dare she chastise and humiliate him in front of everyone. He threw his shoulders back, lifted his chin, and met her gaze with an equally irritating glare.

"I did what I thought was right, Your Grace. Considering his actions, I didn't think a standing ovation was an appropriate response."

"Do not get saucy with me, young man. Do you realize you not only endangered yourself, but your king and everyone in this courtyard as well? Do you not think before you act?"

"Hey, go easy, Slavandria," David said, stepping forward. "You're not being fair. I didn't see anyone else trying to stop that guy. What was he supposed to do? Nothing? If you ask me, that guy should have been knocked to the ground and flattened like a pancake. If

Eric hadn't decked him, I would have, and I was this close, too." He pinched his thumb and forefinger together.

Eric turned to David, his brow lifted in surprise. Why was David standing up for him? It's not like they were friends or for that matter, even liked each other. Whatever the reason, he knew not to turn away welcomed intervention, especially when in an argument with a sorceress. Maybe there was something more to this paladin after all. Only time would tell.

Slavandria's voice cut through him like a blistering cold wind raging through the Domengart Mountains.

"Deserving or not, you do not leap into a pit of venomous snakes without a clue as to how you will get out." Slavandria paused for a moment, her fingertips pressed to her forehead. A sigh escaped her lips as she lowered her hand. "I am not always going to be there to rescue you. They," she pointed to Farnsworth, Gowran, and Crohn, "are not always going to be there to protect you. You have got to learn what battles to fight and which ones to concede. He could have killed you with a single word, do you not understand that?"

Eric's soul seized beneath her stare, her raw, worried expression grating like sandpaper over his heart. Why was she reprimanding him like a small child? He'd stepped up, done what no one else would do. He defended his king. The people of Hirth. His heart swelled with accomplishment. His gut, however, pinched and tugged with guilt. He wanted to shout at her, tell her she was wrong. Open her eyes to what he'd done. Instead, he kicked at the ground and swallowed hard. "I'm sorry," he muttered. "I was only trying to help."

She lifted his chin, and his insides curled and knotted beneath the intensity in her eyes. The love, the fear, the worry … it was almost too much to take in. Why did everyone feel they needed to coddle him? Mother him? He didn't need mothering. He was past that. Over it. Done.

And yet …

"I don't want an apology," Slavandria said. "I want you to be careful." She leaned in and whispered in his ear. "You're not a mere squire anymore, remember?"

Eric nodded, wishing he could forget. It was one thing to discover Trog was his father. It was quite another to learn the man was also the king's brother, which, in turn, made Eric a prince and future heir to the throne of Hirth. His brain curdled at the thought. Him. A king. Ha. Why the notion was about as preposterous as a herring leading a school of pike.

Slavandria glanced over her shoulder at Trog being escorted by the king and queen into the castle. She then turned back to Eric and took his right hand in hers. Warmth, followed by a freezing tingle, oozed into his flesh and bones. She massaged his palm and coaxed his fingers to their full extension. The healing process took all of five minutes. When done, she said as if nothing had occurred, "See to it the healers look after the wounded including the king's guard, then join me in the king's private dining hall." She glanced over her shoulder. "David, come with me. Much has changed since you fell ill, and there are some things we need to discuss before your journey home. Bring Charlotte with you."

Eric's heart flip-flopped like a fish out of water. Home? No. They couldn't go home. Not now. Not when there was still so much to do. He needed David, the paladin, the savior, to help him defeat the dragon, to save their world and win the war. He couldn't do it alone. As for Charlotte. Well, she'd sent him into a blithering conniption with one half of him ready to flee to the hills while the other half commanded him to get tangled up in everything about her. If she went away, he'd never know which side would win. He had to make her—them, stay. The not knowing would drive him mad.

He had to figure out how to do it soon.

Chapter 2

David

David cupped the back of his neck as the king and queen, escorted by their entourage of knights, filed into the small dining hall off the kitchen. His eyes shifted under the weight of their glances, the heat in his cheeks spreading faster than any flame. Who were they, and why did they look at him like he was a pimple on a donkey's ass? He drummed his fingers against his thighs. Charlotte's presence offered some comfort, but not enough to fill the hollowness spreading in his gut.

A look from Slavandria unhinged his thread of security from his side. Charlotte squeezed his hand, and whispered against his neck. "See you inside, Firefox."

Tingles radiated up his spine, turning to heat as they scattered to his neck. She'd used his nickname. She hadn't done that since—since they'd kissed in Chalisdawn.

The memory exploded like fireworks. They'd been so close, their clothes the only barrier between them, and even those had begun to fall away. He'd heard, even felt their heartbeats thrumming in time together, so strong, so erratic. Time slipped away. His insides caught fire. The ice prison he'd erected around his feelings had begun to thaw, and for that one moment, that one blink in time, nothing else mattered. The world could have blown up and he wouldn't have known or cared. All he wanted was to get lost in her. To tell her he loved her. Those elusive three little words formed in his brain. They'd perched on his tongue, waiting, ready to leap.

But they collapsed beneath a cold, steel-plated pile of *what the freak am I doing?*

He remembered the way she'd stared at him, confused. The tear in the corner of her eye that never fell. Later, through a closed door, she told him she loved him, and his heart shattered. He could picture her face—soft, gentle, understanding, like the way she looked at him now.

He released her hand and stepped back, using the nearest column to steady himself. Distance. He needed distance to keep from scooping her in his arms, kissing her, holding her. After all, he had told her then, friends. Only friends. Yet her smile, her presence continued to torment him. If she only knew how she made his breathing uneven and heavy; how she made him ache everywhere, inside and out. How she glued his soul and skin together to keep him from going everywhere at once.

Maybe she did know. Maybe Trog was right when he said she

should be allowed to make up her own mind.

No. This wasn't her battle. She was in Fallhollow because of him. If she hadn't tried to protect him, she'd be home where she would be safe from war and death. Dragons.

She glanced over her shoulder at him, her expression almost sad, before disappearing through the heavy carved doors. His heart oozed into a puddle. He closed his eyes and pumped his fist against his forehead.

"You still haven't told her?"

David lifted his chin and met with Trog's piercing, soul-invading green eyes. Strands of hair, still wet from a quick wash, clung to the knight's face; the shadowmorth wound well-concealed beneath a doublet of blue and gold brocade. He swallowed hard beneath the glare, his thoughts straying for but a second to a balcony in Gable when Trog gave him some fatherly advice. Advice David chose not to take.

"You know the answer to that," David said, "so why ask?"

Trog scratched at the stubble on his cheek. "Oh, I don't know. Just thought after everything the two of you have been through, you might have smartened up a bit, had a change of heart."

David kicked at the tile as the knight's gaze ate into his core. "Yeah, well."

Trog curled a massive hand upon David's shoulder. "Tell her, David, before it's too late. You're not the only boy around here with a charming smile. The last thing you want is to wake up and find your balls have been stolen by someone willing to use them." The knight nodded to Slavandria, then trudged into the dining hall, the door creaking shut behind him.

David snorted and shook his head.

"He's quite an enigma, isn't he?" Slavandria asked, smiling.

"If that's what you want to call it." His eyes met hers. "So, what's up? Why the private pow wow?"

"I made a promise to you and it is time I kept it. I thought after we ate, I would introduce you to your parents, provided that is still what you want."

Her words split the seams of his existence. "M-my parents? They're here?"

Breathe. Just breathe.

Slavandria nodded. "You seem surprised."

"No." He blinked. Ran his fingers through his hair. "Maybe. Yes. I don't know."

He looked away, his heart mortified, stunned. He'd waited for this moment his entire life. He'd wanted nothing more. A family. A dog. A sense of belonging to something bigger than himself. But now? It took everything he had not to run. Scream. Hide. What if they didn't like him? What if he didn't like them? What if reality shattered the dream? He wrung his sweaty palms together. His parents' faces flitted around in his mind, ethereal as ghosts drifting in and out of a heavy fog. His brain hurt. His insides squeezed. A thought skipped across his mind. What if he no longer needed them? What if he never did? Worse yet—what if they never wanted him?

Slavandria touched his arm, and his skin erupted in a thousand goosebumps. He recoiled at the hint of magic.

"You seem distant, perplexed," she said, "as if you've misplaced something."

"I have." He rubbed his arms and walked past her. "My nerve."

"Understandable. Doubt is the greatest warmonger. Give into it, and it will kill your spirit, your heart, and soul."

David hung his head. "I think it already has."

"It hasn't," Slavandria continued. "Trust me. I see you, and I see within you a love for your parents and Charlotte that is so pure, so indestructible. It shines a light within your soul, a light that will always guide you through the darkest times."

"Then why do I feel so afraid? Every inch of me is shivering to the point I feel as if I'm going to explode, and there's nothing I can do to stop it."

"David, you almost died. You're now moments away from meeting your parents after almost seventeen years. Either alone would tangle anyone's nerves. Don't be so hard on yourself." She smiled, and it was warm.

David wandered to a window and stared out onto the hillside, his stomach a hollowed-out bucket. "Have you told them ... about me?"

"No." Soft footsteps sounded behind him. "I felt it best to not say anything until I spoke with you."

David snorted, his rankling gnarling his gut. "Of course, you wouldn't."

"What is that supposed to mean?"

David turned. "Because everything you do or say has to have

some freaking mystery attached to it. *Don't tell anyone this. Don't tell anyone that.* It's irritating and it pisses me off. Why can't you just say what needs to be said and be done with it?"

"I have my reasons."

"Yeah? What are they this time?"

Slavandria steepled her fingers to her lips. "First, let's extinguish the attitude. Second, I needed to confirm your desires. You're not the same person you were a few weeks ago." She paused for a moment before continuing. "I also wanted to ask if you would consider staying in Fallhollow, until the war is over. Einar is not dead. He will attack again. In order for us to defeat him, you and Eric need to remain a team. With Mirith at your side, the three of you are unbeatable. It would also give you time to bond with your parents in their own environment."

David stared at her for a moment as if she'd lost her mind. And then laughed. Loud.

"You've got to be kidding me." More laughter. "Oh my God, no. Just no. I made a deal with you. I've done my part."

"David, please. I beg—"

"No!"

"But the prophesy. Your parents."

"I don't give a damn about your stupid prophesy, and you promised me my parents! This is not my war." He returned her glare with all the confidence of a penguin conversing with an orca before mealtime. And he was the penguin.

"It *is* your war," Slavandria continued. "It's always been your war.

To deny your destiny is to deny who you are. I'm begging you to stay and see it through to the end. Eric, Mirith, Trog, your parents, all of this will perish if you do not."

David pointed his finger at her. "Don't. Don't you dare put that guilt trip on me! I may have started this stupid war by accident, but that doesn't mean I have to end it. I'm done. Finished. I want to go home."

"And what of your parents? What if they do not want to return with you when you go?"

The comment sucker punched David in the gut. Not go? The thought never crossed his mind. He just assumed they'd all leave together. Live as a family while trying to figure out the dynamics. But he also never thought about what would happen to them if they went back. His brain whirred. There would no doubt be an investigation by the cops. Insurance companies. Financial institutions, the Air Force, not to mention the press. Good god, the paparazzi would be all over them. He could hear the questions now. Why did you fake your deaths? Where have you been? Hell, his parents might even be arrested. And Charlotte. They would be ruthless with her. They'd harass her because of her friendship with him, and he wouldn't be able to go anywhere without a camera in his face, reporters scooping up the dirty laundry so they could air it all over the nightly news. He'd rather be chased by a freaking dragon.

His head pounded. When his mouth decided to move, all that came out was, "I guess I'll deal with that when it happens."

"David, please. I rarely beg, but—"

"No." He glared. Worked his jaw.

Slavandria stared back, her eyes searching, pleading. She then sighed. "Very well. However, I need to let you know I cannot guarantee your safety once you return to Havendale."

"You can't guarantee my safety here."

"I have a much better chance here," she said.

"Yeah. I'll remember that the next time I'm stuck in a tree and a dragon is about to eat me."

He opened the doors and stepped into a spacious dining hall, the nearby kitchen bustling with activity and low-pitched conversation. Copper pots shimmered in the morning sunlight flooding through the open windows. A plump cook wiped the sweat from her brow as she slid three loaves of dough into one of two open ovens in the stone walls. Servants plucked feathers from various fowl, and to his right, on the opposite side of the room, in the midst of tapestries and stained-glass windows, sat Charlotte at one of two trestle tables butted together, her elbows on the wood planks, her chin cupped in the heels of her palms. She smiled at him and his heart sank.

Slavandria said she couldn't guarantee his safety in Havendale. That meant she couldn't guarantee Charlotte's either. If they stayed in Fallhollow, Slavandria could keep her tucked away, safe while he and Eric saved the world with his parents. Then they could go home. There would be no other reason to stay.

No! That's exactly what Slavandria wanted. For him to remain a pawn in her game. He wasn't falling for it. He was taking Charlotte home and putting her back with her ex-Black Ops dad. Yeah. He'd keep her safe. No doubt about it.

He swallowed hard and turned his attention on the three hulking men sitting at the table beside her, their log-sized arms folded before them as they conversed with Trog and the king and queen. He strained to listen to their conversation as Slavandria took her seat with them.

Two servants shuttled past him carrying platters of bread, bacon, and scrambled eggs. His stomach growled and begged him to follow, but a resonating voice inside his head cemented him to his spot.

I do wish you would hurry up and decide what to do. Your thoughts are holding mine hostage, and I do not care for being a victim of your emotional terrorism.

David spun around, so caught off guard from the verbal intrusion he forgot about the maelstrom swirling in his brain.

"Mirith!" The dragon, who towered no more than two feet above David, lowered his neck and purred.

David flung his arms around the beast's neck, his face buried in the red and gold feathery mane.

"I thought you were dead," David said, pushing off the dragon's goat-like horns and looking into Mirith's ruby eyes. "You stopped breathing. I felt you slip away. But then I saw you with Charlotte on the Field of Valnor. How? I don't understand."

I did, indeed, straddle the borders of the dead lands for a brief period of time—that is until your intended mate arrived.

My intended what? David followed Mirith's gaze until his sights landed on Charlotte. He snapped back around. *Oh, no. No. She's not my—no, it's not like that. At all.*

Mirth snorted. *You can say the sky is beneath you. It does not make it so.*

David pressed his lips together and stared at the floor. How dare Mirith invade his thoughts, analyze his feelings. Who was he to assume? To judge? So, what if he wanted to torture himself for all eternity. Whose business was it but his own? He locked eyes with the beast.

That's enough. I want you out of my head. Go on. Get out. Please.

Mirith swished his armored tail over the stone floor, the sound screeching up David's spine. *As you wish. Your constant indecision is wearing me thin anyway.* The dragon nuzzled David's cheek, a declaration of a truce. *You should eat. Your belly is rumbling almost as loud as mine.*

The dining hall door opened with a slight creak as Eric stepped inside.

Mirith grumbled. *Ah, the brooding one.*

David chuckled. *Yeah, he is kind of a lot to take in at once. Still, he's a bad ass with a sword. Maybe I just need to give him time to grow on me.*

Fungi takes time to grow on you. That does not make its presence desirable.

David cocked an eyebrow at Mirith. *Wow. That's harsh.*

He's temperamental, impulsive, and has an eye for rare items of beauty. He glanced at the table where Charlotte and the others sat. *Be careful what you discard.*

What the hell does that mean?

Mirith walked away and plopped in a pool of sunshine on the floor. He curled his six-foot tail around his body, his scales glistening in every shade of autumn. *Figure it out*, he said, and the mental connection faded.

David waved off the dragon. *Fine. Be that way.* He sat beside Charlotte at the table.

"You know, that beast refused to leave your side while you were ill," Eric said, sliding onto the bench across from Charlotte and David. He plucked a chunk of bread from a basket on the table and tore at it while he spoke. "Slavandria had to confine him to the pit because he zapped anyone who tried to get near you."

"The pit?" David heaped two spoonfuls of eggs on his plate.

Eric nodded. "It's an old arena just north of here. The former king of Braemar used to torture people there who rebelled against his autocracy."

"That's barbaric," Charlotte said. "Please tell me it isn't used for that anymore."

Eric shook his head. "No. It was abandoned at the end of the Great War."

It is not abandoned, Mirith mumbled, intruding in David's head again. *The souls of the tortured dead live there.*

Tingles crept up David's spine and rushed out of him in a shiver. He dumped a fistful of bacon on his plate. "Wasn't there anywhere else she could have put him? I mean, it sounds so morbid."

Eric tipped a pitcher and poured apple cider into his goblet. "If that was her first resort, I might agree," he said, gulping his drink, "but he blasted out of his suite, destroyed the antechamber in Slavandria's quarters, and froze everything in the dungeon so he could be near you. Where else was she going to put him? Besides, he was only there for two days before Slavandria confined him here."

"Here? To the dining room?"

"Why not? There's food. Warmth." Eric wiped his left hand on a cloth napkin and offered it to Charlotte. "I'm sorry. I don't think we have been properly introduced. I'm Eric Hamden, Trog's squire."

"I know," Charlotte said, ignoring the gesture. "We've spoken before, remember?"

Eric withdrew his hand. "Yes, but please forgive me if I found your words a bit dejecting."

"How so?" Charlotte asked. "We hardly spoke."

"And there lies the reasoning for my dismay. You rejected every effort I made to take the edge from your unhappiness. I was only trying to offer you solace in your time of need, and you all but called me a cad. Why," he jabbed his fist into his chest, as if thrusting a dagger into his heart, "that wounded me to my core."

David rolled his eyes. "You've got to be kidding me."

Charlotte laughed. Her cheeks pinked. "I'm so sorry. I didn't realize."

Eric took a bite of eggs. "I mean, I can't say I blame you for being so short, considering the circumstances. It must have been frightening to you, experiencing the death of your friend, not once, not twice, but three times." He dropped his fork on his plate.

David's heart plummeted to the floor. "What? What do you mean death?"

"Still," Eric continued, ignoring him, "I couldn't help but wonder who you were, are, so please, I must have a name. I can't keep calling you the-girl-who-never-left-his-side." He looked at David and winked.

All sorts of fury bubbled beneath David's skin. Who did this jerk think he was, goading him like that in front of Charlotte?

He has an eye for rare items of beauty. Be careful what you discard.

David focused on his breathing—in through his nose, out through his mouth. Over and over. So that's what Mirith meant. He clenched his jaw, not trusting himself to speak.

Charlotte pressed her foot against David's as if reassuring him, and tucked a few loose strands of hair behind her ear. "It's Charlotte. Charlotte Stine." This time she stretched her hand out to Eric.

He rose to the invitation, and kissed the back of it. "Pleased to meet you, my lady." Eric lowered his butt to the bench and grinned at David, his green eyes vibrant. Mischievous.

David curled his fingers into fists.

"Likewise." Charlotte discretely wiped the kiss on David's leg.

David crunched a slice of bacon between his teeth. *Good. She's not impressed.*

"So, what brings you to Fallhollow, Lady Charlotte?" Eric asked. "Adventure? The breath-taking scenery? Love?"

Charlotte laughed. "No. Nothing like that. More like a series of unfortunate events."

"Sounds intriguing."

"It's a real humdinger, let me tell ya," David said, "and someday you might hear all about it, but can we get back to my dying for a minute?"

"It happened three times in one night," Charlotte said. "The first was after the battle ended and we brought you back here. You were in bed resting. Slavandria and I had just finished a lesson on how to heal bones when you started convulsing. Your heart stopped, and you turned this awful chalky blue.

"Slavandria brought you back, calmed Mirith down and put him in her room, but a few hours later, you stopped breathing again. Mirith freaked out. Slavandria knocked him out with some sort of spell and had him taken to the dungeons, but that still didn't stop him from blasting his way into your room when you, you know, died again. He started doing that scorpion thing with his tail and zapping everyone including Slavandria and me. That's when she made him disappear." Her voice quieted. "I didn't know she sent him to the pit." She glanced over her shoulder at Mirith. "He must have been so scared." Her gaze skipped to David. "I know I was."

Her fingers tightened around his and for a moment David was paralyzed, his soul drowning in two dark pools of Caribbean-blue water. To think he had come so close to never seeing those eyes again. To never hearing her voice or basking in her smile. His heart squeezed to the point of pain, the thought almost unbearable.

"I'm sorry," he said. "I would never do anything to—"

A knock sounded at the door followed by the entrance of a royal guard. He strode with urgency to the king and queen and spoke to them in a low tone.

"What do you think is going on?" Charlotte whispered.

Eric wiped his mouth and heaped his napkin in a bunch on the table. His brow pinched. "Whatever it is, it isn't good."

Gildore nodded, said something to the guard who bowed and retreated in haste. The king stood.

"An unexpected guest has arrived. Eric, you and your friends will join us in the briefing room. Bring the dragon with you."

Chairs scraped across the floor as everyone filed from the room.

David grumbled to Charlotte as they followed. "I guess that means I'm not meeting my parents any time soon." *Any idea what's going on?* he asked Mirith as they turned a corner and headed past the grand staircase.

Servants and courtiers bowed, curtsied, and stared in stunned disbelief as they passed.

I do not, Mirith said.

Okaay, David said, patting the dragon's side. *Thanks for that plethora of information there, buddy.*

They turned left into a wide room, the walls swathed in panels of earthen-toned leather. Colossal oiled paintings hung above two fireplaces. Grandiose maps, swords, and shields adorned the other walls, and with a gentle flourish of Slavandria's wrist, table and floor lamps sprang to light. Gildore closed the door and gestured for everyone to have a seat around an impressive oval table. David pulled out a plush wingback chair and froze, his gaze transfixed on the carving in the center of the table: a bull raised on its hind legs, an eagle poised on its head, wings displayed, all surrounded by a Celtic braid. He touched his fingertips to the identical tattoo on his chest, and glanced at the silver ring on his finger. The one from his father. The one with the same symbol engraved in the lapis stone. What did it all mean? How did he fit into the puzzle? He had to find out. If only anyone would talk.

Charlotte tugged on his sleeve and he sat down. She caressed his arm, her touch like a summer breeze rippling over a river of warm butterscotch. He squeezed her hand, thankful for her presence.

"Bring him in," Gildore said to the guard at the door.

A middle-aged man with mangled, reddish-gray hair and a face in terrible need of a shave entered the room. He wore weathered black trousers tucked into leather boots, a moth-eaten purple shirt, and a black and purple brocade jacket with faded brass buttons and frayed gold braids with tassels at the shoulders. Despite the odd appearance, there was no mistaking those brown, laughing wereman eyes.

Groote!

David breathed in one quick, sharp breath, his lips parted in disbelief.

"Dragon's breath!" Trog rounded the end of the table and embraced the man in a hearty hug. "Stephen Kavenaugh! Look at you, back to normal again. When did this happen?"

"A week ago, maybe two. I don't rightly remember. One minute I was gnawing flesh off a bone, the next I woke on the floor curled up like a baby and naked as a plucked chicken. Thankfully, I had these two around to take care of me." He beckoned toward the door and two creatures stepped inside, their human faces stoic, their dragon wings pressed back.

Charlotte gasped. "It's them! Agimesh and Tacarr! They're all right!"

"You know these creatures?" Eric asked. "How? And who is Stephen Kavenaugh?"

"The captain of the Fauscherian army," David said. "We met him on our way here, but he looked a lot different, trust me."

Groote looked past Trog's shoulder at Slavandria. "Your Grace, I am returning these two shime to your service."

"Thank you for their safe return," Slavandria said, "and you can thank David here for your freedom. He is the one who put an arrow through Avida's heart, thus breaking her spell on you."

David gulped as all eyes turned on him. *Yeah, that's right. Everyone look at the murderer.*

Murderer. That's what he was. It didn't matter why he did it. Killing was killing. Maybe Trog could rationalize it, justify it, but there would never be a base strong enough to neutralize the acid of guilt that ate at his conscience.

Never.

The man formerly known as Groote nodded in David's direction. "I owe you a debt of gratitude, young man. What you did not only saved me but an entire realm. Your courage is most appreciated."

David stared the man in the eye. "I killed someone. It doesn't matter the reason. It's still murder either way you look at it. I don't find anything courageous about that."

Kavenaugh shook his head. "I disagree. You did not go up to someone and kill them for sport. It was survival. Kill or be killed. You've done nothing wrong. Think of it as nothing more than cutting off the head of a venomous snake."

"A human being and a snake are two different things."

"She wasn't human," Slavandria said, her fingers brushing the tops of the chairs as she walked by. "She was evil of the most malignant kind. That doesn't mean you shouldn't feel some sort of guilt or experience a bit of self-condemnation. I'd have some serious concerns about your moral fiber if you didn't. But I hope you will believe me when I say that guilt is misplaced. Had you not killed Avida, Charlotte and many others would be dead. Would you have been able to live with that, knowing you could have done something and didn't?"

David stared at his lap. "No."

"Everything in perspective, boy," Kavenaugh said. "Remember that."

"I couldn't have said it better," Trog said, returning to his seat. "Stephen, I'm sure you remember Sirs Gowran, Crohn, and Farnsworth." He gestured toward the three men sitting to his right.

"Yes, yes, I do," Kavenaugh said, sitting to Trog's left. "And might I add how it pleases me to see I am not the only one who has grown weathered, old, and beaten."

"Speak for yourself, wereman," said Crohn, combing his dark, scraggly hair from his eyes. "I could get me a fair lass if I wanted one."

"Only in a world where an ogre looked like a rabbit and smelled like a rose," quipped the red-haired Gowran. Hearty laughter floated around the room. Even David couldn't keep the chuckle inside.

"So, Captain," Queen Mysterie said, her melodic voice bringing temperance to the room. "What brings you to Gyllen Castle? I would think you would wish to return to Fauscher as soon as possible."

Kavenaugh leaned forward, his hands clasped together on the table. His smile faded, his eyes darkened and his jaw tightened. "Since my recovery, Agimesh, Tacarr, and others have been keeping me abreast of the situation in Fallhollow. It is much more severe than anything you can imagine. Einar is amassing his armies. Dalvarian rebels are infiltrating Berg in large numbers. Other armies, some from as far away as Ochlen and the Mist Vales are moving in from the north and east, taking control of harbor towns between Gable and the Brindle Sea."

"They're annexing the trade routes." Gildore said.

"That's not good," Eric said.

"They've also positioned their headquarters in Tulipakar at the Elthorian Manor in the name of the Dragon King."

David swallowed the rock in this throat.

"No," Charlotte said, shaking her head. "They can't do that! We can't let them. We've got to do something. Twiller's family is there." She clasped David's hand.

A thousand electrifying needles pricked David's skin at her touch. "Ouch!" He jerked his hand away and shook it. "What the hell?"

"Don't be such a baby. You've felt worse." She looked back at

Slavandria. "We have to send in a rescue party."

"And do what, liberate an entire village of gnomes?" Kavenaugh asked. "It's impossible. Shadowmorths, as thick as storm clouds, guard every inch of Tulipakar. An attempt to enter would result in death."

"So, we're going to do nothing?"

"Not necessarily," David said, leaning forward. He glanced at Slavandria. "Why don't we contact Garret and Gertie? I can blink my way in and out of the Inn of the Nesting Owls; tell them what we've learned. They can send Ravenhawk and that other shapeshifter, that fox ... oh what's his name ... Rusty, into the wild. They do it all the time anyway. They can find out what's going on."

"I am afraid that is impossible," Agimesh said. His voice rumbled through David like thunder on a hot summer night. He stepped forward and took a knee, tucking his webbed, lime-green wings tight to his back. The vibrant feathered tips brushed his calves. "Your Grace, if I may have your permission to speak."

"Of course," Slavandria said.

The shime soldier stepped forward, his usual bright, round amethyst eyes now dark in his translucent human-like face. Even his green scales seemed to have lost their glimmer and shine.

"The two humans of which you speak, Garret and Gertie of Gable, were taken prisoner within hours of our departing Gable. They are being held in the Elthorian manor in Tulipakar."

Charlotte gasped, her hand covering her mouth. "No. That can't be."

"The shapeshifting fox, Rusty, of which you have referred, as well as a dozen other shapeshifters have been murdered in their attempts to rescue them."

David's insides went cold, his body trapped in a nightmare he couldn't shake. A half hour ago he was entertaining the thought of meeting his parents and going home with Charlotte, living out as close to a normal life considering all that had happened. Why did something always have to get in the way and puncture holes in his plans?

Trog pounded a fist on the table, rattling David's bones. The knight rose from his chair and turned his back to everyone. He gripped the edge of the mantel, his face dipped toward the floor.

"This is not your fault, Trog," said the knight sitting to the right of Trog's vacant chair. "There is no way you could have known—"

"But I did know, Farnsworth!" Trog rounded on the man. Anger flashed in his eyes. "They knew who I was and I used them! I let them risk everything for us. I should have never allowed them to get involved."

"They knew the chance they were taking and they took it anyway," Farnsworth said.

"He's right, Trog," David said. "They would have done anything for you. We have to do the same for them."

"It's too dangerous," Slavandria said.

"Not if I ferry in," David said. "I've been inside once, I can get in again.

"And what of our discussion this morning?" Slavandria asked.

David drummed his fingers on the table. "I've changed my mind.

I can't go home without trying to rescue them, not after all they did for us. But, I want an introduction with my parents before we set off on this rescue mission. Can we do that?"

Her eyes softened, as if a huge burden had been lifted. "I think that can be arranged."

"Your Grace," Agimesh said, "it would be unwise to ferry anyone into the manor. The shadowmorths will be upon him before you could have a chance to pull him out."

"I have to try," David said. "You've got to figure out a way to make me undetectable."

Eric shifted in his chair. "If David is going on a rescue mission, I'd like to volunteer to join the reconnaissance."

"Absolutely not!" King Gildore said, his tone final.

"Why not?" Eric asked, his jaw tense.

"Because I said so," Gildore replied. "You will see to the weapons and bed rolls and prepare the rations."

Eric's bottom jaw moved from side to side. His fingers balled into fists. "Your Majesty, with all due respect, I feel my skills would be well suited to join them. I am agile, quick with a sword. My injuries are healed. Why not take advantage of that? Let me prove my mettle. Let me use the skills I've been taught."

"Out of the question," Gildore said. "You will do as you have been instructed. Trog, you and I will journey to the Floating Isles and do what we can to convince the Steward to drop its shield of neutrality and join our cause."

"But I don't want to stay here," Eric said, bolting from his seat.

"You have no right keeping me chained to these walls. I know what and who I am and I know what is at stake. I am willing to take the risks and I should be allowed to do so." Infuriating desperation seeped from his eyes which had taken on a strange shade of green. Piercing in an alarming way.

Gildore shook his head. "I'm sorry, Eric, but my answer is no. I need you here."

"But, Your Majesty."

"Eric, your king has spoken," Trog said, his brow furrowed. "That is the end of it."

Eric's gaze locked with Trog's. His nostrils flared, his chest rose and fell in controlled breaths.

David shifted in his seat. His gaze met with Eric's, and he saw the same irritation, the same disgust he'd felt with Slavandria and Lily. He had to fight for him. Stick with him. There was more power in numbers, even if the current number was two.

"Yeah, so I don't know what the scoop is here," David said, standing, his chair scraping across the floor, "and I don't want to know, but I have to agree with Eric."

"David," Trog warned. "This is not your battle."

"Yeah, well none of the battles I've fought in this place have been mine, so I don't see how this is any different. I've seen Eric in action. I know for a fact I wouldn't be here right now if it weren't for him, so maybe having him on your team might not be a bad thing."

"You don't understand the circumstances," Trog said, "and you're out of line. Take a seat."

"With the utmost respect … no."

David took a deep breath to calm the rattle in his nerves. He must be crazy. He had to be to challenge Trog.

"That wasn't a request."

"And you're not listening."

"I said sit. Down."

David stared and seethed. His right eye twitched and the words he wanted to say warbled just below the surface of his lips. The man was so infuriating!

"Do I need to come over there and sit you down myself?"

David snatched his chair and sat down, his heart racing as if he'd run two miles

Trog flicked his gaze to Eric and motioned to him with a finger "Eric?"

"You can't keep treating me like a child!"

"I can, and will do so as long as you continue to act like one. Now sit down."

David took a deep breath. Man, Trog could be a real jerk. He wouldn't even listen. It was his way or no way. Why is it that adults always think they're right? It just burned him to no end.

Eric stared back at Trog. "As you command … *Master*."

"Eric," Gildore said, "one more disrespectful word and I will send you to the kitchens to wash every item of dinnerware in this castle with a rag the size of a lady's handkerchief."

"That's kind of harsh," David mumbled.

Charlotte kicked him.

"Would you like to join him, young man?" King Gildore asked, his gaze pinned on David.

David shook his head. "No sir."

"Coward," Eric said, folding his arms across his chest.

"Jerk," David replied.

"Babies," Charlotte said, smacking them both on the arm. "How old are you anyway? Geez." She shook her head and looked at Slavandria. "I have a question. If we can't go in above ground, why can't we go underground? You've got the Eye of Kedge and the crystals, right? I mean, that's what we all almost died for—getting you that stupid stone. All you have to do is wiggle your fingers, open the tunnels. Boom, we're in and out before anyone knows. That's doable, right?

The room quieted. All eyes on Charlotte for a change. Slavandria stood and paced "Yes, I can activate the tunnels, but doing so comes with a price. Seyekrad, Einar, and whatever demons gather around them will detect the magic in an instant. As we do not know exactly where Garret and Gertie are or what forces surround them, we will need time for reconnaissance once inside. That will take time. Time we do not have. Resistance will come almost instantly, above and below ground. A mage war will no doubt ensue. You must ask yourselves if you have the resources and the stamina to endure such a conflict. Hirth is wounded as is Gyllen Castle. You don't have near enough men, and there is only so much I can do alone. If you haven't noticed, I don't exactly have the assistance of the Mages High Council at my disposal."

"We can't sit here and do nothing," David said.

"I think Charlotte's idea is brilliant," Trog said. "I say we take our chances and fight using the mage tunnels. If it's planned well, if it's planned right, we might be able to succeed. There are thousands of tunnels. I'm sure Slavandria can find a way to mask us for short periods of time to confuse those that might be watching."

The room burst into loud discussion, and before David could blink twice, the knights and the king were strategizing, pulling out maps, spreading them over the tables. Talk over the collection of allied forces, battle routes, reconnaissance, tactical formations melded together into an overwhelming roar. Slavandria conjured an extensive map of the mage tunnels in the air and launched into a discussion over battle plans if met with resistance, escape routes, and ways to ambush the enemy without being discovered.

David's mouth went dry. This wasn't what he wanted, what he suggested. How did a rescue plan change to waging a full-scale battle? The muscles in his arms tightened and a burst of angry heat clawed through his stomach. He stood.

"Umm, hello? Excuse me?"

They continued on, their voices smothering his. He spoke a little louder, this time almost a shout. "Umm, hello? I think you misunderstood me." The room fell quiet again as all eyes turned on him. "I'm not talking about waging an all-out war here. All I want is for Slavandria to get me into the Elthorian Manor, snatch up Gertie and Garrett, and return here. That's it. Plain and simple."

"There is nothing simple about this, David," Slavandria said. "If you use the tunnels, you're going to have to take soldiers with you. I can only mask the magic for maybe a few seconds at a time. That is nowhere near enough to get in and out like what you're thinking."

"But I thought the tunnels shaved time? I thought travel was instant."

"They do, and it is, but as I said, I'm not the only one who can use the tunnels. I can assure you Seyekrad is waiting for me to activate them and when I do, no one inside of them will be safe."

David clenched his fists. "So, you're telling me that with all the magic you possess, there isn't anything you can do to get me in there undetected." It was more of a statement than a question.

"No, there isn't, not without risking your capture and possible murder."

"That's ridiculous."

"David, please," Charlotte, said, taking his hand in hers.

He snatched it away and banged his chair against the table. "You're the great sorceress to ever live," he yelled, pointing at Slavandria. "You're the daughter of Jared, the almighty poobah of all poobah's. I don't care how you do it, but figure out a way that doesn't involve war to get me in there and get them out. Plain and simple. Come find me when you've figured it out."

He stormed from the room, past the grand staircase and out the front door of the castle, ignoring Charlotte's shouts to stop.

Charlotte.

His stomach coiled in a tight knot. He was supposed to protect her. Keep her safe. What a fine job he'd done there. And now he couldn't rescue his other friends without starting World War III. What had he done? Good God, what had he done?

Chapter 3

Eric

Eric ran through the shattered gatehouse, Charlotte close behind, and took off down the dirt road. Far ahead, David disappeared behind a stone wall and into the ravaged, burnt town of Hammershire. Street after street they searched until they finally came upon him sitting on a bench outside a tailor's charred shop, hunched over, his elbows on his knees, his head in his hands.

Charlotte sat on one side, Eric on the other, his hands clasped between his knees. "Are you all right?" he asked.

David straightened and combed his fingers through his hair. "Yeah. I'm fine."

"That was quite a display back there," Charlotte said. "Not exactly the best way to win over—"

Eric caught her eye and shook his head. He knew the monster eating at David. It ate at him, too, and the last thing David needed was a thousand questions and judgments hurled at him. He'd talk when he was ready to talk.

Charlotte combed her fingers through David's hair, her forehead creased with concern. Another glance at Eric and her eyes shifted. She sat back, her hands in her lap, and planted her gaze on something unknown in the distance. Eric's fingers twitched as he tried to look away, to not see her, but her presence tugged at him. He wanted her fingers in his hair, her eyes to look at him the way they looked at David, but why? He was a knight in training. He could have any girl he wanted, as well as the ones he didn't. All he had to do was look at them and they'd swoon and fall at his feet. So what was it about this girl that had him turned upside down?

If only things could go back to the way they were before she showed up, when he was content with trading companionship and love for tournaments and knighthood. It would be so much better than walking around with this feeling that his chest would explode any minute, exposing his beating heart with her name written upon it.

He wondered if David noticed the way the sun glimmered upon her hair, or how sharp her cheekbones had become in her thinning face. Did he see the pale lavender shadows clinging to the puffy skin beneath her eyes or know the story of how the tiny but noticeable scars ended up on her forehead and chin? Did he see the strength and determination in the set of her jaw, in the squareness of her shoulders? Did he know what a precious gem he had?

He wanted to reach out to her, to let her know he understood how difficult it must be to watch her friend in pain, to want to help but know there was nothing she could do. He, too, knew that feeling. He'd experienced it watching Sestian die. No matter how hard he tried, no matter how much he bargained or begged, he couldn't save his best friend. Fate had control over life, not mortal man. And he'd cursed the heavens for it, too, but to what end? Did death care? No, it didn't and it never would. In fact, one day it would come for him. He wondered if anyone would be there in the end to bargain for his life.

David nudged him on the shoulder. "Hey. You want to stop staring at Charlotte and show us around this wreck of a town?"

Heat spattered across Eric's face and his stomach fell over. The look on her face, the sudden unease in her features. He'd let his guard down. He would have to be more careful to not let her see, not let anyone see how broken he really was.

Eric stood and bowed. "I apologize, milady. My thoughts were elsewhere. I meant no disrespect." He flicked a smile at David. "Shall we go?"

As the day wore on, they wandered the streets while Eric shared memories of growing up in the town—all the festivals, his first kiss at the age of six with the haberdasher's daughter, his first glass of ale at the Golden Finch Tavern, an establishment now standing in a lopsided fashion on its scorched frame. They stared at the castle sitting majestically atop the singed hillside. Even in its destruction, its white façade and blue turrets were still a magnificent sight to behold. His belly filled with pride, honor. Gyllen Castle was his home, and he would die defending her.

And, he wasn't alone. He had the paladin on his side, whether David would admit it or not. Twice since daybreak the savior of Hirth had come to his defense. He'd also volunteered for a rescue mission that had a far higher chance of failure than success. And it wasn't the first time David had chosen danger over safety. He'd saved Trog from Bainesworth on the Field of Valnor, and rescued Eric and the king from Berg Castle and Einar's jaws. He'd done so without complaint, yet Eric had berated and chided him, and for what? To make himself look better? Seem more important? What an idiot he'd been. He'd have to find the proper place and time to apologize. Do the knightly thing. Be the man Trog would be proud of.

But now, there was something else he needed to take care of. Someone else he needed to see. They stopped outside a shop on Threadneedle Lane.

"I think this is where I need to take my leave of you. I have something to tend to and I don't want to keep you."

David snorted. "Keep us from what? Going back there," he gestured to the castle, "so I can be yelled at? Maybe thrown in the pit for being a little rebellious and standing up for myself?"

Charlotte rubbed a hand on David's arm. "I think he wants to be alone. Come on. We'll find Mirith. He'll protect you from the big, bad witch." She glanced up at him and smile.

Eric's insides warbled. How could David be so clueless, so unaffected by her?

He rubbed his hands together. "You know what? I'm just going to see my father. Why don't you come with me? I'm sure he wouldn't mind meeting you. And, with everything going on, I'm not sure when I can get back here, so what do you say?"

"Sure," David said with a shrug. "Beats the heck out of the alternative."

"If you're sure he won't mind," Charlotte said. "I hate intruding."

"He won't mind at all. In fact, he'd probably like the distraction."

They made their way through the clothier's shop onto a narrow, dusty road. Eric hurried across the way, shooing chickens from the front door of a small dwelling as he entered.

"Father?" he called out.

The word caught like barbed wire in his throat. His father, but not his father. How long would it take before the truth sank in and stopped boggling his mind?

A girl his age with spirals of red hair emerged from a room in the rear of the home. Eric froze in place.

"Lady Emelia," he breathed, keeping his voice steady. "What are you doing here?" He took a step toward his father's bedroom.

She stepped in front of him, her porcelain face tilted upward, her eyes holding him hostage.

"Your father is ill, Eric." Her nasal voice was almost pleasant. "The physician is confident his ailment isn't life-threatening, but he insists your father get plenty of rest. Since the very stubborn patient refused to stay in the infirmary, I volunteered to stay with him here. I hope you don't mind."

A wad of distrust mixed with a smidgeon of gratitude slid down his throat in a gelatinous gulp. Ever since they were children, she'd been conniving, manipulative. It was if she believed that simply being a baron's daughter and some distant relative to the queen she could have anything she wanted, including Eric. For years he evaded her, discouraged her attentions, but no matter how hard he tried, he always felt like a target and she a lethal arrow. And yet, as she stood before him, caring for his father the way she'd cared for Sestian in his final hour, he had to wonder if the recent attack on Hirth had turned her from shrew to angel, or worse—his perception had been flawed. He needed to be cautious. He squared his shoulders and said, "No. Not at all. May I see him?"

"For a few minutes. I gave him some broth and some herbs that should help him sleep."

"Thank you." He gestured behind him. "Milady, I'd like to introduce you to David and Charlotte. Please be nice and don't spread any lies about me. I have a reputation to keep."

He smiled in jest and strode to his father's room.

His father lay in bed, his head propped on a pillow, a blanket pulled to his chin. There was pallor in his cheeks, a paleness in his lips. His eyes shifted to Eric upon entering. A tear fell as he extended a hand from beneath the covers.

"Eric, my boy."

Eric quickly took his hand and sat on the bed. "Father. How are you feeling? You're burning up."

"Tain't nothin' and I'm much better now that ya here." His father coughed. "I been so worried 'bout ya, ever since you took off outta here." He took back his hand and laid it upon his chest. His gaze traveled over Eric's face. "It looks as if ya've been in a few scrapes."

Eric touched the lingering scabs on his forehead, caught a glimpse of the scars on the back of his hand. "Yes. It's nothing, really. Small run-in with a dragon and a few Bergonian assassins." He paused for a moment and stared at a loose thread in the blanket. "Father, I wanted to see you because … I wanted to tell you something." He lifted his chin and met his father's eyes. "I know the truth about me. You. Trog. Mother. We don't have to pretend anymore."

"Glory be to the heavens." His father took Eric's hand in his again and squeezed. "'Tis about time. I'm sorry it took so long for you ta find out, son."

"No, no, don't be sorry. I'm not angry. At least not anymore. I mean, I was at first, but now I'm trying to sort it all out, make sense of it. But, I guess what I want to say is even though Trog is my … " Eric paused and reeled in the words ready to fly out of his mouth. "You'll always be my father. That'll never change."

A tear rolled down his father's cheek and his grip tightened around Eric's hand. "Thank ya, son. Thank ya. If ya only knew how many times I wanted ta tell ya."

Eric cupped his father's hand in his. "I know. And I'm not upset with you. You did what you thought was best."

"D'not be upset with him, either, son. Everything he done, he done for ya."

Eric stood and walked to the window. He hated the secrecy, the talking in code, but the walls were full of ears, of this much he was sure. "My brain tells me you're right, Father," he said as he watched a baby goat leap on and off an upside-down cart. "I wish it would tell my heart."

"Give it time, son. Give it time." His father coughed.

Silent moments passed before Eric turned to his father. "Father, what was she like? My mother."

A slight smile creased his father's lips. "She was lovely, my boy. An angel." He gestured Eric to him, his voice tapering off to a whisper as Eric sat down. "She loved ya and that master of yours very much."

Eric stared at the bed, his heart swelling and breaking in waves of emotion. "Any ideas who—"

His father squeezed Eric's hand. "We all's got ideas, son, but the fountain … well, it ain't givin' up its secrets. But if I had ta guess—"

His father fell into a violent coughing fit, his face red, his breath difficult to catch. Eric pulled him forward and held him in his arms until the spell subsided.

"Are you all right, Father?"

"He'll be fine," Lady Emelia said, bustling into the room, a steaming cup of broth in hand. "But you should probably go now and let him rest." She stirred an envelope of medicine in the broth, and pressed the cup to his lips so he could drink.

Eric nodded and laid his father back onto the pillow. He brushed the gray hairs from his brow.

His father clasped Eric's hand. "Look to the east, boy, toward the Brindle Sea. Sunrise on Kamill."

"Kamill? What is that? What does it mean?"

The man closed his eyes. "Things always look brighter in the daylight."

"Father, I don't understand. Father?"

"He's sleeping now," Emelia said. "You can come back and see him later."

Three low tones of the castle horns suddenly sounded in the distance, preventing Eric from answering. A warning.

Eric leapt from the bed and hurried from the room. "David! Charlotte! We have to go!"

He ran out of the front door, his friends shouting questions behind him.

The blows of the horns came again. Three times. Low. Drawn out.

"What is that?" David asked.

"There's something wrong," Eric said, running through shops, out onto streets, and out of town. Faster and faster he pushed his feet, his lungs ready to explode, the cooler air drying his throat.

Together the three of them ran through the dilapidated gatehouse. A guard met them as they rushed passed the fountain.

"To the King's chambers. Hurry! Slavandria has been looking everywhere for you!"

"What's wrong?" Eric shouted, taking two steps at a time toward the upper courtyard.

"It's the queen! Hurry!"

They barged through the front doors into the main hall and up the grand staircase. Upon reaching the seventh floor, they were bustled into the royal suites. Trog wheeled around as they entered, his face taut.

"Where have you been?"

Eric gasped for breath, his heart beating fast and hard. "Hammershire. What's happened? Why the warning?"

Slavandria emerged from the sleeping chambers, her expression drawn, distressed. Her eyes widened at seeing Eric, David, and Charlotte.

"Eric! David! Thank the heavens you're all right." She embraced them both, then hugged Charlotte. "My dear, I was so worried."

"About what?" Eric asked.

Slavandria turned to him. "There has been an incident. The queen was attacked with a lethal dose of belladonna."

Eric froze. His heart fell and tumbled, his soul clung to the precipice of a dark, cold abyss. Not the queen. Please, not the queen. She'd always been like a mother to him.

He breathed a sharp breath.

Mother!

His thoughts scattered. Queen Mysterie. Murdered. Like her twin sister, his mother, Gwyndolyn. His heart raced. No. No, it couldn't be.

Charlotte's voice shocked him back to reality. "There must be a mistake!"

"I wish there were. As it was, Mirith must have sensed the poison and blasted the goblet from her hand before she could take more than a sip."

"So, she's not dead?" Eric asked, his heart racing so hard it hurt.

Slavandria cupped his chin, then brushed the hair from his eyes.

"No, she is not dead, however, she is very ill."

"Who would do something like this?" Charlotte asked. "Why?"

Slavandria steepled her fingers beneath her chin. "I believe it was a distraction."

Eric shook his head. "A distraction from what?"

"After the three of you left in a flurry, we carried on without you and devised a plan to rescue your friends by utilizing the tunnels. It was agreed that I would test them first to see what sort of opposition, if any, I encountered. I was waiting for Farnsworth to return with the crystals, but then the girl arrived, her hair and face covered in a veil. She poured the water, then scurried away so fast. Mysterie brought the goblet to her lips. Mirith curled his tail and blasted it from her hand. Sirs Crohn and Gowran assaulted him, but Mirith ran, upending the table and chairs, smashing everything, flinging lightning bolts everywhere. The room was in chaos. Farnsworth returned as Trog scooped the queen in his arms, and revealed the empty box. The crystals were gone. We sounded the horns, hoping you would return quickly."

Emotion clamped Eric's throat shut. Hot tears puddled in the corners of his eyes. "I want to see her. I want to see the queen."

"I've sent her away, Eric, both her and the king, to a place where they are secure and well cared for. I need to do the same to the three of you. You are no longer safe here. The castle has been breached. Secrets within its walls are in jeopardy. All of you are in danger."

Slavandria's gaze cut to Eric. He drew in a heavy breath and heaved it out again. He knew what she spoke of. They were in danger because of him, because of who he was. *Secrets are grave burdens to bear,* Trog once said. No kidding, and if Seyekrad or Einar found out the truth?

His brows drew together, forming a crease between them. "Can't you put up shields or wards? Make it a little more difficult for the castle to, you know, speak?"

A chuckle burst out of David but it held little amusement. "What are you babbling about? What's going on? Why are we in danger?"

"Pawns are being moved. Knights are on the defense, and bishops are in the chancel. At the moment, Hirth is in check. If we are not careful … "

"Checkmate," Eric breathed. The food he'd eaten earlier squished around in his stomach. Reality slapped him a thousand times in the face. The realm was at war. There was no turning away, no denying it, and if Seyekrad or Einar discovered the truth about him being the heir, they would have no mercy on the innocent. They would die. He didn't want that blood splattered on his soul.

"She's right," he said, never surer of anything in his life. "We have to go."

Slavandria slipped a chain from around her neck. Dangling from the end was the Eye of Kedge. The red dragon eye stone, encased in a wreath of filigreed gold, hung in the light, exposed. Dangerous. Coaxing.

"You must go to Finn's," Slavandria said, slipping it around David's neck. "Tell him what has happened. He'll know what to do."

"But what about my parents? You made a promise. That was the deal. If I stayed, you'd introduce me to my parents before I went off and got myself killed. That's what we agreed to!"

"I'm sorry, David. I know how disappointed—"

"Disappointed? Is that what you think I am?"

The floor shook as thunder rumbled through the tile. Charlotte lurched, her expression petrified. Eric clutched her in his arms as Mirith appeared in the doorway, blood dripping from his mouth. A few feathers were missing from his mane and a bump protruded from his head between his horns. He snorted at David, and collapsed.

David took one look at Mirith and continued his rant. "You have lied to me over and over again. You've made promises you never kept. I want you to do what you said you would do. Five minutes. At least give me the courtesy of a 'Hi. Nice to meet you. Gotta go.' Let me put faces with names before I end up dead."

Slavandria wrung her hands. "I can't do that."

"Why? What's the reason this time? Let me see. They have the plague. They've been eaten by ogres. They've turned into ponies and are living somewhere over the rainbow."

Eric quirked an eyebrow. *What?*

"I can't introduce you to them, David, because they're gone. I cannot produce what is not accessible."

David's eyes narrowed. "What do you mean they're gone? Are you implying my parents stole the crystals and have taken off with them?"

"I'm implying nothing of the sort," Slavandria said.

"Are you looking for them?"

"Scouts are preparing to ride as we speak. I'll come to you when they've been found, but for now, you must go. Give the necklace to Finn."

Slavandria said some words that didn't make sense, flipping and twisting her wrists.

Eric turned toward the queen's quarters. His stomach lurched. His breath snagged.

The world spun. Darkened. Elongated.

And Gyllen Castle disappeared into a black abyss.

Chapter 4

David

David slammed into something hard. Pain ripped through his shoulder, his head. Two more thuds landed beside him. A third one hit so hard the ground quaked.

He pushed to his hands and knees, discarded the spindly broken chair clinging to his back like a turtle shell, and stood. He recognized the pots and pans suspended from the ceiling, the prismatic colors flickering off a line of crystals hanging in a sunlit window above a sink. A pewter teapot sat on a wood stove. Bottles of all shapes and sizes, some so dusty he couldn't see their contents, perched on tilted shelves. And up above, nestled between the ceiling and the lopsided cabinets, a black creature with leathery wings stared down at him, its purple eyes watching his every move.

"Hello, Maggot," he muttered under his breath.

It had been two weeks since he'd first laid eyes on the creature.

At the time, Finn called it a familiar, his double, his alter-ego. David called it creepy and wished it would go away. The sentiment hadn't changed.

The gargoyle blinked and turned its gaze on Eric who winced while helping Charlotte to her feet.

He had seen that contorted look of pain on Eric's face once before, in Berg Castle, in the dungeons when they'd first met. A shiver ran up his spine at the sight of Eric's arm dangling precariously at his side.

"It's dislocated again, isn't it?" David asked.

Eric nodded. "Have you got a sash I can use?" He smiled.

David returned the grin. "I wish." He kicked the overturned chairs out of the way and shoved the small table to the side, grimacing as the lanky, twiggy legs grated across the floor. "I do have a wall for you though." He gestured to the partition separating the kitchen from the hall, as if showing off a grand prize on a game show.

"What are you two babbling about?" Charlotte asked. "Where in God's creation are we and what is that thing on top of the cabinets?"

"We're at Finnagin Aginagin's. He's a crazy old magician who's literally as thin as paper with whacky hair and eyes like a lemur. He brought me here the night Einar kidnapped you and I collapsed in the woods. He took care of me and nursed me back to health within hours only to put me through the most insane, spell-casting training you can imagine. Almost twenty-four hours of learning how to pass through solid objects, how to open doors. Perfecting the spells Slavandria gave me. And if that wasn't enough, he tossed me out on my butt the next morning after I had maybe two hours of sleep, and sends me into the belly of Berg Castle. As for that thing up there, his name's Maggot, and he's a gargoyle and probably just about the laziest, most useless creature I've ever seen." David looked around, his brow pinched. "Speaking of creatures, where is Mirith?"

"He can't be too far away," Eric said, one eye on the familiar. "I felt his exorbitant weight shake the whole of Fallhollow, if that is indeed where we are."

"Oh, yeah. We're still in Fallhollow," David said. He found a stained but clean cloth in a drawer and handed it to Eric. "Here. Is there enough there to keep you from biting off your tongue?"

Eric nodded. "Thank you, however, I must say with a great amount of certainty, I am not looking forward to this." He squared off with the wall, and shoved the cloth in his mouth.

"What is he doing?" Charlotte asked, her eyes wide. Scared.

Eric shot forward, turning his body at the last minute so that his shoulder connected with the door jam. A loud pop, followed by an excruciating yell sent Maggot scampering across the cabinets to the darkest corner of the room. Eric spun and pressed his back to the wall. Sweat dripped from his forehead.

David squeezed his eyes tight at the bellow of pain. He couldn't begin to imagine it. He hoped he never would.

Charlotte shouted, "What did you do? Why?" She approached Eric, her expression one of anger and perplexity. "What in the devil's name possessed you do such a thing?"

"My arm was out of its socket. I had to put it back. Otherwise, I would be unable to protect you from such dangerous creatures as the one hovering in the shadows above you."

David chuckled. "He's not dangerous. Besides, what are you going to protect her with, your charming smile and daring personality?" He grinned. "That is unless you have an invisible sword you can wield."

Eric glanced down at his side and cursed beneath his breath. "Fantastic." He pointed to David. "Looks as if you are without armament as well."

"Which is all the more reason to find Finn. Shall we? He'll know what to do."

They strode down a narrow hallway littered with stacks of papers and small tables topped with knick-knacks. The corridor emptied into a large room lit by a single lamp, tassels hanging from the rim of its pointed shade. Slanted bookshelves hung on the walls. Stacks of papers were piled high to the ceiling. Crystal balls, potions, and bizarre, miniature animals, some striped, some spotted, wandered around tables and over open books as if it were the most natural thing in the world. In a shadowed corner at the far end of the room, David spotted his host slumped in an overstuffed chair.

"Finn," David said, hurrying to his side, "it's David. Wake up. Come on, buddy. Snap out of it."

"What are you doing?" Charlotte asked. "Why don't you let him sleep?"

"He's a sestra, and sestras don't sleep. Ever," David said. He shook Finn by the shoulders. "Finn. Come on. Wake up."

"He's a what?" Eric asked, stepping over strewn parchments and leather-bound books splayed like birds in flight.

Both Eric's and Charlotte's gasps nearly sucked all the air from the room as their gazes fell upon the man in the chair.

"What in dragon's breath did you say he was?" Eric asked, staring at the man with flesh as pale as moon glow, bugged eyes, and eyebrows that appeared half-eaten by a goat. Blades of grass-green hair spiked at every angle, while flat, paper-thin arms and hands protruded from the bell sleeves of his embroidered robe. "He's as thin as a feather. Literally. Why, you could turn him sideways and lose him all together."

David nodded. "I know. I thought the same thing when I first saw him."

"Is he really a sestra, an emissary of the mages?"

"Yep, so he says." A wave of confusion swept through David's. "Wait a minute. Are you telling me you've never seen one before?"

Eric shook his head. "I always thought they were feigned, creatures of hope made up for bedtime stories to ward off evil dreams." Eric reached out and touched Finn's arm. "This is remarkable." His gaze traveled down Finn's body, all the way to his paper-thin feet. "I wonder how he moves, how he breathes. There's nothing to him."

"I could say the same about you, sprout," Finn said, bolting upright. "Didn't your elders ever teach you it's impolite to gawk and comment on others' appearances? I may look scrawny and weak, but I could send you into another universe before you could utter a sound."

Eric laughed, his nerves playing havoc on the sound coming out of his throat. He stood, not taking his hand off of Finn. "I'm sure you could, Sir. No offense meant."

"None taken. I'm only giving you grief." The sestra grasped David's hand and patted it. "I'm glad to see you survived the attack. The paladin lives to fight another day."

"Yeah. Whatever," David said, wishing someone else would claim the job. "What happened to you? Why were you sleeping?"

Finn rubbed his forehead. "It wasn't sleeping, young man, of that I can assure you. I was working on a project when I heard this strange noise coming from the hallway. An instant later, I became quite disoriented and took a seat in hopes the feeling would dissipate. I passed out. Quite different from sleeping."

David stood still, every inch of him taut with tension. Something wasn't right. Finn sensed everything. Nothing got by him, yet something dulled his mind. Wiped his senses. Had someone cast a spell upon him, and if so, why? He remembered the Eye of Kedge dangling from his neck. Could it be whomever stole the crystals came looking for the pendant?

Finn snapped his paper-thin fingers in David's face. "What's got you so serious, boy?" He headed toward the kitchen without a look back.

"Finn, I think someone may have drugged you or used magic on you."

"To what end?"

"To get their hands on this." David pulled the Eye of Kedge from beneath his doublet.

"Bring it here by the window so as I can get a better look."

David slipped the necklace over his head and handed it to Finn.

"Slavandria said to give it to you. That you would know what to do with it."

Finn held it up to the sunlight streaming in through the kitchen window. He examined it backwards, forwards, and upside down. His only words were "Umm hmm. Hmm. Umm hum." After intense inspection, he turned to Eric who stood beside the kitchen table wearing a most perplexed look.

Finn shook his head and motioned to Eric. "Sit, sit, boy. No need to gawk. I know I'm a bit much to take in, but your brain might explode if you don't give it a rest."

"Explode?"

"Yes, yes," Finn said. "It happened once, you know. Right here in this very room. I was talking to a young boy about your age and he couldn't stop staring. Soon, his eyes got bigger and bigger until they bulged from their sockets. All of a sudden," he mimicked an explosion with his fingers, "his head popped." He paused for a few moments, long enough to prepare four mugs of tea, then continued. "It was a nasty mess, I have to tell you. There was brain matter everywhere. If it wasn't for Maggot helping out, I might still be cleaning up the remnants."

"Finn," David said, folding his arms across his chest, "you're so full of crap."

Eric sipped and swallowed his tea. His gaze flitted from Finn to Charlotte then back to Finn. "I apologize, sir. It was not my intention to stare. I-it's just you're a sestra. A real, live sestra."

"Well, we'd be in a bit of a pickle if I were a dead one now, wouldn't we?" He turned to David. "Are you going to introduce me? It's rather rude to drop in unannounced and not introduce your playmates."

"They're not playmates," David said, taking a seat.

"Semantics. Get to it."

"Fine." David sat back in his chair. "Eric, this is Finnegan Aginagin, but you can call him Finn. Finn, this is Eric, and my best friend in any world, Charlotte. And somewhere around here is Mirith, my pet dragon."

"So that's who's making the ruckus in the basement," Finn said. He glanced up at the gargoyle. "Maggot doesn't like dragons."

David snorted and said, "Kind of an oxymoron, considering where you live."

"Why do you say that?" Eric asked.

"Go look out the window."

Eric rose and walked to the window. Within seconds, his face turned red. Anger pinched his brow as he balled his fingers into fists. "That's Berg Castle." He glared at David. "Why are we at Berg Castle? Didn't you get enough of this place?"

"Hey, I didn't pick the vacation destination, remember. Thank Slavandria for that one."

"Does she want to see us dead?"

"I don't think so," David said. "In fact, I'm pretty sure she sent us here so we'd be safe."

"Safe?" Eric's hands began to shake. "We are within a stone's throw of Einar's lair, a place where King Gildore and I were held captive and beaten." A black, wispy shadow passed outside the glass. Eric's eyes widened. He pointed at the window. "Did you see that? Did you? It was a shadowmorth! Do you remember those? Trog almost died from one of them. I was scraped by one and thought I would die."

David took a deep breath. "Yes, I remember, but they don't know we're here. The cottage is concealed. Finn's got it under control, so relax. Trust me, there's no one here who wants to beat you up or hurt you, unless you want to keep acting like a deranged mental patient, at which time I'd be happy to knock you on your butt."

"You? Knock me on my butt?" Eric laughed loud and hard. "I'd like to see you try."

"Children," Charlotte moaned, "chill out. Sheesh."

Finn tapped the pendant in his palm. His brow furrowed and his eyes changed from black to a strange shade of forest green. "David, what has happened to the crystals?"

"They've been stolen," David said.

"When?"

"We're not sure, but if I had to guess, I'd say this morning about the same time someone tried to poison the queen."

Finn's eyes got bigger, if that was even possible. "A distraction."

David nodded. "And even though Slavandria denied it, I think my parents might have been the ones to take them."

"What would your parents need with them?" Finn asked.

"I was hoping you could tell me."

"Do I look like a mind reader, boy? Now tell me what happened at Gyllen, and maybe I'll decide if I can help you."

***

Finn paced the room as he listened, his forefinger tapping his lips. Back and forth. Back and forth, even when the story was through.

Eric smacked the table. "Will you please quit pounding the floor and tell us what you're thinking?"

Finn stopped and flattened his palms on the kitchen table, his face inches from Eric's. "I know who all of you are. I know what roles you are to play. You think you understand what has happened, what will happen, but you know nothing. Destinies have been set into motion. The three of you are players in a game of perpetuity. You will not endure here, not while the Seekers hunt for the one who controls the Eye." His gaze turned to David. "I know why Slavandria sent you to me. I know why I must send you away." Finn turned away.

David drummed his fingers on the table and bit his bottom lip, choosing his next words carefully.

"Do you plan on telling us what you know?"

Finn moved to the sink and stared out the window. "It was written seasons ago in the Book of Telling that no harm should come to the Hirth or Fallhollow so long as the protectors of Hirth remained in the realm together. Sadly, to protect the realm, the king of Hirth entered into a sorcerer's agreement, nullifying the sacred words, and the protectors of Hirth were separated."

David's stomach flipped and hitched a ride to what-the-hell island. Why would the king do that? What could have been so sacred he would make such a bargain?

"Now, they have rejoined," Finn continued, "thus breaking the sorcerer's concordance." He turned around, facing them once more. "He and the Dragon King will never stop searching for you. They will tear this world upside down to find you. You must leave. Go where he cannot touch you."

"What about the crystals?" Charlotte asked. "What about Gertie and Garrett? We have to get them back."

"And you will, when the fates allow."

Eric snorted. The muscles in his arms flexed. "I don't know about you, but I'm not going anywhere."

"Do you want to die?" Finn asked.

"No, of course not," Eric said, his voice cool and measured, "but if you think I'm going to run while everyone else stays to fight, you're wrong."

Finn pushed back from the table. "What makes you think you're running from a fight? How do you know you're not running into one?"

"But you just said—"

"I said what I said. You construed the rest." He placed the necklace with the medallion around his neck. "Come with me. All of you."

Chairs scraped across the floor.

They turned left out of the kitchen, down another narrow hallway into a room as dark and musty as the one they'd found Finn in. David shook his head at the tilted shelves. Did Finn not believe in anything being flat and level? He flinched as Maggot scuttled past him and jumped up on a credenza stacked high with parchments, books, and odd glass globes filled with water and model cities. Finn pushed his way through piles of broken chairs, picture frames, and strange metal contraptions until he reached a roll-topped desk in the center of the room. Raising the tambour, he removed a round metallic ball, red as an apple and half the size.

"What's that?" David asked.

"A rutseer. A very handy device for where you're going."

"Where are we going?" David asked.

Finn tossed the ball once and caught it. "Wherever the crystals are."

He laid the Eye of Kedge upside down on a table. David and the others moved closer as Finn pressed the rutseer into an indentation in the back. A glow swelled from deep within the ball, turning it into a fiery globe.

"What is it doing?" Charlotte asked.

"Finding the crystals."

The ball began to spin, slow at first, then increasing in speed until it began to hum. The top opened, emitting a shard of light which faded, leaving behind a projected map hanging in the air.

Eric gasped, his mouth hung open. "This is incredible."

"It's a hologram," David said, "and the image looks familiar."

"It should," Finn said. "It's—"

BOOM!

Eric shoved Charlotte to the ground, his body shielding hers as a door blasted from its hinges and flew from across the hallway into the room, crashing into an ocean of spindles and broken chairs. Mirith's shape filled the doorway, his sizzling tail arched over his back, his teeth exposed. Behind him, Maggot crouched on a table, rows of flesh-ripping teeth exposed within a guttural growl.

"No, no," Finn said, panic saturating his voice. Incantations slipped from his tongue. Tingles invaded David's body as the spells shot by him, one after the other. Maggot roared as the powers bounced off his body, now covered in plates of stone. "David, do something with your dragon! The two together are as volatile as gunpowder and fire!"

David called out to Mirith in his mind. *Stop, Mirith! Back away. You're going to get us killed.*

The plea slammed into an invisible wall. The dragon had mentally turned himself off.

A string of curses flew from David's lips.

Another growl, this one so deep it rumbled the floor. Blue sparks sizzled overhead.

Maggot roared.

Eric covered Charlotte once more as another bolt exploded the desk behind them, raining splinters of wood.

"Get off of me!" Charlotte said. Sparks danced off her fingertips and into Eric's arms.

"Oww! Dragon's breath, you just shocked me!"

Charlotte shimmied away on her belly. "Sorry. Next time, don't assume I need—" Her words were lost in Maggot's screech.

David covered his ears, the high-pitch painful.

Maggot leapt and latched onto Mirith's head. His long talons dug into the dragon's face, his angular teeth ripping out feathers.

Mirith shrieked, his ruby eyes rolling back in their sockets.

"Stop!" David shouted. "Get off of him!" He bent down, grabbed a broken table leg, and hit Maggot in the back.

The gargoyle released his grip and turned toward his attacker, his amethyst eyes glowing.

"Yeah, okay, that was stupid," David said. "Eric! Get Charlotte out of here. Go!"

Maggot dived.

David swung. The table leg broke upon impact. Shards of wood flew in the air. He ducked and half ran, half stumbled toward the hallway.

Mirith burst after him, shattering the doorframe. He pivoted around, cocked his tail over his head, and aimed at Maggot.

"David, you must control your dragon!" Finn yelled, grabbing David's arm. "If he hurls anymore bolts, he'll shatter the barrier around the cottage. He'll expose everything!"

"Now you tell me, Finn!"

Charlotte disappeared under a couch.

"David," Eric shouted. "Get Mirith. I'll hold off Maggot. Ready?"

David nodded. "Just like old times, right? Go!"

The two charged, yelling like madmen. Mirith whipped his head around as David and Eric clambered over the wreckage.

David jumped in front of Mirith, his hands in the air. "Stop. You're going to give us away. The shadowmorths. They're going to find us. Einar will find us. Please. Stop."

Another bolt lit up the room.

"David, that one almost hit me," Eric yelled, diving onto Maggot's back and latching on to the beast's ears.

The gargoyle growled, reared, and with a violent shake, sent Eric flying through the air. He crashed into a desk, bringing the contents down on him.

"Mirith, please," David yelled. "He's not worth it. He's just a gargoyle. You're going to get us killed."

Eric's hiding place disappeared, the heavy piece of furniture smashing into pieces behind him. Maggot hovered over him, his nails stretched out like an eagle's talons ready to pluck a fish from a lake.

Eric swallowed, his breathing heavy and uneven. A rod of light zoomed across the room, exploding across Maggot's back. The gargoyle turned and flapped toward Mirith.

One.

Two.

Three more bolts.

The room burst into flames.

A fourth bolt blew the roof off.

Sunlight streamed into darkness.

Outside came an ear-splitting screech.

"Shadowmorths!" Eric screamed.

Eric bounded over the piles of shattered wood as the swarms

entered overhead. "David, get those spells ready!"

"Thanks, Mirith, you stupid dragon," David yelled.

The window in the kitchen shattered. Shadowmorths screamed their way into the cottage, their appendages snapping.

Charlotte screamed.

Maggot soared overhead, plunging and diving into the fray. Purple droplets of blood rained down.

Mirith bounded into the room, his tail zapping the wispy clouds of death.

"David!" Finn yelled. "The necklace. The rutseer."

Two shadowmorths swarmed Finn and sliced his mid-section. He met David's gaze and said, "Go," before he collapsed to the floor.

"No!" David yelled.

Maggot circled and screeched. Mirith shot off more bolts.

Charlotte scrambled across the room, grabbing the necklace and rutseer now rolling across the floor. "Guys, we have to go!"

"I can't leave him!" David wailed. "I have to save Finn!"

"There's nothing we can do!" Charlotte yelled. "We have to go!"

Eric and David grasped her hands as shadowmorths swarmed. David clasped the necklace and rutseer in between their palms.

A familiar grip tugged at David's gut as they went spinning down a familiar black swirling hole.

Again.

Chapter 5

David

David gasped, his breathing ragged as his starving lungs sucked in every bit of air they could find. He clung to the nearest object—a countertop—and stood, his legs like two lead posts cemented in wet sand. His brain swirled in a fog. His vision skewed as if trying to see the world through oil drenched, opaque glass. Other raspy breaths chorused to each side of him, a higher, softer pitch to his left, a deeper, more resonating tone to his right.

Charlotte.

Eric.

At least he hoped.

He blinked once, twice, three times, a desperate attempt to shove the disorientation aside. Never had he felt so discombobulated. So out of sorts. He needed—no *had* to pull it together.

He took several deep breaths. Slowed his breathing, and glanced around the room.

A Wurlitzer jukebox in the corner. Black and white checkered floor tiles. Rounded stainless steel refrigerator, and red appliances.

No. It can't be.

He knew this place all too well. He'd been here a hundred times. His first root beer float was served to him at the chromatic kitchen table with the red-cushioned chairs, the one near the window, beneath a rare autographed picture of a grinning nineteen-year-old Elvis Presley standing with his arm around a waiter from some bar called the Dive Bomber. That waiter was Francis Winston Loudermilk ... a.k.a. Seyekrad.

In hindsight, it all made sense: the neighborly history teacher slash friend slash father figure who disappeared from sight. Rumor had it he'd become very, very ill and was going to die. Then one day, he emerged from his home, his clothes and hair all askew. He'd sit outside and stare at David's home. He'd mumble things at David as he walked by the house. The man he respected had turned into a deranged lunatic. So uncomfortably creepy and weird. It had been a long time since David stepped foot in Mr. Loudermilk's house. His skin tingled, not from excitement, not from flooding memories, but from ...

Panic.

Terror.

The rutseer! Finn coded it to find the crystals, which meant ...

They're here and Seyekrad has them!

Charlotte stumbled into David, her legs wobbling like rubber stilts. David caught her and pressed a finger to his lips.

Eric pulled himself up and balanced against the center island. "Why? Why is that the only way you know how to travel?"

"Shh," David said. "We're not in a happy place. We've got to get out of here. Follow me." He took a step toward the side door.

The house rumbled as if moving over rolling logs. David, Charlotte, and Eric froze. A voice filtered from a distant room. "Silence, you mollycoddled dullard. I'll only be a moment."

"Oh, no! Not good!" David shoved Charlotte and Eric through a door next to the refrigerator, and pulled it to without a sound. "Shh," he whispered again, "and pray whoever is on the other side doesn't need anything out of here."

David fidgeted with the ring on his forefinger. Footsteps padded across the floor on the other side, stopping just shy of their hiding place. *Go away*, David prayed, his heart ready to leap from his chest.

The refrigerator door opened. There was the rattling of ice, the clink of cubes hitting a glass. Water turned on and off in the sink. And then the footsteps retreated, fading into nothing.

David exhaled. "Good God, that was close."

"Who was that?" Eric asked. His tone suggested he already knew but was looking for confirmation.

"I'll give you one guess," David said. "This house used to belong to my neighbor before Seyekrad nached his body. Now it's his."

"Which means, if we're here, and the rutseer knows what it's doing, Seyekrad has the crystals," Charlotte said.

"Exactly," David said.

"If that's true, why are we standing around in this pantry hissing in each other's ears?" Eric quipped. "Let's find them and get back to Fallhollow."

"Wait." David pressed his ear to the door. He pushed it open enough to confirm the kitchen was empty, then motioned everyone out.

"Who do you think he was talking to?" Charlotte whispered.

David shook his head. "I don't know."

Eric pulled the chrome handle on the red refrigerator and peered inside. He shut the door. "What is this thing? How does it work? What's its purpose?"

"It's a refrigerator," David answered, "and it keeps food fresh and cold. I'll explain later. Right now, I'd like to know how he didn't sense us hiding in the pantry."

"That is curious," Eric said. "Even more so is what caused that massive rumble."

David shrugged. "Let's go find out."

Charlotte grabbed both their arms. "I have a better idea. Let's suppose Seyekrad *does* know we're here and he's luring us into a trap? I say we go to my house, talk about it, and come up with a plan that won't get us killed."

Eric and David looked at each other and shook their heads. "No," they said in unison.

David smiled. "I'm starting to like you more and more." He held up his hand, his palm facing Eric.

Eric paused, a perplexed look on his face. "What are you doing?

Why are we stopping? We haven't gone anywhere."

David suppressed a chuckle. "No. It's called a high-five. You take your palm and slap it against mine."

"Why?"

"It's a symbol of celebration when something good is said or done."

"And to what are we high-fiving?"

David lowered his hand and glanced at Charlotte, who smiled at him in return.

"Never mind, buddy," he said, patting Eric on the back. "Let's go hunt for some crystals."

David led them down a hallway trimmed with display cases housing medieval weapons, armor, and antique books. He grinned at Eric's wide-eyed expression. If he only knew how many other artifacts the ex-history teacher had in private collections and museums around the world.

The living room at the end of the hall looked exactly as it had when he'd last seen it. Lime green shag carpet. A white couch with pale pink rose buds on vines. An upholstered chair with white and lime green stripes.

And to his right, a wall lay open, revealing a stone wall lit with torches.

David's body locked. His brain seized in some sort of stoned paralysis.

"Looks like we found the source of the rumble," Eric said.

David willed his feet to move forward. "That wasn't here before."

Voices wafted on a breath of cool air from below.

The lair of the beast.

His stomach and heart swapped places. His pulse thumped in his ears.

"Crystals," Charlotte whispered, her voice rippling through him. "Betcha a duck against a donut they're down there with him."

Eric sidled around her and peered down the dark passage. He glanced over his shoulder and met David's gaze. *Ready?* he mouthed.

David nodded.

Cool air snapped against his face as he entered the chamber. The breath of death. He admonished the thought and followed the ramp downward, stopping short of entering a dimly lit room at the bottom. The aroma of pipe tobacco lingered in the air. David listened. The voices came from another room far away. He held his breath and stepped inside.

The room was immense. Built of stone, it spanned the length of the house. Wrought iron chandeliers hung from wood beams anchored to a high ceiling. Old, worn books stuffed the grand bookshelves, and papers, yellowed and crumbling with age, lay in stacks on the floor beside an overstuffed chair. Above the massive fireplace hung a vibrant tapestry, at least fifteen feet wide by fifteen feet tall, depicting peacocks, unicorns, and knights on horseback; goblets, chalices, and vases cluttered the mantel. Two arched doorways, separated by a scenic carving of dueling dragons and knights, punctuated the wall across from them, expanding the chamber even deeper still under the backyard.

"This is sick," Charlotte said.

"You're telling me," David replied.

Eric edged into the room, his gaze focused on a massive table topped with ancient scrolls, blueprints, and various sized parchments He took several steps toward it.

David's finger pulsed with warmth. He glanced down at his ring, now aglow in a vibrant blue. Two voices approached from the corridor furthest away.

Eric grabbed Charlotte and dived behind a sofa. David followed, tucking his legs to his chest as a door opened and two people stepped inside.

"I see you have acquired a new addition since yesterday afternoon," said a man as he sat on a cushion above Charlotte's head. She closed her eyes tight and covered her mouth. "Where did you get it?"

Eric's eyes narrowed. His jaw clenched. Anger settled on his brow. There was no doubt he knew who the voice belonged to, and more importantly, he was an enemy.

"Why, your father, the Baron von Stuegler, of course," said Seyekrad as he walked toward a hutch.

The man's nauseating voice blasted chills up David's spine.

"It was to have been a gift to you, Bainesworth, upon your claiming the Hirthinian throne. But you failed and now it's mine, a token for saving your insignificant life."

Bainesworth! David repeated in his head. *But I killed him! I put an arrow through him. He fell.*

"There are far more insignificant lives than mine who owe you favors and debts of gratitude, Seyekrad. Are you going to cash in on all of them?"

"When the time comes," he said. "Care for a brandy?"

"I'd love one."

Bainesworth rose and walked over to Seyekrad. Glasses clinked and there was a moment of silence before Bainesworth ordered another.

Liquid gurgled into a glass. "You gulped that down fast enough. What has you in such a dither?" Seyekrad asked. There was an edge of suspicion in his voice.

"An ill feeling, as if being watched." There was a brief moment of silence before Bainesworth continued. "Pay no mind. It must be my suspicious mind running away with me, as I am certain your mighty sorcery would detect anything or anyone out of ordinary."

David gulped, his heart beating in his throat.

"Quite right," Seyekrad said.

More liquid spilled into glasses.

"So, if you don't mind my asking, what is this mess strewn about the table?" Bainesworth asked.

"Papers that are of little consequence to you."

A glass clunked on the table. "You know, Seyekrad, I am getting rather irritated at your lack of trust in me. Remember, you were the one who approached me to help find and kill the paladin. As it is, you have nixed all of my ideas, and remarkably failed at every one of yours."

"I have not failed!" Another glass banged on the table. "You wait.

The rutseer I enchanted will find its way into the Eye of Kedge, and that bratty thorn of a paladin will have no choice but to bring it home. When he returns, I'll collect the Eye and you can remove his head."

David cringed. He didn't want to lose his head. He was, after all, rather partial to it. Maybe he should take Bainesworth's head, instead.

No, one side of his brain said. *That would-be murder.*

No, it wouldn't, the other side retaliated. *It would be self-defense.*

But.

No buts.

And so, it went, his conscience fighting with itself until Bainesworth silenced it.

"I look forward to ending his life after what he did to me, and Sir Trogsdill will be next. You have no idea how much I loathe his existence."

"You will have your chance to suffocate the life from him as well, provided you remain on my good side. You know how I detest disobedience, especially by those whose lives I've pulled from the abyss of death." Seyekrad stepped closer to his guest. "I can always return you to the place from whence you came."

"Do not threaten me, Seyekrad. You need me. Besides, it would be a shame for the Dragon King to discover there was a plot afoot, and his trusted advisor and confidant was being held against his will by the likes of you. I do not think that would bode well, do you?"

Seyekrad chuckled. "My, my. You do know how to play this game."

"Better than you can imagine," Bainesworth replied. "Now, what are these papers?"

"Nothing much. Historical documents and such, but here is what pleases me the most."

"Well, well," Bainesworth said, "an elaborate map of the Dragon King's prison beneath Lake Sturtle. Oh, I think this might suit our plans quite well."

Seyekrad laughed. "The Dragon King will have a long time to contemplate his *position* once we eliminate the paladin and the heir, and turn Gyllen and Berg castles over to their rightful scions."

Bainesworth chuckled. "Indeed." He lifted his glass in a toast. "To the demise of Hirth and the Dragon King."

The clink of glasses rippled through David's body. His hands turned cold. So they were in cahoots with each other to take over two kingdoms. But at the same time, they continued to do Einar's biddings. What was up with that? Were they really stupid enough to think they could betray Einar in such a way and live? And did they really think they could return the dragon back to the lair beneath Lake Sturtle? The thought almost made him laugh.

The men remained in the room for hours, eating, talking, conspiring, before extinguishing the lights and retreating down different hallways of the sanctum.

David, Charlotte, and Eric groaned as they stretched the stiffness from their bodies.

Upstairs, the wall rumbled closed.

"Oh, no!" Charlotte said. "No, no, no, no!"

"How did he close the door?" Eric asked, army-crawling from beneath the couch.

"Magic," David said, emerging from their hiding space after Charlotte. "How else?"

Rumble.

Rumble.

"No! Don't close!" Charlotte breathed, scrambling to her feet.

They ran up the ramp. Go!

Go!

Closer.

Closer.

Freedom.

So close. So close.

They hit the landing.

The door shut.

"No!" David banged his fist on the wall.

"You've got to be kidding me!" Charlotte said. "What the freak do we do now?"

"Look for a mechanism of some sort," Eric said. "All secret passageways have a device to make them open."

"Unless they're built by a sorcerer!"

The three of them felt along the walls, searching for a button, a switch, anything that would slide the door open.

David froze, his brain firing warnings. "Stop!" he whispered. "We can't do this. Even if we found the button or lever or whatever it is, this wall isn't exactly quiet. If this thing starts to open and Seyekrad didn't do it, he'll be on top of us like flies on crap."

"And if he comes around that corner down there and finds us here?" Charlotte asked. "Uh uh, wiener whiner. You can sit around and wait for that magical zip zap party if you want, but I'm getting out of here." She continued scanning the wall.

Eric smiled. "Fiery lass, this one is. I like her."

"Yeah, I bet you do," David muttered to himself. He rolled his fingers into fists and faced the back wall, enraged by the green beast coiling around his gut again. Gah! He hated feeling angry and jealous. It was not like him, but he couldn't stand the way Eric looked at her … or the way she looked at him. He should have told her how he felt a long time ago. Maybe there was still time. Once they got out of Seyekrad's dungeon and …

A door slammed shut downstairs. A light flicked on.

Panic held David's breath hostage. Who was it? Seyekrad? Bainesworth? He wiped his sweaty palms on his britches. Eric stood beside him, shielding Charlotte from whoever came around the corner.

Bare feet pattered across the floor below.

"Come on. Open the door," Eric whispered.

The wall rumbled.

David's mind raced. His heart thudded. *That's it. Come on.*

He jerked Charlotte in front of him and motioned for her to get ready to run.

She nodded.

A sliver of moonlight seeped through the narrow opening. A

shadow appeared on the wall below.

Charlotte slipped sideways through the opening, followed by Eric, then David. They ran in the direction from which they came, down the hall. Through the kitchen. Charlotte escaped through the side door.

Eric's foot caught the leg of a chair.

It hit the floor with a bang.

"Klutz!" David grasped Eric by an arm. One, two, three steps and they were outside and sailing over the porch railing. They disappeared into the woods and ducked behind a fallen log just as a wide beam of light illuminated the yard and trees.

Waves of energy distorted the air, bending. Pulsing. Seeking. Magic at its max. Minutes later the grounds fell dark, and the kitchen door slammed shut and locked.

David rolled to his back, his heart galloping like a racehorse vying for a win at the Kentucky Derby. "Whew, that was close."

"Too close," Eric said, getting to his feet. He glanced around. "Where's Charlotte?"

Alarm spread through David's body. She'd fled out the door before they did. He didn't see where she went.

A half a dozen flashlight beams, maybe more, swept the side yards between Mr. Loudermilk's and Mrs. Fenton's houses.

"Get down!" David said, tugging on Eric's pants.

He dropped to the ground and peeked over the log. "Who are they?"

"Police." David slid all the way down. "Get as low to the ground as you can and hope they don't have dogs."

The beams of light cut through the trees directly above them, lingering far too long on the area where they lay. An owl hooted to their right. David listened for Charlotte, but it was as if she'd disappeared.

The police combed both lawns, coming as far as the tree line, their lights illuminating the forest. Finding nothing, they retreated.

David waited before standing. He cupped his hands together, placed them to his lips, and whistled a dove call. He waited a few minutes and repeated.

"What are cops?" Eric asked, standing beside him, brushing leaves from his pants.

"Peace-keepers. They investigate crimes and disturbances, and arrest those committing them."

Footsteps approached from behind them. Leaves crunched beneath each step.

"David, Eric," Charlotte whispered. "What are you doing? Do you *want* someone to see you? Get in here."

David expelled a sigh of relief. "Charlotte!" He scrambled toward her.

Eric followed. "Are you all right, my lady?"

"I'm fine."

"Are you certain? You gave us quite a scare. If I may, might I suggest you do not do so again."

"Yeah, sure. Whatever. David, I followed the trail to the back of your house. There are cops everywhere. We've got to find somewhere else to hide. I thought about my parents', but to be honest, I think I'd totally freak them out, not to mention there are probably detectives living in my bedroom."

David ran his fingers through his hair and stared off into the darkness. An idea plowed into his head. He grasped her hand.

"I know just the place. This way."

Chapter 6

Eric

They moved as fast as the forest and the moonlight would allow. Trails disappeared beneath layers of leaves, and shadows danced among the trees, giving Eric reason to pause more than once. The land rose and fell, and small creeks and streams challenged them along the way. After some time, they emerged onto a road, its foundation unlike anything Eric had ever seen. He stood upon it, marveling at its smooth rigidity.

David called it pavement. He said most roads were covered with it, that it made it easier for the cars to travel on. When he asked what cars were, David ended the discussion with, "You'll find out soon enough." While Eric didn't care for the abrupt end to the conversation, the mystery intrigued him nonetheless.

They crossed the road and ran down a hill toward a metal fence. Off in the distance was a sprawling building, a couple of floors high.

"Really, David," Charlotte said. "We're going to hide in the school?"

"That is a school?" Eric asked, his heart thumping wildly. "For higher learning?"

David chuckled. "Not exactly. That's Havendale High. It's where Charlotte and I go to high school. If you lived here, that's where you would go, too."

"Fascinating."

"Yeah. Totally." David and Charlotte smiled at one another as David linked his fingers together, his palms up. "Up and over, missy."

Charlotte placed a hand on David's shoulder. "You do realize if anyone catches us, we're toast, right? We'll never find the crystals, or save Garrett and Gertie or Twiller's family. And how are we going to explain these clothes? We look like escapees from a Renaissance Faire."

"First, let's not become toast. Second, we will rescue Gertie and Garrett, and third, I don't think if anyone catches us, their first reaction will be, *Where did you get those clothes?* Now up and over."

Charlotte took the boost and jumped over to the other side.

David went next.

"Toast? What does that mean?" Eric asked, clambering over the fence.

"It means we'll be in deep trouble," David said.

"Oh. Then I agree. Let us not become toast."

They took off across the open field where two posts shaped similarly to Y's stood in the ground opposite each other. "Football,"

David said. "Don't ask." Eric didn't, but he would, eventually.

They rounded the side of the building and stopped.

Sprawling before them was a town with a road that went through the middle and stretched off so far in both directions, it got lost in the darkness. There was another road to the left, intersecting the main one. Gray lights dangled overhead on a line of some sort, taking turns flashing red, yellow, and green colors. Riding on the roads were a handful of loud, growling, metal contraptions of all shapes, sizes, and colors, each with four strange wheels and bright lights.

Cars, Charlotte pointed out, and while not dangerous on their own, the people driving them could be. He had no reason to doubt her.

Lining the roads were trees and establishments, most of which seemed to be closed for the night. The light changed and the few cars on the main road moved on, leaving the streets empty and quiet. Crouching, David led them down a small incline and onto what Charlotte called a sidewalk. Eric marveled at the surface and imagined how much easier it would be to get around if Fallhollow had similar structures. He'd have to find out how to make them and teach the king's architects once the war was over.

At the intersection, they crossed Main Street and headed down Clairmont. David jogged ahead and stopped before a small brick, two-story building with a large sign shaped like a cup, the words Java Joe's written in big letters across the front. The building was dark except for the right upstairs window. A shadow moved past the drawn curtains.

David scoured the ground, picked up a couple of pebbles and walked to the darker side of the building. He took aim and tossed a pebble at the side window. The stone pinged off the glass and fell to the ground. He tossed another. That one garnered attention.

A boy with dark skin shoved the curtain aside and opened the window. "Who's there? What do you want?"

"Jackson, it's me, David. David Heiland. I need your help."

Jackson leaned out the window. "David? Holy beeswax!" He spoke just a tad above a whisper. "Where have you been? You've got the whole world looking for you."

"I, we, need your help. Can you let us in?"

"Sure. Meet me around back."

The sash shut. The shadow of the boy vanished.

"Come on." David led them down the alleyway, turning the bend around what could only be a large garbage bin judging by its smell. Jackson opened the door.

"Oh my God, dude, where have you been?" He embraced David in a hearty hug and stood back. "And what is that you're wearing?"

Charlotte shot David a sideways glance. "See. I told you."

"Yeah, okay. Bite me. Jackson, you remember Charlotte. And this is my friend, Eric. He's not from around here so go easy on him."

"Can't promise anything. Come on in."

"Where are your folks?"

"Bristol. They're attending some coffee bean expo for the weekend. They'll be back tomorrow night."

Jackson led them down the hallway into a spacious room with

bright, colorful couches, plush chairs, and weird but interesting artwork on the walls.

"You want some joe?" Jackson asked.

"Good heavens, yes," David said, falling into a couch. "Nothing special, just make it hot and delicious."

Jackson grinned. "Charlotte, Eric, want anything?"

Charlotte yawned. "Tea for me, please, and a blueberry muffin if you have one."

"I'll take some tea as well," Eric said. "Black."

"Sure nuff. My Uncle Charles likes to drink black tea. He lives in Stevenage. Where abouts in the U.K. are you from?"

"He's not from the U.K.," David said.

"Oh. I'm sorry. I assumed by the accent you were British. Accept my apologies." Jackson addressed David. "Brazilian or Columbian?"

"Brazilian, please. Medium grind."

Within minutes, Eric fell hostage to the most aromatic scent he'd ever experienced. "What is that? I have never smelled anything so bold. So intoxicating."

"That," Jackson said, "is coffee, or what we around here call joe. Wanna change your order?"

Eric inhaled deep. "Yes, please. I'd like a cup of joe, instead." He doubted it would be the last time he drank it.

"Coming right up. Cream's in the fridge, sugar's on the counter."

"I'll get it," Charlotte said, winking at Eric as she passed.

He smiled, and his heart flipped. Was she being flirtatious? No. Certainly not. It was clear by the way she looked at David how much she adored him. But, there was something in the wink. A twinkle in her eye. A softness in her smile. *Ah, what are you gandering about, Eric? It was nothing more than a gesture of friendship and comfort, two things a man out of time and place needs. Maybe more so than the air in your lungs.* Still, he relished in the gesture, thankful he even had one to ponder.

A few minutes later, they were all sitting around in a circle, sipping, nibbling, and trying to sort out the world as it applied to them.

"Okay, so you've got to tell me what's going on." Jackson set his coffee mug down. "I swear to God, we have had so many cops and FBI agents swarming around this town over the last eight weeks. I mean—"

"What?" David gulped the sip he'd taken, and sat forward, almost dropping his cup on the short table they sat around.

"What?" Charlotte said. Clearly, it wasn't good news to them. "Did you say eight weeks? That's impossible. I figured it up this morning. You were out of it for two weeks and it took us two weeks to do everything else."

Jackson sipped his coffee and chuckled. "I don't know what time clock you've been looking at, kitten, but seein' as you guys disappeared January 4, and today's the last day of February, I'm thinkin' eight weeks."

David stared at the floor, his expression blank. "How? How is it even possible to manipulate time? Twiller never said anything about—"

"Who's Twiller?" Eric asked. "You've mentioned him a few times."

"He's a meadow—" Charlotte began, her voice, her expression lost in a daze.

David tapped her leg with his.

Charlotte brought her tea to her lips. "He lives in the same town where Garret and Gertie are. The last I heard he was on a sailboat with Jared and Mangus."

Eric swallowed hard. Mangus Grythorn. The general of the mage army. Jared's right-hand man. He'd said they were going on a diplomatic mission. More like they'd gone to collect allies willing to fight another war.

Jackson chuckled again. "The three of ya look like I just told you your favorite dog died. You wanna fill me in on what you guys are babbling about?"

"Sorry, buddy," David said. "We're tired. I guess days ran into each other and more time got away from us than we thought." He collected his coffee and pressed back into the cushion. "You were saying about the cops?"

"Yeah, right," Jackson continued. "Anyway, it's been like something out of a who-done-it novel around here. And school. Good God. Everyone is like flipping out, wondering if the two of you are dead or something. Military's been here, too. Air Force folk. Helicopters. Planes. Search teams probing the forest. They were called off about a week ago. And forget the track team. Dude, we haven't won a single freaking race without you. Not one."

"Sorry," David said. "It hasn't been a picnic where we've been, either."

"Yeah, and where has that been? Comic-Con? Pennsic? I mean, I like Ren Fest, too, but come on, dude. You couldn't change your threads?"

Eric sipped his coffee and set it on the table beside him. "That is the second reference you have made to our attire. Do you find it offensive?"

Jackson laughed. "No, dude. It'd take something really weird, and I mean *really* weird to offend me. But I can tell you it's not the norm, know what I mean? Jeans, tees, and sneakers. That's the norm."

Eric had no idea what he meant. Any of it.

"We had to borrow some clothes," David said. "It's a very long story, and one I'd love to share, but we're kind of in a situation. What we do need is a huge favor and you're the first person that popped in my head."

"Name it, man. Anything."

"We need to get into my house, but there are cops crawling everywhere."

Jackson grinned. Big. "And you need a distraction."

"Think you can provide one? I hate to ask. If my friend, Mirith, was around, I wouldn't have to."

Eric bit his tongue. If it hadn't been for Mirith, they wouldn't be where they were at the moment. Stupid dragon. Stupid, stupid dragon.

"They don't call me Jackson the Distraction for nothing."

David snorted. "No one calls you that."

"Hey, don't go hurtin' the feelings, man. Do I need to remind you? Homecoming. 2014. Bare Ass High versus their mighty rival, the Havendale Warriors."

"Bearss," David corrected with a grin.

"Hey, when you're telling the story you can tell it like you want." Jackson leaned back, his arm in the air, painting a picture as he spoke. "It was a cool autumn evening. Gentle breeze. Almost a full moon. Their king and queen had just been crowned and everyone was fanning their tears when suddenly, out of the nowhere—"

Eric's ears perked up. They had kings and queens in this place? They'd attended a coronation? He would have to get details.

Charlotte broke into laughter. "Oh my gosh, that was you? You were the pilot who flew over the field and unleashed all those rolls of toilet paper on their Homecoming Court?"

Jackson stood and bowed. "Pilot extraordinaire at your service."

Her laughter lit up the room.

Eric melted.

"Oh my gosh, I contributed to the t.p. fund!" she said. "You're a legend!"

"He's a criminal." David chuckled. "He was arrested as soon as he landed for stealing his dad's plane, and was sentenced to sixty days in a nursing home cleaning out bedpans."

"Well worth it, my dear," Jackson said, taking his seat. "Well worth it."

Eric sat back, listened, and laughed, even though he had no idea what a plane, a pilot, or toilet paper was. He had his suspicions on the latter, and hoped against hope it had been of the unused kind.

David scratched his temple and leaned forward. "Well, we're not going to need anything so grand tonight, just something distracting enough to draw all the cops from my backyard to the front yard. Have any ideas?"

Jackson smiled. "Oh yeah. Do I ever. Give me one hour, and I'll give you your distraction."

David gulped down the rest of his coffee and stood. "Thanks, man. I can't thank you enough." The two friends hugged again, this time with hearty smacks to the backs. "I don't think I need to tell you to keep this all a secret. You never saw us, okay?"

"Well, I didn't think you were asking me to distract them so you could stand on the roof and yell, 'Here I am!'" Jackson punched David on the shoulder. "Get outta here, man. Stay safe. And one day, you better fill me in on all this, okay? Something tells me you're going to be a legend, too."

"Yeah, we'll see."

Eric rose and clasped Jackson's outstretched arm. "Thank you for your assistance. I hope we meet again someday."

"I'm sure we will." Jackson turned to Charlotte and hugged her. Strings of electrical currents arced between her fingers and his arms. He arched his back and yelled, "Ouch! Damn, woman! What kind of personal power grid are you housing there?"

Charlotte's cheeks turned red. "I'm sorry. It's been happening every now and then. I don't know why. I hope you're okay."

"Are you kidding? I'm rock solid. It'd take a bit more than a few lightning bolts like those to knock me on my feet."

"You're so full of it," David said.

"Hey, dude, it's my story. I'll tell it like I want." Jackson smiled at Charlotte. "Keep my team captain safe, and if you ever need a place … "

"Thanks for everything," Charlotte said, pecking him on his cheek. No sparks from her lips. "We owe you one."

"Eeh. Your hand in marriage would be payment enough. We'll discuss the terms of your surrender when I'm the last man alive."

Laughter. A joke. Eric breathed a sigh of relief.

***

They scurried back toward David's home the way they came. The cool air bit at Eric's face as he pondered different distractions Jackson could pull off by himself. There weren't many he could think of. In fact, there were none. David, however, appeared quite confident that his very odd friend with the incredible joe could pull off such feat with no problem. Time would tell, and Eric reveled in the possibilities.

The hike back also provided a brief education in track and field, and football, the latter of which seemed almost as barbaric and entertaining as jousting. But why anyone would want to run for a sport seemed peculiar; however, the archery part appealed to him immensely, especially since it is where David seemed to excel. He challenged his newfound friend to a tournament, upon which, David laughed and said, "You're on, but be prepared to lose." Eric smiled. What a cocky fellow David could be.

They topped a small incline and David motioned for silence. In the distance, a majestic white manor, rich with massive columns and gargantuan windows, appeared like an apparition, sprawling tall and wide across a rolling landscape. A thick wall of hedges, at least fifteen-feet high, guarded the left side of the home, the line ending at the forest's edge. A huge fountain of a goddess, her arms outstretched to three jumping fish, graced an elaborate courtyard still sleeping from winter's chill. To the right was a sprawling brick cottage veiled in thick ivy. Beyond it—a spatial greenhouse with arched windows and an ornate glass dome.

And walking the grounds were three men dressed in uniforms.

They kept to the shadows amidst a thick cluster of oaks and hickory trees.

Charlotte pressed her back to a tree. "David, don't you find this strange? I mean, if we've been gone eight weeks, why are there still cops here? Why haven't they moved on to something else? Surely, we're not the only Havendale crime they have to solve."

"I don't know," David answered. "It is kind of weird now that you mention it."

"Not really." Eric said. "Where is the first place you'd probe if you wanted to ensnare someone?" He glanced at the men walking the grounds. "I doubt they are who you think they are."

"Great," Charlotte said, throwing up her hands. "You had to point that out, didn't you?"

David patted him on the back. "Thanks, buddy. I feel so much better now."

"Happy to be of service." Eric smiled. He looked over his shoulder at the house. "You know, I have to say, I never imagined you living in such opulence. You seem so … provincial." He kicked at the ground, a grin stretched wide on his face. David laughed and shook his head. "Better watch tossing out those insults, buckaroo. This hillbilly hick throws them right back."

Eric had no idea what a hillbilly hick was and he wasn't about to ask, but he liked that David could make fun of himself. There was hope for the chap yet.

But now it was time to get serious.

"I don't remember. Why do we need to get inside your home again?" Eric asked.

David scratched his nose. "Clothes, food, stuff we're going to need if we're going to hunt crystals. I also need to talk to Lily. I've got a gazillion questions."

Charlotte snorted. "Don't we all." She bit her bottom lip while she thought. "How are we planning to get inside?"

"When Jackson does his distraction thing, we're going to haul butt across the yard to the back door and pray to God the spare key is still inside the turtle's butt."

"Excuse me?" Eric asked, his brow tweaked. A horrible image fixed in his mind. He couldn't be serious, could he?

"It's a statue, dude, not a real turtle," David said.

"What about the alarm?" Charlotte asked.

"I'll take care of that. Once inside, you and Eric take the servant's stairs and go to my room. No lights."

"You have servant stairs?" Eric asked. The surprises never ended.

"Among a few other things."

"Hey, guys, we've got company," Charlotte said.

Three cops were heading their way.

They dropped to the ground behind a small slope

Beams of light cut across the forest.

Behind them, more footsteps.

Eric's heart skipped, flipped and flopped. He closed his eyes and listened. The gait. It was light, measured, an animal of some sort. Large, but gentle. No threat. He exhaled and opened his eyes. One of the cops unhinged a black object from his hip and aimed it into the dark.

"You in there! Come out with your hands up!"

The forest grew quiet. Still. The beam sliced over Eric's head and came to rest upon the face of a young buck standing a few feet away. The animal twitched its ears and bolted into the forest.

Eric gulped, his pulse racing.

The cop returned the object to his hip and the three headed back toward the house, their discussion on deer season, or rather the lack thereof, the topic of reflection and laughter.

Eric exhaled, his heart ready to take off after the deer.

"Wow, that was close," David whispered, rolling onto his back. "I can't believe he pulled a gun."

"What is a gun? What does it do?" Eric asked, his eyes still on the men, now halfway to the house.

"What's a … " David retorted. "Oh, that's right, you wouldn't know. They're weapons. They shoot these things called bullets that can kill you. Those cops, if they really are cops, they're experts, trained very well on how to use them, and they won't hesitate to do so."

"Then I won't give them reason to."

A loud boom vibrated the air and a blue flash streaked across the sky. It exploded into a crackling waterfall and fizzled out. More booms and cracks followed lighting the sky in an array of colors. "Oh, no," Charlotte said. "Please tell me he didn't."

David chuckled. "Oh yes he did. Oh, Jackson, you're a genius."

"What did he do?" Eric asked. "What are those things?"

"Fireworks," David said. "Are you ready to run?"

Boom!

Boom!

Boom!

The cops ran to the front of the house.

"Go! Now!" David grabbed Eric by the sleeve. "Run! You can watch them from my room!"

Eric ran, David and Charlotte puffing at his side. Around the fountain. Up the walkway. Onto the porch.

Boom!

Boom!

David grabbed a turtle statue from a table and fished a key from its butt. He unlocked and opened the door.

A loud, repetitive *Honk! Honk! Honk!* split the air.

Eric covered his ears.

"It's the alarm!" David shouted. "Char, get him upstairs!"

A tall woman with auburn hair and turquoise eyes ran at them through a doorway to the left, her eyes and mouth open wide.

"David! Charlotte! What are you doing here?" She embraced David for a moment before she pushed him back. "Never mind. You've got to go. Upstairs. Now. Through the music room. You know where. Go! Before they see you!"

A knock hammered at the front door. "Ms. Perish, open the door!"

Footsteps pounded the front porch. Shadows appeared in the windows.

David drew in a breath. He tugged at Charlotte and Eric. "Follow me."

They crouched and hurried down the hall into a spacious room. A strange looking harpsichord stood in one corner, a floor harp in another. Violins and a cello graced another corner. David lifted a wand from a music stand and inserted the thick end in a round hole obscured behind a gilded picture on a wall. A door opened inward revealing steps leading up.

"Are you freaking kidding me?" Charlotte asked. "I've known you how long and you've never told me about this!" She stepped inside.

"Never needed to." David pulled a cord, a mechanism on the wall turned, and the door closed.

More pounding on the front door.

"I'm coming!" Lily shouted. The alarm shut off.

"Bless the pixies of Halair that sound is done." Eric said.

They ran to the top of the stairs and exited through a wall into an elongated room that smelled of cedar. Eric paused for a moment, taking in the racks of clothes and shelves of shoes that surrounded them. In the center of the room were two small plush seats, and on the floor, a plush blue carpet littered with clothing.

Downstairs, Lily shouted, "You cannot barge into my home without a warrant! I demand you get out."

David thrust aside some clothes in what looked to be a dressing room, twisted an overhead light fixture, and pushed on the wall. Overhead, the ceiling moved, and a set of steps descended, leading upward to an attic.

"Well, this house is just full of all kinds of surprises you never told me about," Charlotte said, climbing up first.

Lily's stern voice could be heard again, this time a bit closer than before. "I did not give you permission to go upstairs or traipse through my house. I beg you to leave."

A man's voice answered. "Your alarm went off, ma'am. We have to—"

"I already told you, the alarm went off by accident, probably due to the fireworks still rattling my home and everyone else's in the vicinity. Why don't you find the culprit responsible for the ruckus instead of violating my privacy and intruding in my home?"

David urged Eric not to stick around to hear more of the conversation.

Like ants, they retreated into the darkness. David turned a knob in the floor and the steps retracted.

"David Arwen Highland," Charlotte said, standing in the middle of the dark room, her hands on her hips. "You and I need to have a serious conversation. What's with the secret rooms and those NASA sized telescopes by the window, huh? Whose antique bed is this?"

"Shh," he said.

Muffled voices entered his bedroom.

"Ms. Perish, please get out of the way."

"But there is no one here, Officer, and I don't appreciate the intrusion. I know my rights. You can't just barge in here on whatever whim you think is valid."

Doors opened and closed. Someone banged on a wall.

"There were others in the house," a man said. "Where are they? We saw shadows moving in the hallway through the window."

"There is no one else here. I don't know how many times I have to tell you. Now get out!"

Another man spoke from what sounded to be a room away. "We checked everywhere. There's no one else here."

"Just like I told you, *Officer*," Lily said. "Now get out of my house and off my property before I call the chief of police!"

The first man harrumphed. "Pardon our intrusion, Miss."

"I will not *pardon it*, and the next time you want to search my home, get a warrant."

"Oh, I'll do that, Ms. Perish. Have no worries about that."

Footsteps retreated. David dashed to a window and cracked opened the shutters. Four policemen and two plain-clothes cops got in their cars at the end of the cul-de-sac.

"More cops?" Eric asked, standing over David.

"Yes. And maybe an FBI agent or two."

"Explain."

Charlotte sat on the foot of the antique bed and ran her hands over the yellowed eyelet bedspread. "The FBI investigates missing person's cases."

Another boom, followed by a shower of gold and red sparks lit up the sky, this one further away.

The cars pulled out down the street, their lights flashing.

"Why do they think you're missing?" Eric asked. "Didn't you leave on your own accord?"

"No, they did not," Lily said.

David and Charlotte spun around.

Eric jumped at her presence.

"They were taken," she continued. She pulled David into her arms.

"Hi, honey." She kissed his temple. "How are you? How are you feeling?"

David stepped back. "I'm fine. Slavandria said I'm almost as good as new. When did you come back here?"

"The night you fell ill. I wanted to stay with you, but I had to return here to not raise suspicion. Forgive me?"

"There's nothing to forgive. I get it." David turned back to the window. "Who were they, those men?"

Lily swept the back of her hand across her brow and finger-combed the hair from her face. "There are two men that work undercover for Charlotte's father whom I know and trust, neither of which were here tonight. I've never seen those men before. They've been hovering around like vultures all day."

"Seyekrad's spies," David said.

"I didn't sense any magic about them, but that means nothing. I actually thought the same thing. Seyekrad could mask himself from me for months. Either my powers are getting weaker, or he has some black magic the devil himself wouldn't want to use."

Eric ignored the sudden sickness in his stomach. He hated being right. Sometimes.

Lily turned to Charlotte, her arms outstretched. "Hi, honey."

Charlotte hurried into her open arms. "Hi, Lily. How are you? How are Mom and Daddy?"

"Good." Lily brushed the hair from Charlotte's eyes. "We're all fine, but I'm a bit confused." Her eyes shifted from Charlotte, to Eric, to David. "What are you doing here? Slavandria didn't inform me you would be arriving."

"That's because she didn't know," David said. "We're here because Finn ferried us. Well, not exactly, but I'll get to that in a second. First, you've got to help Jackson. If they catch him, he'll be in so much trouble, and I don't want him to get in trouble for helping us."

"So that's who is responsible for all the racket." Lily smiled as if she should have known. "I'll be right back."

She vanished with a swish of her hand.

Eric's mouth quirked to the side. "She seems pleasant. How did you come into her care?"

David walked to the window and stared out. "She's my godmother, and Slavandria's sister."

Eric dropped his gaze. Of all the answers he expected, that wasn't one of them. It made sense, however, as he thought of it. Who better to hold the position of paladin than someone in the care of the most powerful mage family to ever exist? But how had the alliance been made? Who were David's parents? Why did David live in Havendale, in a world away, rather than in Fallhollow? What was the connection?

His thoughts scattered as Lily materialized in almost the same spot from which she disappeared. She wore a satisfied smile.

"Jackson is safe and sound and the café has been tidied. He wanted me to tell you it was the most fun he's had in months." She glanced between Eric and David and grinned. "Don't worry. He won't remember speaking to me. In fact, he won't remember anything from this evening. It's best that way."

Eric nodded even though his stomach turned. To think she could erase someone's memory at the snap of a finger didn't seem right. It was an invasion of the most personal kind, and yet, he knew deep down Lily was right. No one could risk the exposure, especially Jackson.

Lily sat on the edge of the bed. "So, tell me, David, why are you here? Did you meet your parents?"

David shook his head. "There was an incident. The queen was attacked, the crystals were stolen, and my parents are missing."

Lily frowned. "I'm sorry—what?"

David, Charlotte, and Eric sat on the bed and rehashed the day's events, from Trog's almost arrest to Seyekrad and their narrow escape from Mr. Loudermilk's house. Lily paced the floor, flicking her fingers around the room, setting magical boundaries as she listened. When they finished, she stood still, her back to them. With the flick of her wrist, an antique table lamp flicked on, casting a golden glow about the attic.

"Well?" David asked. "What are we going to do? How do we get the crystals back from Seyekrad without him killing us?"

"We have to find them first, David." She fingered the pendant around David's neck. "Rutseers, such as this one, are mere homing devices. They place the seeker within a certain radius of a missing item, not on top of it. They could be anywhere in Havendale, though it would make sense for Seyekrad to keep them close. From the sounds of it, he's set up an elaborate maze beneath that house. Without seeing the atelier, without testing its magical limitations, I couldn't and wouldn't give you a definitive answer to any of your questions. But I can tell you this, we're going to need some help and lots of it, and I know just the person."

"Who?" David, Charlotte, and Eric hooted together.

Lily smiled. "My sister, of course. Who else?"

Chapter 7

Eric

E ric sat on a plush couch almost twice his length and ran his hands over the sage green suede material. It was soft, but not overly so, comfortable yet troubling to the mind, like everything else in the house. Lights that came on with a flip of a switch. Rectangular black boxes on the walls that, when turned on, played sounds and moving pictures. Television, Charlotte called it. A form of entertainment. But it was too much noise, too much to take in, so he asked her to turn it off.

He wandered into the adjoining kitchen where David was busy smearing a light brown spread on multiple slices of bread he pulled from a clear bag. Eric looked around. "I am quite confused. Where is the bread from the oven? Come to think of it, where is your oven?" All that loomed around him were cabinets and steel boxes, some short, some tall, wedged in between them.

"The oven is right there on the wall, two of them stacked one on top of the other."

Eric pulled on the metal handle of the top box and peered inside at the smooth, shiny blue interior and metal racks. "This is strange. Where do you put your wood? Does that go in the one below?" He pulled open the oven door below only to become more confused.

"It's electric," David said, "like the lights, the alarm. Not many people have wood stoves anymore." He thrust a plate toward Eric. "Have a sandwich."

Eric hesitated, staring at the thin-sliced, uniform bread stacked three high with unrecognizable stuff in between, before taking it. "What do you call this concoction?" Eric held the sandwich to his nose and sniffed. Interesting. It was nutty. Delectable, even.

"A triple decker pb and j," David said, "and you're eating that one since you stuck your nose in it. I have extra strawberry, grape, or apricot preserves if you want some."

"Do you have hurtleberries?"

"Umm, that would be a big nugatory since I don't even know what a hurtleberry is."

"Then how do you know if you don't have one?"

"They're blueberries," Lily said, returning from the library with an over-sized black, leather-bound book in her arms, "and we don't have any, but I'll pick some up for you tomorrow." She made her way to the green couch and set the book down on the coffee table, shaking out her arms from the weight. "I've placed wards around the house to keep prying eyes or ears from seeing or hearing any of you, but keep up your guard. Vigilance is a must. Always." She sat in a plush chair beside the couch, and thumbed through the pages.

"What is that you're reading?" Eric asked, leaving David to construct his iffy edible masterpieces. The book looked familiar. Too familiar. He sat on the other side of Lily, his food on the table before him.

"It is called the Book of Telling, and it was given to me by my father many, many years ago for safekeeping."

Eric clipped his breathing. He swallowed to get his heart out of his throat. "You have the sacred mage book? I thought it was at Gyllen."

Lily shook her head. "There is a forgery at Gyllen. Close enough to appear to be the real thing, but upon careful examination one would see it is a humorous substitution." Lily smiled and leaned toward Eric. "My father can be quite the jokester."

"Your father is an evil warlord who enjoys inflicting pain on helpless, innocent souls." David set down two plates on what he called a coffee table. He returned to the kitchen and came back with three glasses filled with a dark, fizzing liquid and ice cubes he snagged from a large silver box standing upright against a wall. The refrigerator. "He grabbed me at the base of my neck and I thought I was going to die."

"And yet you're still here." Eric smiled. He couldn't help himself.

"Yeah, because he knew you wouldn't survive without my awesome archery skills and superior intellect," David retorted. A smile twitched at his lips.

Eric laughed, and it felt good. "I shall remember that, Sir Bow Man."

"You better," David said, taking a bite of his sandwich, "or I might have to kick your ass." He swigged back half his drink and belched.

Eric laughed again. "I'd like to see you try."

"David," Lily warned. "Watch your language."

"He started it," David said. "And ten-year-olds say worse stuff than that."

She gave him *the look* without lifting her face from the book. "I don't think I opened the topic for debate, did I?"

Eric smiled, the type of conversation all too familiar. Do this. Don't do that. Watch your posture. Be polite. It was exasperating. He brought the glass of the fizzy liquid to his lips. Intrigued by the tiny bubbles popping against his nose, he took a sip.

He spewed the drink halfway across the room. "Dragon's breath, that is retched!" He set the glass on the table, the liquid sloshing over the edge. He wiped the sticky fluid from his hand onto his pants. "You cannot seriously expect me to drink this!"

Charlotte held out a few paper towels. "No, but you can clean up your disgusting mess while I get you some water." She picked up his glass and took it to the kitchen.

Eric dabbed at the puddle on the table. "I am sorry, my lady. I assure you my manners are far more impeccable than this."

"No harm done," Lily said, "and please, call me Lily."

Her smile was like sunlight peeking through dark, uncompromising rain clouds. He allowed the warmth to flow over him, through him, thankful for the slight reprieve from the storm swirling within him. She returned to flipping through the massive book, each page of parchment crinkling as they turned.

He glanced over his shoulder at Charlotte. "Do you have a cloth of some sort? These paper things you gave me are flimsy and fail at their task." He placed them on the edge of his plate.

A small towel sailed across the room, thumping him in the face. Charlotte laughed. "Sorry."

Eric returned her smile. "I'll remember that one." He glanced at Lily while he wiped the table. "You seem intense. What are you looking for?"

Charlotte set down his glass with ice water beside his untouched sandwich and returned to her place beside Lily.

"I am almost certain there is a section in here related to finding and retrieving the crystals should they ever become lost or stolen. I know synching the key to the rutseer is the first step, but there are many more undertakings which involve spells and enchantments. I need to find them."

"And when you're done, let me read it so I can understand all this crap that has happened to me," David said. "It's all in there, right? Why I was chosen? Why I have this tattoo, which, by the way, has been super quiet."

"Be thankful for that," Lily said. "When it starts aching again, you'll know Einar is on the move."

"So, this thing on my chest is nothing but an early warning system?"

"That, and a summoner."

David choked and coughed. "A summoner?" David asked, spittle dripping from the corner of his bottom lip. "Of what?"

"Spells. Magic," Lily said. "Together the ring and the mark wield great power, but only when the time is right. It is nothing you can control, so do not go seeking it."

Eric nudged David. "Well, aren't you the lucky one."

Charlotte rolled her eyes and tucked her legs beneath her. "Lily, why do you think Seyekrad was oblivious to us in his house?"

"I was wondering that myself," David said. "He's never had difficulty sniffing me out before."

"It is odd," Lily said. "Odder still is that I didn't detect any of you, either. I thought perhaps Seyekrad had put an anti-detection charm over the area, but he wouldn't have included the three of you in the protection. It doesn't make sense."

Charlotte laid back, her hair draped over the back of the couch, her eyes closed. "Nothing makes sense, including why Seyekrad would want to steal the crystals."

"That's easy," Eric said. "If he has them, he controls the war. He can use them as leverage. The mages will not want him to use them. Einar will, but not under Seyekrad's terms."

"He'll also use them to bring David into the open," Lily said. "You've got to remember, he's playing both sides against the middle, appeasing both Einar and Bainesworth to get what he wants."

"Like a typical mage," Eric said, bitterness curling his tongue. "Always interfering where he shouldn't."

"Not all mages interfere," Lily said.

Eric cast a sideways glance at her. "Really? Because my experience says otherwise, as does David's."

"What my sister and I have done is not the same thing as what Seyekrad or the High Council is doing." Her voice carried a sharp edge. "Are there any other assumptions you'd like to make?"

Her tone, the dipped eyebrows, the piercing eyes, they all boiled his blood. He wanted to tell her she wasn't supposed to interfere with the affairs of men, ever, whether asked to or not, and yet she and Slavandria did, on a regular basis, just like the other mages. Just because they did good deeds didn't change the fact they weren't supposed to intercede at all. Not that he minded the help. In fact, he welcomed it, but to lie about it and then pretend they weren't breaking their own rules was a gross hypocrisy. Still, he kept his mouth shut. After all, turning his only ally in this world against him would be harebrained at best. This fight he would be happy to concede.

"No, ma'am," he said with a sincerity that surprised even him. "I apologize for overstepping."

David shook his head and snorted.

Lily placed a hand on Eric's leg. "I know what you're thinking and I understand. But sometimes we all must step outside the lines to do what is right. To state you have not done the same as Trog's squire would be duplicitous, wouldn't you agree?" She withdrew her hand and didn't wait for an answer. "As I was saying, we now know that Seyekrad has a motive. He wants Hirth for himself. To do that, he needs to eliminate the one person who can stop him, and that's you, David."

"Thanks," David said. He ran his palms over his face and yawned. "You're such a joy to talk to lately." He stretched his arms above his head.

"I only speak the truth. You are the paladin, and that means a great deal to Einar and Seyekrad. If they eliminate you, then they are one step closer to absolute power."

"You know, I keep hearing that, but I'm not the one who can kill Einar. Only the heir to the throne of Hirth or Einar's offspring can do that, and I'm pretty sure Mirith is probably dead because of some stupid gargoyle."

"Don't underestimate him," Charlotte said. "That little dragon is tough. Maggot is probably wishing he'd never tangled with him." She glanced at Lily. "But David is right. You'd think Seyekrad would be chasing this heir person, too, and not just David."

"That's because Seyekrad doesn't know who he is … yet," Eric said, "and I mean to keep that way."

Charlotte sat forward. "You know who the heir is? Why didn't you tell us?"

"Because, it didn't seem important until now."

David eyed him speculatively. Moments ticked by. "Well, who is it? Is it someone we know?"

"Be careful, Eric," Lily warned. "The fewer that know, the better for all involved."

"No," David said. "He brought it up. He needs to finish it." David sat forward his hands clasped between his knees. "We're waiting. Who's the heir?"

Eric held Lily's gaze, hoping she would see the plea in his eyes and come to his aid, but she sat back, her lips closed, her fingertips tapping on the chair arms.

What a conundrum he was in. If he told them his secret, he would betray Trog's trust, not to mention, he'd put all of them in danger. But withholding the secret was tearing him apart. Trog had once said secrets were grave burdens to bear, and he wasn't lying. Maybe Trog could hold secrets for years, but he needed to share it with someone. He needed to unload the heavy burden. If Sestian were around, he'd confide in him. But Sestian was gone. He had new friends now. Friends he needed to trust. Friends who he hoped would understand, and never betray him. He had to take the chance. He had to risk it all. So far, his instincts had been right. He had to trust himself. He had to follow his gut. He picked up the sandwich, and said in the most nonchalant tone he could muster, "I am," then took a bite.

Silence drowned in his revelation.

Then came the disbelieving nervous laughter.

"You? The heir?" David said.

"It's true," Lily said, fixing him with steely eyes.

"But how is that possible?"

"Long story," Eric said.

"We're listening." David shifted in his seat.

Eric took another bite of his sandwich, and another, taking his time to decide how much to reveal. After all, they didn't need to know everything. He still didn't know everything. But talking about it was helping to sort it out. Maybe if he didn't act as if it were a giant thing, they'd be willing to take what he wanted to share, and leave the rest alone until he was ready to tell them more. "It's not a big thing, really." He sucked the remnants from his fingers. "My father is the king's brother. I'm the next in line." Clean. Simple. To the point.

"Funny," Charlotte said, sitting forward, "I was in that castle for two weeks and never did I hear one word about the king having a brother."

"Yeah," David said. "And if you're a prince, the hallowed heir to the throne, why are you Trog's squire? That's like one of the most dangerous positions there is. I mean, you go to war. That's what you do. It's not like you can throw your hands up and go, '*Nope, I've decided to sit this war out because I'm a prince. Have fun on the battlefield. Ta Ta. I'll be in my room reading.*'"

Eric's jaw flexed. "That goes to show how much you know. *Because* of who I am, I was never allowed to do anything that would put me in harm's way. I have been sheltered and treated like a child my entire life, only allowed to do certain things, and all under the watchful eye of four knights and my king. I have jousted. I have been in tournaments. I sharpen and shine blades and armor, but that's about as close as I've been to anything remotely life-threatening. Well, except for almost being killed by the mages in Avaleen, or being plucked from my horse by Einar, or the day we escaped from Berg, but trust me, if any of my overseers had their way, I wouldn't have been there that day. Their constant attention has been stifling, annoying, and belittling, and I hated every second of it."

"That must have been horrible for you," Charlotte said, "being trained for a role you couldn't play."

He looked into her eyes and the wall he'd constructed around himself rattled at its foundation.

Eric tried to swallow, but his swelling emotions made it difficult. Did she really understand? "It was. That's why I came looking for you." He shifted his eyes to David. "You see, my friend Sestian and I thought if we could team up with the almighty paladin, we could get our masters to notice us for something more than lackeys. Imagine my surprise to find out the paladin was nothing more than a magician's apprentice, and my life was nothing more than a lie." He dropped his gaze to the floor.

"I know what you mean," David said. "It sucks being lied to. Manipulated. At least you know who your parents are."

Eric frowned and nodded. "Trust me. That bit of knowledge brings its own plethora of problems."

"You can say that again," Charlotte said, unfurling her legs and sitting forward. "Parents are strange creatures, puppies one minute, and piranhas the next. That's why it's nice to have friends you can confide in." She reached for her glass and sparks crackled from her fingertips. She yanked back her hand and shook it. "Ouch! Gosh darnit that hurts. I hate it when it happens."

"How long has that been going on?" Lily asked.

"I don't know. A few weeks I guess, but I don't want to talk about it right now." She turned back to Eric. "So, how about it? Spill it. Who's your daddy?"

A wave of unease washed over Eric. His mouth dried into a desert. He stood with casual ease, thankful no one could see his insides trembling like a string of bones rattling in a gale force wind.

There were too many eyes on him. So much silence.

Such absolute silence.

Except for the ticking of the clock on the wall and the rapid ba boom, ba boom of his heart.

He had to tell them. It was the right thing to do. David and Charlotte deserved to know. But the truth was a dangerous thing, to him and to everyone who knew it. It was also difficult to utter aloud, as if doing so would bring death to all of them.

"We're waiting," Charlotte said, getting up and going into the kitchen. She put more ice cubes in her glass and added water from the big silver box.

"I'm trying, but it's not easy," Eric said.

"We're your friends," Charlotte said. "There's nothing you can't tell us."

"You don't understand. This is … *complicated.*" Panic skittered through his bones. He wasn't prepared for this. Not now. Not ever. Why did he have to open his mouth? Why did he have to say anything?

"You're stalling." She raised her glass to her lips.

"It's all right," Lily said, taking his hand and giving it a gentle squeeze. He hadn't even noticed she'd stood or moved beside him. "You've come this far. You acted on your initial instinct. Now you must see it through." She let him go and entered the kitchen where she stood, her arms wrapped tight to her.

Eric blinked, considering, debating with himself. "Fine. Fine," he finally said. "You want to know who my father is?" *Go ahead. Say it. Release the beast.* He licked his lips. "It's Sir Trogsdill Domnall, Master and General of the King's army extraordinaire." *The man you love and hate. The man who kept this secret, made me love him, and then hate him for his lies. The man who tortured me for years, making my life a living hell, but protected me with his life.* "Are you happy now?"

There he was, open and exposed. Naked. Vulnerable. He wished he could wake up and find the whole conversation to be a bad dream.

David's jaw fell open.

Charlotte dropped her glass.

It shattered across the universe.

***

Eric retreated to David's bedroom and collapsed on the bed, unable to stop the flow of tears. He'd held them in for far too long. Sestian's death. His life. War. It was all too much. He'd tried to remain strong. Resilient. He was, after all, a squire. Squires didn't cry. Squires didn't show weakness or emotion. They were responsible for absorbing everyone else's pain and grief, to provide solutions, not exasperate a problem. They weren't allowed to break, and yet, as he lay there staring at the ceiling, he'd never felt more damaged, fragmented, as parts of him he used to know vanished into oblivion. His innocence, his playfulness. Gone. Destroyed by a beast who felt he could take whatever he wanted, when he wanted, with no regard to life.

He was thankful David and Charlotte didn't follow him. They probably needed as much time as he did to process the truth, and while it was difficult to force the truth from his mouth, he was glad he'd done so. Now the burden wasn't only his to carry.

Time passed, as did the sorrow. Eric sat on the edge of the bed and studied the room flooded in moonlight. On the nightstand were two framed pictures, one of a woman with shimmering blond hair and a radiant smile; the other of a clean-cut, stately man with dark hair standing beside a sleek, metallic winged vessel. David's parents perhaps? He studied the picture for quite a while before noticing the larger, more colorful pictures on the walls of the same craft. He picked up the picture and walked around the room, reading the words on each vivid display.

F-22 Raptor.

Air Supremacy.

Strength.

Stealth. Shoot before seen.

There were people sitting inside the flying machines. He glanced down at the picture in his hand.

His heart fluttered. Every butterfly in all the worlds migrated to his stomach. Could these mechanical wonders fight dragons? Could they win? Did David's father know how to fly one of these steel dragons? Was that why he was in Fallhollow, to inform the mages of these magnificent machines?

He put the picture back where he got it and turned his attention to the trophies in the corner, all with archers on the top. There must have been three dozen if not more, all different sizes and colors. A smile tugged at his mouth. So, David *was* as good as he said.

On a couch he found two cases, one empty, the other housed an exquisite longbow of kingwood and oak. He plucked it from its case and held it up, the string pulled back to his cheek. It felt light. Smooth. Perfect. A paladin's weapon.

Sitting on shelves above the couch were framed papers: National AP Scholar Award, U.S. Presidential Scholars Award, National Honor Society, American Citizenship Award, and they went on and on, some duplicates, but the dates were different, and none of them coincided with dates in Fallhollow. How was that even possible? How could time be so similar yet so different? It was no wonder David felt so out of his realm, so confused while in Fallhollow. Time had a way of changing everything, even perceived reality.

He continued his way around the room, examining every item, his interest piqued more and more with every discovery. Pens with built-in tubes of ink. Fans that spun in the ceiling.

He kicked at the items on the floor, moving them aside so he didn't step on them. There was another television like the one downstairs, hanging on the wall, and a shiver crept up his spine. He knew what that did and wanted no part of it. Beside his feet was a dark brown seat of some sort that crinkled at his touch. Curious, he sat down in it and smiled at the way it engulfed him. He wiggled his butt in and stretched out his legs, his arms dangling over the side. Something hard dug into his hip. He shifted a bit and withdrew a black rectangular object with multiple colored buttons buried in the folds of the seat. There were strange words stamped upon each one.

VOL. CH. REW. FF. 3D. AUX. STEREO. POWER.

Hmm. What do these do?

Eric started pushing buttons.

Noise, loud and wailing, blasted from two boxes on either side of the television. He scrambled to his feet his palms to his ears. *Turn it off!* He picked up the culprit and pressed every button. One of them had to work.

The television sprang to life. A moving picture of a guy dragging a creature in a large sack with strings appeared. Two thin, flat black boxes turned on. A sleek silver box whirred and a black tray popped out.

The door to the bedroom flew open. David rushed inside, grabbed the object from Eric's hand and turned everything off.

"H-how did you do that?" Eric stuttered, his ears still ringing.

David pointed to the power button. "This one. It controls the off and on." He tossed it back into the squishy chair where Eric was sitting. "Are you okay?" he asked, his concern genuine.

Eric shook his head. "Yes. No. I don't know. What was that noise that assaulted my ears?"

"Noise? Dude, that was Led Zeppelin, possibly the greatest rock band known to mankind."

"It is one of our many versions of music," Charlotte said, standing in the doorway. She flicked a switch on the wall and lamps on either side of the bed came on.

"Music? I heard nothing but caterwauling," Eric said.

David laughed. "Remind me not to play you any Metallica."

Eric sat on the bed, his breathing returning to normal. He pointed at the lamp beside the bed. "How does that work?"

"Electricity," David said. "Just like the oven. It powers just about everything in our world."

"Even them?" He pointed to the replica of the F-22 dangling from the ceiling fan.

"No. Those aren't real. They just hang there looking all bad."

"But they are models of real ones, right? Do real ones use electricity?"

"Yeah, kind of, but those are a lot more complicated."

"How so?"

"They require fuel, and not just any kind of fuel. It's like kerosene, but better. But it's not the fuel that makes these babies supreme." He opened a drawer in a nightstand and withdrew another plane identical to the ones hanging.

"Oh, Lord, here we go." Charlotte plopped on the bed and curled up with a pillow.

David ignored her. "These planes are like the Jared's of all planes. They have incredible stealth capabilities and can maneuver like nothing you've ever seen. The sensors, they allow the pilots to track, identify, shoot, and kill air-to-air threats before being detected. And you know what the great thing is? They're damn near impossible to detect on radar. Plus, they have super cruise capabilities, which means they don't have to use the afterburners to go the speed of sound."

"S-speed of sound? That's impossible." Nothing could travel that fast.

"Yep, and these babies can pretty much blow anything out of the air and off the ground before anyone sees them coming. They don't call them F-22 Raptors for nothing."

"Can they blow up a dragon?"

David froze, the animation in his face gone. "What?"

"Can it destroy a dragon?"

Charlotte sat up, her face twisted in confusion. "You've got to be kidding me. Is he thinking what I think he's thinking?"

"I don't know. Are you thinking what we think you're thinking?"

"Answer the question. Can these things kill Einar?"

"Umm, I suppose so, but that's kind of impossible at the moment," David said.

"Why? I thought you said they had all these fighting capabilities."

David put the plane in the drawer and shut it. "They do, but … "

"But what? Can they or can they not destroy Einar?"

"Yeah, I'm pretty sure they can destroy ten Einars before they knew what hit them, but that's not the problem."

"What is?"

"One," Charlotte said, "how are you going to get one into Fallhollow? Two, even if we figured that one out, you don't just walk onto an Air Force base and ask to borrow one of the most expensive military planes ever built. Third, we don't know anyone who could fly one."

"My dad could," David said.

"Well then," Eric said. "I suppose we need to get busy and find your father, don't we?"

132

Chapter 8

David

David rolled over and stared at the model F-22 dangling from the ceiling fan, Eric's preposterous idea turning over in his mind. The guy had only been in this world for less that twenty-four hours and already wanted to steal a billion-dollar aircraft, somehow take it back to Fallhollow, and blow up Einar with it. While David had no problem with the result, pulling it off would be next to impossible. It was an insane idea, yet ...

The smell of coffee and bacon begged him to get up, but he'd forgotten what it felt like to sleep in his own bed, with a real pillow and all the luxuries of home. Never again would he take it for granted. While the fineries at Gyllen Castle were extraordinary, they had nothing on memory foam beds, hot showers, or disposable razors.

He wondered how Eric managed through his first night in the 21st century. Did he feel as out of place as David felt his first night in Fallhollow? It was difficult enough going back in time. Going forward in time must have its own WTF moments, too. He rolled out of bed and padded out onto the landing and down the hallway to Eric's room. The door opened after a single knock.

David yawned. "I was just checking on you. Seeing how you slept."

"All right, for the most part." Eric scratched his head all over. "I like the bed, though I'm not too fond of the floral décor."

"Yeah, I get that. Sorry. I should have probably searched out a better room. It's just this one was the closest to mine."

Eric stretched and flexed his arms over his head. A scar, at least eight inches in diameter puckered like a full moon in the center of his back. He tried to imagine what had caused it, the pain he must have suffered. And it wasn't the only one. There were many, each with their own story.

David glanced at the floor and rubbed the back of his neck. "I take it you found the bathroom okay and figured it all out? I guess I should have given you the ten-cent tour of how that all worked."

Eric faced David, his shirt wadded in his hands. "Einar did it. The scar on my back. He skewered me with a talon."

"I'm sorry. I didn't mean—"

"It's okay, and to answer your question, yes, I figured out the toilet. It's brilliant."

David swallowed. He could almost feel the wound deep in his chest as it ripped open. The agony. It must have been … there was no word to describe it. And how had he survived? By all reasoning, Eric should be dead, but he wasn't.

His brain throbbed with questions begging for answers that had no logical explanations. Perhaps someday the mysteries would unravel. Right now, he needed air.

"Good, good. Umm, I need to take a shower, get dressed. If you want, you can rummage through my closet and find something clean to wear. I think you and I are about the same size. If you want to take a shower, feel free to. It's in the bathroom behind the glass doors. Just pull out on the knob and turn the handle to get the right temperature of water. There's soap and shampoo. I'm sure you'll figure it out."

Eric smiled. "I'm sure I will, but thanks."

David nodded and retreated to his room. He shut the bathroom door a moment later and lingered in the shower until the water turned cold, his mind a knotted mess of worry over his parents, Gertie and Garret, Mirith, Finn, the crystals. When would the nightmare ever end? When would life return to normal? Was there such a thing?

He dressed in a t-shirt and a pair of jeans and took the servant's steps to the kitchen, following the laughter and chatter to the formal dining room. He turned the corner and jolted to a stop.

Slavandria sat at the head of the dressed table, her elbows on the arms of her chair and her fingers steepled to her lips, waiting. At the serving table stood Eric and Charlotte, both dressed in jeans, t-shirts, and sneakers. They both glanced his way as he entered the room. As always, Charlotte greeted him with a smile that melted the very fabric of his being. He pushed the emotion aside and returned a half-smile. The days of pining for her were over, the decision made in the middle of the night upon waking from a horrid nightmare in which his indecision left her dead. The thought was more than he could bear. He had to move on without her. He had to. To protect her from the danger that followed him. She was home, and he'd do everything he could to see she stayed here, even if it meant leaving her and everything he treasured, behind.

Eric dipped his chin in acknowledgement, and raised a glass of orange juice.

In that instant, David *saw* Eric and Trog. They had the same square jaw, the same eyes, only Eric's were a darker green. The same build. While other features were different, there was no mistaking he was Trog's son. He wished he could wrap his head around the fact Trog had a family. A son.

Eric probably did, too.

David eyed Slavandria as he pulled out a chair and sat down. So Lily had summoned her to help with the crystals. How sisterly. In the center of the table lay his bow and quiver, and Eric's sword and scabbard. His stomach twisted. Their presence only meant one thing, and he was pretty sure it had nothing to do with playing the roles of archer and swordsman in a local Renaissance faire.

Lily approached from behind and placed a hand on his back. "You might want to get something to eat. We have a lot to discuss."

Eric and Charlotte sat down across from him, their plates stacked with pancakes, bacon, scrambled eggs, and fruit. Lily poured coffee from an ornate silver coffee pot that had never seen the outside of a china cabinet, at least not since David could remember. It had been polished to a mirrored shine, their reflections distorted. Creepy. Like a funhouse mirror.

He made his way to the buffet table and listened to the small talk behind him as he loaded his plate. Eric marveled at how strange but comfortable his clothes were, and how well he slept. Charlotte thanked Lily for the fresh squeezed orange juice and the change of clothes. But despite the laughter and lightness to the conversation, there was a palpable tension and unease that hung in the air like a thick, toxic fog. Breathe too deep, and one might die from the strain.

There was no doubt this meeting was important. Slavandria's presence made it so. He had to admit there was a part of him that craved the answers only she had, but how willing would she be to give up the knowledge? That was the grand question. He returned to his seat and picked up his fork.

"I am happy to see the three of you are all right," Slavandria said, her lavender hair shimmering in the sunlight from the window. "As you can see, I brought some items you left behind due to your rapid departure from Fallhollow." Her gaze fell to the weapons on the table. She glanced to her left. "How are you feeling, Charlotte? Anything unusual going on?"

Charlotte wiped her mouth and shook her head. "I'm fine. In fact, I was telling Eric this morning that I never felt better. Stronger almost. I am having some weird tingles shooting throughout my arms and legs which sometimes makes me shock people when I touch them, but when I talked to Lily before I went to bed last night, she said she's pretty sure it'll wear off."

Slavandria nodded, her eyes on Lily. "Yes, I agree. More than likely it's a remnant of some leftover magic you came in contact with."

Charlotte dragged a piece of egg around on her plate with her fork. "I'm not too worried about it. Have you heard from Finn? Is he okay?"

"No, I haven't heard from him," Slavandria said, sipping her coffee. "By the time I arrived at the cottage, there was nothing left but a shell of a home. An *indicium* spell revealed an intense skirmish with the three of you being hurled out of there by a powerful *expulso* spell. Finn, Mirith, and Maggot vanished separately. I have yet to locate them, but sestras have an entire realm of magic I don't understand. I can only hope they are safe."

Charlotte laid down her fork. "That makes me feel better."

David picked at the food on his plate. Why had Slavandria brought attention to Charlotte's *shocking* side effects? And what was with the odd exchange of glances between Slavandria and Lily? Was there something more they weren't revealing? It wouldn't be the first time. Either way, he'd have to keep an eye on Charlotte. Maybe it was residual magic, but he didn't think so. If only she remembered when it started.

"Thank you for bringing our things to us," David said, "but we all know that's not why you're here." He gave Slavandria a flat stare. They sat in silence for a brief moment, the only sound that of knives and forks scraping over china.

"No, it is not." Slavandria leaned back in her chair. "However, Charlotte's shocking health problem has my curiosity piqued. I want to hear all about it as well as how you escaped the Elastine Forest."

Charlotte paused, her cheeks stuffed like a hamster's. "Wha'?" She swallowed her food and gulped her juice.

Eric's eyes widened. A smile of disbelief lit his face. "Is that true? You escaped from the Elastine Forest?"

Charlotte snorted. "You make it sound like I won the Noble Peace Prize." She placed her napkin on the table and hunched over, her hands in her lap. "I didn't do anything, really. It was Mirith. He was the one who got us out of there."

Slavandria leaned forward, her arms folded on the table. "Mirith was on the brink of death, weak and unresponsive. Queen Mysterie said she was struggling to hold onto hope until you came. She said it was you who saved them, but she could not shed any light on the mystery."

"I swear to you I didn't do anything. It was Mirith. He blasted a hole in the invisible barrier around the forest."

"How, Charlotte? I must know every detail. Please don't make me extract the information the hard way. I think you would find it most unpleasant."

Her threat jumped on David's back and clung to his spine like an alien creature, its fingernails raking across David's throat, choking his words. Surely, she must know she'd have to kill him first if she wished to bring any harm to Charlotte.

"I'm telling you what I know. He popped his tail over his head and launched a lightning bolt."

"Think," Lily said. "Tell us the story. Tell us what happened. Even down to the smallest detail you don't think matters. It is an inescapable prison, protected by magic so dark, our own father cannot go near the wood's edge without suffering severe nose and eye bleeds. Perhaps the secret of your escape will uncover Einar's weakness."

Charlotte gathered her hair over one shoulder. "Oh my gosh. Fine. Okay. I'll tell you the story. It all started when Trog was taking us to Gyllen Castle."

David closed his eyes and listened to a story he'd never forget.

Chapter 9

Charlotte

Charlotte fell from great heights and crashed through the trees, smashing limbs as she plummeted to the ground. She hit the earth like a garbage bag filled with pea soup, her body as broken as the trail of branches she left behind. She stared at the stars twinkling through the hole in the canopy as darkness overcame her.

Minutes or hours later, she wasn't sure which, she woke, the sky black as tar, sprinkled with shimmering sequins. She lay there for the longest time, at first unable to move, and then too scared to do so. Finally, she rolled onto all fours and with laboring breaths, stood. The cool air brushed over her scraped and bloodied arms and the grass was icy wet beneath her. She cupped her bruised ribs, baffled as to how she wasn't broken into a thousand pieces. A breeze lifted her hair and soft bells chimed all around her. She followed the sound, her gaze pinned to the ground.

All around her on the forest floor was a carpet of dark purple. Thousands of stems bearing white flowers shaped like bells protruded from within the tapestry. With every light breeze, the bells would sway and the purple pendulous stamens would circle the inside of the delicate petals, each patch of flowers playing a different note, all coming together in a haunting, melodious tune. Charlotte turned around, taking in her surroundings where the foliage was a strange bluish-green and tiny, flighty, winged creatures fluttered from tree to tree with a wild, free sound that filled the forest.

"Where the heck am I?"

"The Elastine Forest," said a female voice behind her. "It is where Einar imprisons all women and children he captures."

Charlotte startled and turned, her gaze falling upon a graceful woman with long black hair and gray clothing. She was standing in a sliver of moonlight, her face was soft, her eyes gentle despite the drawn features. She walked toward Charlotte with the grace of a gazelle and said, "My name is Mysterie." She offered her hand to Charlotte.

Charlotte's mouth hung open. "I-I'm Charlotte," she said. "Y-you're the queen of Hirth."

The woman smiled. "Yes, I am."

"Oh my gosh! Everyone is looking for you. We've got to get you out of here. We've got to get you back to Hirth."

The woman laughed softly. "If only we could. Four days I've walked the perimeter looking for a way out, but this fortress is well sealed."

"But that's impossible. There's always a way out, even if it means we go over or under."

"I've tried digging, but the soil burned my hands." Mysterie held out her blistered palms for Charlotte to see. "Climbing the trees is out of the question. Once you climb so high, they bend and stretch like soft taffy, and of course, they only bend inward." She smiled and it held a hint of sadness. "I had hoped the dragon could help, but I fear he's dead."

Charlotte's eyes widened. "What dragon?"

"He arrived a short while before you. Strange looking creature. He's over here."

Charlotte followed Mysterie deeper into the woods, stepping over and through the underbrush. She could see nothing, but she was well aware of life growing all around her. A ground mist appeared and grew thicker with each step. Ahead, a tawny glow appeared through the trees. The drumming of her heart grew louder, so much she was sure the entire forest could hear it. They arrived at a clearing where a small dragon lay on his side among gold and red leaves.

"Mirith!"

Charlotte took a step toward him, but Mysterie grasped her arm. "Shhh." Her eyes darted, her finger to her lips. "We need to hide," she whispered. "They're coming."

"Who's coming?" Charlotte asked, unable to mask the alarm growing within.

Mysterie smiled. "Dryads. Watch."

They hid behind a cluster of boulders covered in a carpet of vibrant green moss.

From the depths of the forest emerged seven enormous humanesque creatures with bright green foliage for hair, branches for arms, and skin the color of pumpkins."

Charlotte's pulse quickened. "Oh. My. God."

"I've heard of them all my life," Mysterie whispered, "but never witnessed one until the day Einar cast me here. I was broken. Ill. They cured me. It is said they hold the power to understand and heal all sentient beings. If anyone can breathe a spark into that poor creature, it will be them."

"So, why are we hiding?"

"Legend says the visible presence of humans during a blessing inhibits the power of healing, and in that vulnerable state, the sins of the watchful transfer into the souls of the weak. I'm not a bad person, but I'd rather not take the chance of transferring what sins I do have into a dragon, would you?"

Charlotte crouched and watched as an older-looking and larger dryad stepped forward and raised her branchlike arms to the sky. Her voice rang out clear and strong. "Let all who are gathered bear witness to the awakening. Let our life force settle within the boundaries of this body and spring forth new life."

The other dryads raised their arms and swayed and moaned. A cool breeze swept through the trees. The bells chimed. The dryad spoke again. "Behold the veil of life. Rise and walk the mist young creature of life. Cross the River of Existence and pursue the spirits of the earth. Seek the song of the life sprites. Come hither. Rise from the darkness. Let the drums of life beat within your heart." Two of her branches thumped the ground.

Bum. Bum.

Bum. Bum.

The other dryads stepped forward and formed a circle, their branches to the sky. The small, fluttering creatures joined in, rising and falling like sparks from a campfire. The chant grew louder. Stronger. Faster.

Bum. Bum.

Bum. Bum.

The earth vibrated. A chill ran through Charlotte. Her skin prickled with excitement.

The drumming grew louder and louder until the air boomed like thunder.

The aroma of baked apples and cinnamon filled the night air. Charlotte squeezed Mysterie's hand. "Do you smell it?" Charlotte whispered. "That's him. That's what Mirith smells like." A tear fell down her cheek. "He's alive!"

The dryads clasped branches and swayed to the left and to the right. A wispy vortex formed around Mirith, lifting him from the ground. Charlotte's and Mysterie's hair whipped in their faces. Twigs and leaves blew past. They both flattened to the ground until the wind died. Slowly, they peered over the boulders.

Mirith stood in the center of the clearing. He shook his head and puffed his scales.

The elder dryad stepped forward, breaking apart the ring. "Young beast of the earth. You have tasted death and now you breathe life once more. Your destiny awaits. Seek it. Find it. Command it. Peace be upon you, our young friend."

The dryads turned and slipped away, flowing into the forest, leaving Mirith all alone. Charlotte waited a few moments to make sure they were gone, and stepped out from the forest's edge.

Mirith's gaze snapped in her direction. A brief moment of fear held Charlotte to her spot. "It's me, Mirith," Charlotte said, holding out her hand.

"How do you know him?" Mysterie asked.

"He came to me and David and Trog in the Field of Palinar."

Mysterie clasped her hands to her heart. "Trog? He's safe? He's not dead?" Tears swelled in her eyes.

"I don't know. We were almost to the Field of Valnor when Einar attacked. Mirith battled him and we thought he died. David and I ran, but then David and I broke apart. Einar captured me. I don't know what happened to Trog or David. I do know, though, if anyone can help us get out of this place, it's Mirith. I just hope he remembers me."

"Then might I suggest you begin convincing him." Mysterie looked off in the distance toward a rustle, slowly drawing closer. "The forest trolls are on their way and they'll be here soon."

Charlotte's heart fell into her feet. "Trolls?"

"Hurry," Mysterie whispered.

Charlotte moved into the glade, thankful for the moonlight to guide her steps. "Hey Mirith," she said, her hand out. "Do you remember me? Charlotte? I'm David's friend."

Mirith's tail swished the ground.

"We met on the Field of Palinar. I was with Sir Trogsdill and David. Do you remember?"

Mirith flattened his scales and his feathered mane. He cocked his head from side to side and took a step closer, sniffing, then stopped, his neck careened to his left as if listening. He snorted and bounded toward Charlotte and Mysterie, tossing his head about while snorting.

"Oh, my," Mysterie said, fear seizing her voice. "He's attacking."

Charlotte shook her head as Mirith fled past. "No. He wants us to follow him." Charlotte grabbed Mysterie's hand. "Let's go!"

They ran deep into the forest where the air was dank and heavy with the scent of upturned soil. Mirith slowed to a trot, his head held high, his nose to the wind. Nearing the edge of a stream, he turned and flashed his feathered mane. Charlotte and Mysterie stopped, their breathing hard and fast.

Mirith set about ripping aside brush and undergrowth. Charlotte and Mysterie huddled close together, the stomping and growling of the trolls drawing closer. Wood splintered and crashed to the ground, stirring up the night creatures and sending them squawking into the night sky. Anxious moments passed before the mouth of a cave emerged from all of Mirith's steady work.

Mirith trotted to her side and nudged her toward the dark, gaping mouth in the earth.

The stomping drew nearer, the growls of the trolls louder.

"Come on," Mysterie said, clasping Charlotte's hand. "I'm not too fond of what might be waiting for us inside there, but it has to be better than what is coming for us out here."

They crawled into the darkness, the ground moist and spongy. The air had a sweet, earthy tinge to it, like orange blossoms and fresh cut grass. They sat across from each other, their knees drawn to their chests. Outside, Mirith scurried about raking the brush over the cave's door.

Boom. Boom. Boom.

The ground shook with the trolls' approach.

"No, Mirith," Charlotte said, scuttling toward him on her hands and knees. "Come inside, before they see you."

He arched his tail and threw a bolt toward her. The rock above her exploded. Pebbles rained down in sheets.

Charlotte backed up, her chest rising and falling with the rapid beat of her heart. More brush kicked up around the opening until there was nothing more than a sliver of moonlight shining through.

Branches splintered. The forest floor crunched.

Peering through the slit, Charlotte clasped a hand over her mouth as three enormous creatures pounded from the forest, swinging clubs the size of battering rams. They were broad of shoulder with yellow-green skin, and at least twelve feet tall, with round black eyes, jagged teeth, and bald heads. Pustules oozed on their faces, and they wore a horrid stench of death and decay.

Mirith took up his attack stance, his scales shimmering of fire in the moonlight.

The trolls spoke, their voices gruff and throaty. They laughed, and the trees trembled.

Mirith pawed at the ground, a bull ready to fight.

The trolls roared and thundered toward him, their clubs raised, their teeth exposed.

Mirith threw a bolt. It landed on the ground at their feet.

A warning.

The trolls roared louder.

Lightning bolts erupted in the night sky.

One.

Two.

Three.

Howls of pain tore through the forest.

A troll stumbled and fell. The earth trembled as he hit the ground. His face lay mere feet from the cave, nostrils flaring. His eyes shifted, looking. Staring. At Charlotte. He stretched out an arm and tossed aside all of the brush Mirith had built.

"No!" Charlotte said. She grasped Mysterie's arm and scurried deeper into the cave, but it was only so deep and the troll's arm was long. "Mirith, do something!" Charlotte yelled as the beast's hand found them pressed to the rear wall.

Charlotte beat at the thick, green fingers as they wrapped around her. "Let. Go. Of me!"

The troll dragged her toward his wretched face, his arm dragging along the cave floor. She ducked as he pulled her through the opening.

One lightning bolt after another flew through the sky, striking the standing trolls and bursting them into flames. They howled and fell upon each other, a pyre of writhing, rancid flesh. Burning. Scorching.

Charlotte coughed, the smoke choking her lungs. Tears fell, her eyes burning from the rank, sulfurous odor and fumes. The troll's grip tightened around her as he pulled to his hands and knees.

Her ribs quaked beneath the pressure, bones ready to snap any minute.

Stay calm. Relax. Play dead.

The troll roared at Mirith.

Trees bent from the gale force. Mirith tumbled backwards from the blast.

The troll stood, held Charlotte by her legs like a club, and stomped toward Mirith, Charlotte swinging like a pendulum.

She squeezed her eyes shut tight and pictured a thousand fiery needles lodged into the troll's eyes.

Flashes of light penetrated her closed lids.

The howl ripped across her nerves.

The troll's grip loosened and Charlotte plummeted to the ground. She crab-walked backwards as the creature weaved, his fingers dug into his eyes. Blood streamed down his forearms. Thick, heavy drops plopped to the forest floor. Mirith grasped her by the arm and dragged her into the cave, away from the faltering feet. Blind, the giant creature failed his arms about, smashing the forest into kindling. Mirith snorted and emerged from the cage, his tail poised for one final blow. The bolt flew from the tip of his tail and found its mark at the base of the troll's neck. One final bellow, one last stumble, and the troll toppled to the ground, falling dead upon his smoldering companions. His body burst into flames.

With little prodding from the dragon, Mysterie and Charlotte fled from the scene, happy to be away from the stench of trolls and death. They hiked for hours along the stream until they arrived in a glade of plush grass and yellow flowers as pungent as jasmine on a spring night. Mirith moved toward the other side of the clearing, his steps methodic, cautious.

"What is it, boy?" Charlotte asked, following behind.

Mirith swiped his tail across the ground, back and forth, back and forth, until the tip turned blue. With a sideways flip, he flung a dagger of ice at the tree line. It met with an invisible membrane and plunked to the ground.

A lightning bolt followed only to sizzle and disintegrate on impact.

Charlotte and Mysterie threw rocks, twigs, anything they could find, but the results were the same. Mirith sat on his haunches, his head tilted to one side as if deep in though. Tired, Charlotte yawned, sat cross-legged, and leaned against him.

Pain shot through her body like lighting through a rod. Sparks flew from her skin. Raging fire surged through her body. She blew off his side like a bullet from a gun and crash-landed a few feet away.

She moaned and stood. "What the heck? That freaking hurt." She brushed at the tingles scurrying up her arms, like an army of fire ants marching over ice.

Mirith stared at her, at the wall, then back at her. His eyes grew dark—two garnets shimmering from the depths of a well—and calculating. He stepped toward her, swishing his tail, his eyes flitting from her to the barrier.

Charlotte swallowed, her saliva like bubblegum in her throat. "You want me to touch you again, don't you?"

Mirith made a loon sound, spun in a circle, then sat and wagged his tail.

Charlotte looked toward the cloaked borderline and hugged herself. "I don't know, Mirith. That was some messed up shit, pardon my French."

He scrambled to his feet and bowed, the whites of his eyes turned up to her. Begging. Pleading. His tail swished.

"Oh, no. Don't you dare start that cute crap with me! There is no way I'm going through Torture 101 again. I learned everything I needed to learn from that class."

He growled, walked up to the unseen wall, and blew on it, encrusting the invisible frame in a frosty sheet. With a powerful sideways flick of his tail, he shot a lightning bolt into the target. The ice cracked, shattered into thousands of pieces, but the barrier remained.

Mysterie grasped Charlotte's hand. "I think I understand. He can't break the barrier on his own. He needs you to help him."

"How can I help him? I don't have any magic."

"Maybe not, but something happened when you touched him. Maybe if you do it again, it will have some effect."

"What? You mean be his catalyst?" Charlotte shook her head.

"No, no, no. I'm not going to deliberately inflict that kind of pain on myself ever again. It was as if I my bones were frozen, but my flesh was searing in flames."

"You have to try." Mysterie squeezed Charlotte's hand with motherly tenderness. "I know it's a lot to ask, but if it will grant our freedom … "

Ahh, damn it, why did she have to be logical? She was right, though. They were prisoners of Einar's and they would die in this forest if they didn't find a way out. She thought of her brother. Daniel didn't question his duties, his missions. He didn't chicken out because he was scared of pain or death. He knew the risks and flew into them anyway, and it wasn't even his freedom he was seeking. He stared into the face of the ultimate sacrifice with strength and determination. If he could do it, so could she. After all, what was a little pain?

She mumbled under her breath and kicked at the ground. "Fine, Mirith." The little dragon bound toward her. "I'll do it, but you better not make me hold onto you longer than I have to, got it?"

Charlotte mounted the dragon, and screamed.

The pain cascaded through her, one part sun flare, the other negative fifty degrees cold. Both burning, blistering her from the inside out.

Mirith spun around twice, inhaled a deep breath, and arched his tail.

"Now!" Charlotte yelled, her voice muffled and distant to her own ears.

Mirith exhaled a long-winded breath. The shield turned into a large sheet of ice.

Charlotte squinted against the intense white around her. She'd become a human sparkler, sizzling and popping, while the heat inside of her continued to build, a pain bordering on insanity.

"Hurry, Mirith!" Charlotte shouted. "I can't hold on much longer!"

Mirith stomped at the ground, arced his tail, and fired the largest lightning bolt she'd ever seen.

WHAM!

Crack!

Pop!

Sizzle!

Shatter!

Charlotte catapulted through the air, her pain cooling, fading, and spiraling off in an orange trail behind her. She landed with a thud several feet from Mirith.

Mysterie ran to her side and embraced Charlotte in a hug. "You did it! Look!" Her smile lit up her face.

Charlotte rose up on her elbows and stared at the broken membrane hanging like burned flesh from a corpse.

"Whoa. That's insane. It worked. It really worked." Charlotte stood and brushed herself off. She was on the other side of the Elastine Forest looking in at Mirith who was admiring his handy work.

A crackling sound drew Charlotte's gaze upward. The membrane was beginning to heal itself like a zipper pulling two sides together.

She looked back at the dragon.

"Mirith! Come on! It's mending! We have to go!"

Mirith followed her gaze, his eyes following the crease as it melded back together. He galloped as fast as he could go, leaping through the opening just before the last part of the rip mended.

Charlotte hugged his neck, not thinking, but touching his feathers didn't affect her in the least.

"Come on, buddy. Let's get out of here. I've got a feeling Einar will figure this out and come looking for us. How far is the castle from here, Mysterie?"

"I'm not sure." She peered at the sky. "Maybe a half-day walk if we hurry."

"Then let's get walking. I sure could use a hot bath."

"As could I," Mysterie replied with a smile.

The three trudged northward.

Freedom never felt so good.

Chapter 10

Eric

"Your story has them ruffled." Eric leaned forward, his arms folded on the table, his eyes on Slavandria and Lily conversing quietly in the kitchen. "Something tells me they think there's more to your tingles than leftover magic."

"That's ridiculous," Charlotte replied.

"Is it?" David asked. He, too, leaned forward, his voice low. "Slavandria gave you healing powers in Tulipakar. What if she gave something else to you, something you don't know about?"

"I don't think she would do that." Charlotte propped her elbows on the table, her chin resting on the heels of her palms. "She was very honest that day about what she was *bestowing* upon us. She would have no reason to lie or keep something like that from us."

Eric laughed. "I disagree, but if you feel that way," he tilted his face her way, "that only leaves one other explanation and that is you hold some sort of magical powers naturally."

"Bite your tongue." Charlotte scoffed. "Honestly, I think Mirith has something in his scales that reacts when humans touch him. Have you ever touched his back?" She glanced across the table at David. "Have you? Huh?"

They both shook their heads.

"No," Eric said with a smile. "I have done my best to stay clear of the beast, never mind laying my hands on him."

"Come to think of it," David said, "I haven't touched his back either, only his neck and feathers."

"Well, there you go," Charlotte said with a huff. She sat back, her fingers drumming the chair arms.

"Regardless," Eric said, "you were quite brave and you suffered immeasurable pain in order to free yourself and my queen from Einar's clutches. For that I shall be eternally grateful."

Charlotte glanced down at her lap. "Thank you. I'm glad Mysterie is all right. She's very sweet and kind."

Eric nodded. "That she is. She's also very wise. I wish Trog had taken her advice. We might have avoided the rift that fell between us."

"It must have been so weird to find out Trog's your dad." Charlotte said. "Almost like a blessing and a nightmare rolled into one."

"It was quite shocking. I'd always looked up to him like a father. I always wanted to be like him, honorable and unfeigned. He always prided himself on honesty and he paraded it around for all to see, not in a boisterous way, mind you. That's not how he is. I trusted him and put every ounce of my faith into him. I never dreamed he would ever lie to me. To find out he did about something so important shattered my entire perception of him."

"I can imagine. I guess that's what happens when you love someone so much. You can't see, or maybe you choose not to see, that person's flaws."

"Oh, no, my lady, I saw his flaws all right. He's closed-off and stubborn. He thrives off of giving evasive answers all under the guise of education. What he doesn't realize, or maybe he does, is that all you want to do is hurl a shoe at his departing backside."

David laughed. "Ain't that the truth. I've never met anyone who has a way of getting under your skin and pushing all the wrong buttons the way he does."

"Did he ever tell you why he kept the secret for so long?" Charlotte asked.

"He said it was to protect me. One of Einar's henchmen already killed my mother. He wasn't going to allow the same thing to happen to me, so he gave me away to be raised by the farrier."

Charlotte touched his arm. "That was an amazing sacrifice, you know that, right? To put your safety above his own needs. That's like the deepest, most unselfish kind of love I've ever heard of. Can you imagine the torture he must have gone through every day for all these years? Seeing you every day, wanting to hold you, be a father to you and he couldn't? I can't even imagine that sort of agony."

Eric blinked back the emotion swelling in his chest. For so long, he'd been so wrapped up in how the lie had affected him he didn't want to consider how it affected Trog. How selfish of him to only consider his pain and suffering. He covered Charlotte's hand with his.

"Nor can I. Thank you for showing me what I could not see."

Charlotte's gaze lingered on his face, his eyes. "He loves you, Eric. Don't ever forget that."

"I won't." He squeezed her hand.

An arc of electricity zapped his hand away.

"Sorry," Charlotte said. "I wish I could make it stop."

"It's okay," he said, rubbing his palm. That one really stung.

Charlotte slipped her hand into her lap. He took a deep breath and lifted his chin, his gaze pinned to Slavandria and Lily as they entered the room.

David careened his neck in their direction, his thumbs tumbling over one another.

"Well?" he asked.

Slavandria wrapped her slender fingers around the spindles of a high-back chair. "Lily and I have gone over the story several times, and have evaluated the vibes emanating from Charlotte, and we believe with almost one hundred percent certainty she held no sway in the escape."

Charlotte released a huge sigh. "See, I told you I had nothing to do with it."

Slavandria smiled and glanced down at Charlotte. "We also agree that your tingles are nothing to be concerned with and will vanish in time."

"I hope so because they're really annoying."

"So, where does that leave us?" Eric asked, turning his glass ever so slowly on the tablecloth. "What do we do now? What's the plan to get the crystals back and rescue this Gertie and Garret from Tulipakar?"

Lily clasped her hands together and brought them to her lips. "Slavandria and I have decided to pursue the collection of the crystals. We feel it best if the three of you return to Gyllen where you will be safe."

Eric tapped on the table. "No." There was no way he was going to come so far only to be cast back into the nursery with a pack of over-protective nursemaids with beards.

Lily continued. "Slavandria placed a few weaves around the castle before she departed that should deter any unsavory beings from entering the grounds. Farnsworth, Gowran, and Crohn are—"

"I said no." Eric pushed his chair from the table and stood. He collected his scabbard and sword and strapped them to his hips.

"This isn't up for a vote," Slavandria said.

"You're right. It's not." Eric met her gaze, his left hand gripping the hilt of his sword. "We're here to find the crystals and I'm not going home until I have them."

"You will do as we instruct," Slavandria said.

"No, I won't. I know who and what I am. It's time I acted like it, which means, as Prince to the throne of Hirth, you listen to me, not the other way around."

Charlotte pushed her chair back and stood. "I'm not going

anywhere, either."

"You're right about that," David said, standing. "Havendale is your home, and this is where you're going to stay. Eric and I will find the crystals and return them to Gyllen."

"Um, I don't think so, Mr. I Got This," Charlotte said. "You can't tell me what to do. I'm just as much a part of this team as you are."

David snatched his bow and quiver of arrows. "No, you're not. Not this time. Havendale is where you belong."

"*Belong*? Are you serious? Who put you in charge of me, because I sure as hell didn't."

"That's not what I meant, Char, and you know it."

"Really, because what I heard was you trying to tell me where my place is in all this insanity."

"I thought this is what you wanted, to go home, to be back with your family. We're here. You're safe. Go. Live a happy life without dragons. You don't have to be in danger anymore."

"And what would you have me do, David Alwyn Heiland, cry myself to sleep every night because I don't know if you're alive or dead? I suppose you want me to go to the mall, get my nails done, kick my feet up, and forget that the two of you may or may not come back."

"If that's what it takes so you're not in danger, then go for it."

Eric kept the expression from his face, but underneath, he was smiling. What a snarky little thing Lady Charlotte had become. Unafraid. Determined. And while he did not want her wrath aimed at him, he loved her spark and poise. He doubted, however, if the royal court would view her in the same light.

"And what about what I want?" Charlotte continued. "Do you even care about that?" Charlotte rounded the table and stood chest to chest with David. "I'll tell you what I want. I want to be seen as something more than a fragile little girl who needs protection from mommy and daddy and wannabe heroes. I want the freedom to make my own choices. I want you to put aside your skewed obsessions and look at me. See me. See the fire within me and not be afraid to play with it. Can you do that?"

Charlotte turned and stormed from the room, leaving behind a mess of silence.

Eric stared at the floor then smiled. He glanced up at Slavandria and Lily, laughter hanging in his throat. "Well, I guess we know where she stands on the matter." He pushed in his and Charlotte's chairs and walked around Slavandria and Lily. "It is my stand as well. No more coddling. No more protecting. We have a job to do and we're going to do it, with or without your help." He left the room.

"Eric, come back here," Slavandria said.

He chuckled at her obligatory, non-commanding tone and kept walking.

David tossed his cloth napkin on the table and hurried after them.

"You all right?" Eric asked, as David breezed around him.

"Yeah. Never better."

David darted up the sweeping stairs, taking two steps at a time. He opened the door to his room and called out Charlotte's name.

Eric scooted in behind and peered in the dressing room, unsurprised to find the steps to the secret room exposed.

"In here," he said.

***

David

David climbed the steps to find Charlotte sitting cross-legged on the bed, her head hung, her hands buried in her hair.

Eric dragged an old wooden chair across the floor and sat down.

David dropped his bow and quiver on the bed and took a seat at the foot, the mattress squeaking beneath his weight.

Charlotte glared at him, her lips quivering. She wiped a tear from her cheek. "Go away. Don't even talk to me."

"Aww, come on, Char, don't be that way."

"There you go again, telling me how to be and not to be. You're not the keeper of me."

"You're right. I'm not, and I'm not trying to be, but can you please listen to me for a minute? Please?"

Charlotte shrugged. "Fine. Go for it."

"I'm sorry," David began. "I didn't mean to upset you."

"Yeah, well, what you mean to do and what you end up doing are two different things." She walked to the small, shuttered window, her arms crossed.

"Hey, don't get pissed off at me for wanting to keep you safe."

"I don't have a problem with that, David, but you have no right to tell me what I should and shouldn't do or where I should or shouldn't belong. You're not my dad. Stop being so overprotective and just be my friend, since it's obvious you want nothing more of me or us."

David pinched the bridge of his nose. He paused for a moment, collecting the right words to say and shoving aside the ones he shouldn't. He wished Eric would leave, go away. Instead, Eric moved to a dark area of the room and leaned against a post, trying not to be obvious.

After what seemed an impossible silence, David rose from the bed and strode toward her, taking her hands in his. "Char, please try to understand. You're the most amazing person I've ever met. You're like the glue that holds me together. I adore you. All I've thought about since all of this started was how could I get you home, back to your family where you would be safe. When Twiller yanked you from my house, I went nuts. And that look of horror on your face when Agimesh and Tacarr killed those men. Damn it, Char, I'll never forget it. You should have never experienced that and you wouldn't have if it hadn't been for me.

"I got you into this mess. Hell, I even battled a freaking dragon to bring you home. I can't even sort that out in my head, and saying it aloud only makes me sound insane, but it's the truth." He cupped her face in his hands. "The reason I don't want you to go back to Fallhollow is not because I don't want you with me. It's because if anything happened to you, I'd never forgive myself. It would kill me.

So please forgive me if I'm overprotective. Forgive me for being an ass. Forgive me for wanting the moon and the stars and the universe for you. If I could give them to you, I would, but I can't. I'm not sure if I ever will."

Charlotte looked into his eyes, and his heart puddled. "So, I guess this means we're friends, nothing more."

"I can't give you any more than that. Not now. I'm sorry. Maybe, when all of this is over, things will be different."

Charlotte pressed two fingers to his lips, her eyes looking deep into his. "Don't. I understand. Friends." She ran her fingers through his hair. A slight smile creased her face. "So does that mean I can date other guys and if they treat me wrong, you'll whoop their ass?"

David smiled, stroking her hair from her face. "You betcha. All day long."

He wiped a tear that rambled down her cheek. Why did he have to hurt her? His heart cracked. A chunk broke off and floated away. He almost reached for it, but stopped. The damage was done. No sense in repeating it.

Charlotte wrapped her arms around his neck. "I think you're amazing, too." She let go of him and stepped back. "But that doesn't mean you can tell me what to do. I've been with you from the beginning of this insanity, and I will be with you until the end of it. That's what friends do. They don't abandon each other when the crap splatters, so don't ask me to. Got it?"

"Char—"

She touched her forefinger to his lips. "Got it?"

David closed his eyes and sighed, defeated. He shook his head and looked her in the eye. "Yeah. I've got it."

"Good." Charlotte smiled. "So, how do we get these crystals back?"

Eric walked over to the steps and pulled them up into their hiding spot. "We need to get the necklace and the rutseer back." He latched the door. "Right now, they're in the possession of the two most powerful sorceresses who ever lived, who happen to be downstairs."

"Yeah, speaking of that, why haven't we been tossed back into Fallhollow already? Slavandria's not one to waste time."

"I think we might have an ally in your godmother, Lily," Eric said. "While you two were—you know—Slavandria and Lily were in a heated argument. I didn't hear everything they said, but Lily was not standing for Slavandria's bullying. If we do indeed have Lily on our side, I don't know how long she can hold her sister off, or how to retrieve the rutseer. What I do know is we can't stay here, and Lily seems to be giving us the time we need to leave."

"Where do we go?" Charlotte asked. "It's not like we can go to any of our friends."

"We'll go into the woods," Eric said. He looked at David. "They are expansive, yes?"

David snorted. "Yeah. It's the Cherokee National Forest. More than one thousand square miles of wilderness begging for three teens to get lost."

"Have you got a map of the forest?" Eric asked.

David nodded. "Sure. I can get one off the internet. What kind do you want? Trails? Roads? Campsites?"

"All," Eric said.

"Wait." Charlotte's eyes almost closed, her face twisted in confusion. "I'm up for a good camping trip, too, but how are we going to get out of the house?"

Eric looked at David. "Can you use your invisibility spell here?"

"I don't know. I haven't tried." David closed his eyes, shook out his arms and legs, and took a deep breath. "*Ibidem Evanescere.*"

"Nothing," Eric said. "We can still see you. Try again."

"Come on, David," Charlotte said. "You can do it."

This time the words remained silent on David's moving lips. Still nothing.

"Well, this clogs the wheel a bit," Eric said, pounding a beam with his fist.

As if in answer, a warm light surged within a glass globe sitting on a table near the window. Second by second, it grew brighter until its glow obscured the miniature village nestled between cliffs and sea inside. Eric shielded his eyes against the glare.

"What is that thing?" he asked. "Turn it off."

"I can't," David said, his arm a barrier against the light. "It's not a lamp."

The globe sizzled. Dancing threads of lightning arced from its rim.

"Ouch!" Charlotte jumped back, rubbing her arm. "That thing just zapped me!"

David swiped a blanket from a rocking chair and tossed it over the globe. The room darkened. He turned to Charlotte. "Are you all right?"

"Yeah, I think so." She blew on the red spot forming on her arm. "Oww, oww, oww, oww, oww."

David examined her arm. "Whoa. That damn thing burned you. It's already starting to blister. I'll be right back. I'm going to run downstairs and get the silver sulfadiazine from the fridge." He put his nose in the air. "What is that smell?"

Eric's gaze settled on the globe, the blanket now engulfed in flames. "Move!" He leaped forward, yanked the fabric to the ground, and stomped on it. The globe, burning bright as a star on a summer night, clunked to the floor. Sizzling arcs sprayed outward, their threads long and chaotic.

"What the hell is that thing?" Eric shouted.

David backed up. "I don't know. It's never done this before."

The doorway to the secret stairs flung open.

Eric drew his sword from his scabbard.

Slavandria appeared first, followed by Lily. Terror clung to her eyes.

"Give it to them, Van. Now, before it's too late!" Lily dashed to the globe and scooped it in her arms. Her body folded in half, her face nocked in pain.

Slavandria shook her head. "No. They have to go back to Gyllen." She spoke a string of strange words. A hole in space and time opened behind her, its outer membrane pulsed like a giant heart. "Go. Now," she said, her eyes on David, "while there is time."

David shook his head. "I'm not going anywhere!" He reached for Lily. She dodged his touch. The globe tumbled from her arms and rolled across the floor, its light blinding and hot. It landed in a crevice in the floor. Tendrils of light waved from it, searching, reaching …

For Charlotte.

"Van, give him the Eye. He must have it!" Lily straightened, her face contorted in pain.

David's words caught in his throat at the sight of the round burnt marks on her arms. He took a tight breath and clenched his shaking fingers. What sort of wizardry could do such a thing?

"No," Slavandria said, her arm extended before her. Magic swirled in her palm. "Let him go. Let me send them where they will be safe."

"We don't have time to argue about this." Lily's eyes turned a strange shade of lavender, the pupils swirling like a storm upon a sea. Sparks danced on the tips of her fingers. Sizzling threads of magic exploded from her left hand.

Charlotte grasped Eric's and David's hands as the spell blasted past them and into Slavandria.

Another braided thread flew from Lily, the spell unraveling into a hand before ripping the Eye of Kedge from around Slavandria's neck. Lily thrust it around David's neck.

"Go! Get out of here!"

The globe began to hum and rock back and forth, almost angry, its tentacles of sparking light whipping in the air.

David grabbed his bow and quiver.

"Valla, don't!"

It was the last thing David heard before time split, and the world disappeared.

Chapter 11

Eric

Eric rolled like a pill bug, bumping over dirt, roots, and splintered planks. He winced as he stood and rubbed at the pain gnarling like an angry dog at his hip and thigh.

Charlotte hurdled past him and creamed into a stone wall, her arms the only thing saving her from a serious face-plant. She moaned and clutched an elbow, her face twisted in agony.

David lurched out of nothingness, his legs like rubber bands, his arms stretched out to his sides like rudders. He spilled to a stop, catching himself before toppling out a window edged in braided vines, moss, and beetles. Pushing off the cracked sill, he turned around, his wild-eyed gaze flitting over his entire surrounds.

"Shit. Holy shit," he said, gasping for air.

"What is this place?" Eric asked, his heart thumping. He bent over, his hands on his knees.

Charlotte exhaled a long breath and pressed her back to the wall. "The grist mill. We're in the old grist mill." She placed a hand to her side and steadied her breathing.

David righted himself and held up the necklace. The Eye of Kedge dangled from its chain, the rutseer nice and tight in its back.

Eric straightened. "I don't believe it. She attacked her own sister to get it for you."

"Yeah." David placed the chain around his neck, and turned away, his face drawn.

Eric knew that look. He suspected he wore the same. It would be hard not to. Jared's daughters were at war with each other and David was the prize. Or was he the pawn? If the latter, what was the game? What was at stake? Was David the sacrifice or the savior? And what were his and Charlotte's roles in his demise or salvation? He balled his fingers into fists. He hated being manipulated.

He felt a nudge and met with Charlotte's blue-eyed gaze.

"Penny for your thoughts?" she asked.

He glanced down at her outstretched palm, a coin in the center. She laughed. "I know, it's silly, but I had to do something. You were getting too serious. My head ached from watching yours and David's faces, the way your eyes squinted and your brows furrowed together. It was like watching anger in visual stereo."

"My lady, do you not understand what happened back there? It *was* serious. Do you not see that?"

Charlotte stepped into the middle of the ruins. "No. You know what I see? We have the rutseer. We can find the crystals now. That was our quest, right? So, let's get questing."

"It's not that easy," David said, walking toward her. "There's something going on between Slavandria and Lily. A power play. They're tugging against one another."

"That's typical," Charlotte said. "They're sisters."

"It's more than that," Eric said. "Did you see the way Lily protected that globe? Even after what it did to you? To David?"

"You noticed that, too, huh?" David asked.

"She wasn't protecting *it*," Charlotte said, looking at David. "She was protecting you from all those sparking octopus-tendril things. I swear, it was coming after you, like it wanted to grab a hold of you and suck you inside."

Eric felt his stomach sink through the damp, earthen floor. What if that was what the globe wanted, to rip David from this world and imprison him inside, in a room, in a dark attic where no one ever went? He glanced up at David. "What is that room?" he asked. "What is its significance?"

David walked to the window, his hands gripping the sill. "According to Lily, my mother spent a lot of time in that room while pregnant with me. There's a skylight of sorts that once slid open above the bed. Lily said my mother would lie there at night for several months after my father died, and stare at the stars and wonder where he was. Was he looking down on her, protecting her? Watching over her? When my mother passed away, Lily sealed off the skylight. She said it was a painful reminder of what once was." David turned around. "Of course, now I know it was all a lie and my parents aren't really dead, so that's that."

Eric rubbed his chin. "Not necessarily. What if that skylight was a portal? What if that was the way your mother transported to Fallhollow? What if Lily sealed it shut so you would never find it and accidentally transport yourself?"

David gulped. His eyes widened. "Holy crap, I never thought of that. That's why Slavandria couldn't zap us out of there."

"I don't understand," Charlotte said.

"It's something Twiller explained to me once. There are natural portals all over the various worlds. But if they've just been used or sealed, a new portal must be made. That's why I couldn't follow you, Char, when Twiller took you. The natural portal was hot so he had to create a new one for me to go through, which dumped us off in a different place. If Eric's right, and the skylight was a deactivated portal, then the only way Slavandria could ferry us from the room and perhaps from the house itself, was to create a new portal."

"It still doesn't explain why Lily and Slavandria are feuding over David's destiny," Eric said, "or why they showed up in your room when they did. I think they sensed the danger. I think they knew whatever was lurking in that globe came to find you."

"But Lily put up wards," Charlotte said.

"Yes, to keep non-magic folk out. But what if Seyekrad placed a detection spell in your home, something that would alert him to your arrival?"

"How would he do that?" Charlotte asked.

Eric paced. "It's something I learned in my history of magic classes. Using magic displaces time, even for a minute second. It's like a door opening and closing. If two opposing spells meet, neither will penetrate the other side. That's how the mages can disarm one another. Strike. Counterstrike. However, if a wizard is using magic to clean his home, and another wizard wants to steal something, Wizard Two could place a sleeping spell over the home, off to la la land Wizard One would go, and Wizard Two would be free to pillage at his leisure."

"So, you're saying when Lily placed the wards on the house, Seyekrad snuck in and let loose a detection spell to find me."

Eric nodded. "Not just any detection spell. A snatcher."

A visible shiver wiggled out of David.

"Wait. So, if that was a snatcher spell, why wouldn't Lily want David to be protected? Why keep him here? You'd think she'd want him, us, to go where we'd be safe."

"Because we have work to do," Eric said. "We have the rutseer. Whatever magic Finn put in that thing, Seyekrad can't find us, not as long as David has that thing around his neck and we stick close to him."

"We can truly move in the shadows," Charlotte said. Her eyes turned an electric blue, bright and clear. There was an itch to her stance. Excitement in her voice. "We're going to need some stuff—camping gear, a phone, a solar charger, food."

"I've got all that stuff in my room," David said, "well, except for the food."

"You haven't time for that," Lily said, materializing before them.

Eric's heart skipped. He hated how she could materialize out of thin air.

David spun around. "Lily! What? How?"

She entered their dark, dank refuge. "Shh, no questions. You've got to get out of here."

"No, no, no," Charlotte said, rushing forward. "Not yet. Where's Slavandria? What did you do with that globe thing? Why was it trying to attack David?"

"Slavandria's returned to Fallhollow but she'll be back and I want you far away by then. As for the globe, it was trying to ensnare you, not David."

Eric's pulse thumped in his throat. Panic clutched at his heart.

Charlotte's eyes widened, her face dripped with horror. "Me? Why me? What did I do?"

"You are an influencer to the ones who can save or destroy Fallhollow. The orbalisk sensed your presence as a threat, someone that must be contained."

There was that word. Contained. Ensnared. Imprisoned. Inside a globe. Eric gulped.

Charlotte stuttered. "Why? Why would you have such a thing in your home?"

"It was a gift, one I never suspected held dark magic. The scene is from my home in Felindil. It has been years since I've been there, and it's brought me great comfort. As I spent so much time in the room with David's mother before she left, I placed it beside the bed to bring me solace. I never gave it a thought. I didn't know."

"Who was the gift from?" Eric asked.

"That doesn't matter."

"Who was it from?" he asked again, his tone stern. He wasn't going to let her get away from this one.

She paused for a moment. "Seyekrad," she said. She reached out and touched David's arm. "But it was long ago, when he still had honor and love in his heart."

A flip switched inside Eric. He couldn't believe what he was hearing.

David exploded. "Love? Honor? Do you hear yourself? He gave you a cursed object! Does that sound like love and honor to you?"

"He wasn't always bad, David."

"Oh my God, Lily. He tried to kill me and your sister! How can you defend him?"

"I'm not defending him."

"To hell you're not, and now you're telling us that you allowed his loving and honorable magic into our home!"

"How dare you pass judgment on me! Slavandria and I didn't know it was hexed until you did. It was just a water globe, no more filled with magic than the floor you're standing on."

David ran his fingers through his hair. Cupped the back of his neck. "How is that even possible? You and Slavandria are supposed to be these all-knowing, all-powerful sorceresses."

"According to whom? We may be strong in many aspects, David, but we don't know all magic, especially dark magic, nor how to defeat it. We are also not perfect. We make mistakes, the same as you, so don't stand there and point fingers and chastise."

Uncomfortable silence stretched between them.

Blood surged through Eric's veins, rushing like a raging river. White caps of heat and fury rose and tumbled in the ripping current. Once again, the mages had interfered and it had almost cost him his friend's life. There should be laws against such meddlesomeness. Wait. There were, set by Jared himself. Apparently, his daughters felt as if the rules didn't apply to them. Sanctimonious witches.

Charlotte's fingers brushed David's. He shirked her touch. "Don't. I might infect you with an unhealthy dose of anger and resentment."

"Stop being an ass," Lily said, "and don't take out your displeasure with me on Charlotte." She glared at him, her eyes intense. "I know you've had a lot thrust on you in a short period of time. I know the dangers you've faced, and I know you're angry. You have every right to be, but you need to focus." She took his hands in hers. "Look at me. This isn't over. Far from it. I need," she glanced at Eric and Charlotte, "they need you to be calm, rational. You're their leader. You're the paladin. As much as you want to fall apart and scream and yell and blame the universe, you have to hold it together. Think smart. Not with your emotions but with your brain. This is war. You are the general of your army. They are looking to you for guidance, not anarchy."

David laughed. "The general of my army? Are you nuts, Lily? Look around. I don't have an army. I have Charlotte and a guy who thinks I'm about as useful as a ripped umbrella in a downpour."

Lily squeezed his hands. "None of us can choose our destiny, and none of us can escape it. Every moment you don't do what's right is a moment the enemy gains ground. You cannot afford to lose this war. It may only be the three of you, but you're strong in ways you can't imagine. Why else does Seyekrad want you out of the picture? He knows you can defeat him."

"Why don't you defeat him?" Charlotte asked. "Why does David have to fight your battles? I mean, it seems kind of lame to drag him into your problems."

"David and Eric are obligated by birth and decree to protect and defend Fallhollow. I cannot change that. No one can. Did Slavandria and I pray these dark days would never come? Yes. We prayed with all our might, but our prayers were not enough. Greed, malcontent, evil, they all triumphed, but they won't for long. The chosen ones have been summoned and they will win the day. If you do not, then Fallhollow will be lost and this world will follow."

"What is that supposed to mean?" David asked.

She reached into her pockets and pulled out a bundle of money, keys, something she called a cell phone, and handed them to David. "I know this sounds crazy, but please, I'm begging the three of you to trust me. Go to Kingsport, to Charlotte's grandfather's house. He's a very wise man."

"I don't understand," Charlotte said. "What does my grandfather have to do with this?"

Lily ignored her question. "Your car is in the Conroy's barn off 421. I've already alerted them that someone would be coming by to pick it up. Go. Now. Do not stray from the course. Fallhollow and

Havendale are depending on you."

"Lily, you sound crazy."

She collected David's bow and quiver from the ground and handed them to him. "You don't have much time before Slavandria returns. Oh, and here." She withdrew a leather rope necklace from around her neck and placed it in David's hand. A small orb, not much bigger than a dime and filled with what looked like swirling smoke, lay cool in his palm. "It holds the answer to some of your questions. Charlotte's grandfather will know what to do with it. Keep it safe. Now go. Hurry. All of you."

David snagged her in a big hug. "I love you, Lily. Thanks for everything."

"I love you, too, honey." She leaned back and cupped his face in her hands. "Be kind to each other." Her eyes searched his face.

"I'll see you again, Lily. I promise." He glanced over his shoulder at Eric and Charlotte. "Come on. Let's go."

Lily grasped Eric's hand as he passed, and whispered, "Guard them. Protect them. Their fates rest on the blade you carry. Wield it well."

And then she was gone.

Chapter 12

David

David led the way through the heavily forested hills for more than an hour before emerging onto a flat terrain of farmlands, pastures, and scattered clusters of woodlands. In the distance, a road cut through the landscape. State Road 421. But how far away were they from the Conroy's barn?

He pulled his phone from his pocket and typed in their address the best he could remember. The map showed they weren't far away, maybe a twenty-minute hike to the north.

"What is that contraption?" Eric asked.

"It's a cell phone. You talk to people with it, play games. Even find cars in barns." He shared a smile with Charlotte.

"May I see it?" Eric asked.

David shook his head. "Not just yet. I don't want to lose my GPS. When we get where we're going, I'll let you check it out, okay?"

And in that instant, he sounded like Lily did when he was five years old. He'd have to work on that.

"Agreed," Eric replied. "What does this car of yours look like?"

"It's a black '67 Mustang GT500, not that that means anything to you, but in my world, it's a big deal. There were only a handful of these models made, so it's sort of a rarity. You'll flip out when you see it. It's sleek and rumbles like a—"

David's words froze in his throat. He crumpled to his knees and clutched his chest.

Pain.

Burning, horrific pain.

"David!" Charlotte dropped beside him. "What's wrong?"

"I … don't … know. Hot … in my chest."

"Eric, help me get his shirt off!"

Fabric flew from David's body. Cool air brushed his skin, but not cool enough. The agony.

"What … is … it? What's … wrong … with me?"

Charlotte shook her head. "The rutseer. It's glowing red like fire. So is your tattoo!" She reached for the pendent.

"No!" Eric smacked her hand out of the way. "It might burn you."

Eric gathered David's shirt and slid it between the Eye and the tattoo. In an instant, the rutseer cooled to a dark red, and David began to breathe.

He lay there, his chest rising and falling, his hand clasped around the pendent, his eyes focused on a cloud that changed from a rabbit to a cat to the makings of whatever his imagination came up with next.

"Are you better?" Eric asked.

David nodded. "That was wicked painful. I can't even begin to describe it. It felt like someone set my body on fire."

"I think maybe somebody did," Eric said.

"What?" David's heart skipped. He dared not move.

"I think Seyekrad's trying to find you. If you had removed the Eye, I think he would have succeeded."

Charlotte gasped and stood. "You can't mean that?"

Eric nodded. "I do. Seyekrad wants the Eye. He needs it or the crystals are worthless. The thing is, he can't find David. There's something about that rutseer that makes him blind to us, and if I were him, I'd be desperate about now, trying anything I could to make David reveal it. What better way than causing so much pain that it would force him to remove it?"

David sat up and stared at Eric. "How do you come up with this stuff? I mean, it makes total sense, but I am in awe that you thought of it."

Eric gave David a wan smile. "I had a friend once who saw life through a menagerie of colors. He believed all experiences were nothing more than puzzle pieces that needed to be sorted and put together to make the final big picture. All we needed to do was get out of our own way and open our minds to see it. The more I follow his thinking, the more I think he's right."

Eric stood and offered David a hand. "Make sure you wear that garish thing on the outside of your shirt until we can find something to wrap it with."

David clasped Eric's hand and pulled to his feet. "No problem. Trust me. I don't want a repeat." He bent over, allowing the pendent to hang away from his body, and pulled the t-shirt over his head, ensuring the necklace remained outside, away from his skin. He straightened and took his phone from Charlotte. "Thank you. Both of you," he said. "I'm sorry for being such a pain."

"Don't apologize," Eric said. "The day you aren't a pain I'll know there is something terribly wrong with you."

"You've got that straight." David smiled, took a deep breath and exhaled. "Are we ready?"

David referred to the GPS one more time and started walking. Behind him, Eric apologized for smacking Charlotte's hand, and she forgave him. They started talking about many things, including Eric's friend, Sestian. Some recollections were funny, others sad, and while David enjoyed the stories and the companionship, an ache gnawed at his heart. Charlotte was bonding with Eric, whether she knew it or not. As much as he wanted to, he couldn't blame her. He was a good-looking guy as guys went, smart, and he oozed charm and class. He was perfect in every way. A prince. Literally.

But Eric would break her heart. It was inevitable. There's no way he would move to Havendale, and he was pretty sure Charlotte would never agree to stay in Fallhollow, which meant he'd have to stand by and help mend the broken pieces when the fairytale fell apart. It tore at his soul to think of her miserable. He saw the way she was when her brother, Daniel, died. The heartache was unbearable to watch. There were no words to dissolve the pain. There was nothing he could offer to fill the void. That kind of hurt never goes away. It only gets covered up with layers of emotional bandages until one learns how to block it out. Until one learns not to feel.

He didn't want Charlotte to stop feeling. But what could he do? They were just friends. It was official. He'd made it so. She would have to sort her feelings on her own, and he would have to watch and wait.

Idiot.

He glanced at the map on his phone again and stopped. "We're here," he said, pointing to a large red barn on a parcel of land partitioned off by a white wood fence.

They ran across the yard toward the structure. A cow hung his head over the planks and mooed. David slid open the door and froze, his mouth wide open.

Charlotte came around his right side and gasped.

"It's blue," she said.

David linked his fingers behind his head. "Silver blue," he said, his throat as dry as a sandbox. He shook out his arms. "It's okay. It can be fixed."

Eric leaned in toward Charlotte. "I thought he said it was black."

"It was," she replied. "Lily must have changed it."

"License plate's been changed, too," David said, walking around his car. He stopped and stared at it, his palms pressed to the sides of his head. "Why, Lily? Of all the colors in the world, why this one?"

"I think it looks nice," Eric said.

David's brow creased. His eyes narrowed. His lips pursed. "Of course, you'd think it looks nice. You didn't see it before. It was sick. Now it's, it's … freaking blue!"

"Why is that so upsetting?" Eric asked. "Is it no longer useable?"

"Of course, it's useable. Paint color doesn't change that, but for crying out loud. It's a '67 Shelby GT500. There's a 428 V-8 engine under that hood. That's three hundred and fifty-five horsepower. You don't paint something that powerful blue. It would be like painting your sword green. It defies logic. Speaking of which," he unlocked the trunk and raised it into the air, "put your sword back here. You can't have it up front." He tossed his bow and quiver inside.

"But I never travel on the road without my sword. What if we stumble upon bandits?"

"We won't, but if we do, knock them out with that glowing smile."

"I fail to see how my smile can be seen as a—"

"Oh my god! Just put your sword in the back. Please."

Eric removed his weapon and set it beside the bow. "I'm going to ignore your temper seeing as you are upset about your—"

"Car. It's a car."

"Yes. I know. But if it doesn't affect its performance, I say we get in it and go to Charlotte's grandfather's."

"You're right," David said, scratching the back of his head. "You're absolutely right. She probably did it so no one would recognize it. She was only trying to help. I'll stop being a dick now."

"What's a dick?" Eric asked.

"Never mind," Charlotte said. "Just get in the car before David can teach you more bad language."

"Yeah, you do that." David's gaze swept over the car again and his face cringed. "Why blue? What's wrong with red?"

"Too conspicuous," Charlotte said. "Eric, you sit up front. More leg room. I'll hop in the back." She opened the driver door, leaned the seat forward, and got in. "Come on, David. Stop whining about your car and let's roll."

Eric watched the way David got in on his side and slid in the same way.

"If you're knees are too far up, reach under your seat," David said. "You'll find a lever. Slide it to your right and it'll slide the seat back."

Eric felt around, found the mechanism, and pulled. His breath hitched as the seat moved back.

Charlotte laughed. "You okay there?"

Eric let out a long breath and gulped. "Yes. I think so. I wasn't expecting that."

"Now you know," Charlotte said, leaning over the seat, her voice in his ear. "Now lean forward and close the door."

Sweat popped out on his forehead as he slammed the door closed. The color left his face.

"What's the matter there?" David asked. "You don't look like you're feeling good."

"To tell the truth, I am not. I'm very much confined. My heart feels as if it will dart from my chest and run off without me. I don't know if I can do this, David." He gripped the armrest, his knuckles white.

"Try not to think about it. First times are always scary." David inserted the key into the ignition and turned it. The beast roared to life.

A startled cry flew from Eric's mouth as the Mustang rumbled beneath them. He pressed his head to the headrest, his eyes closed.

"I can't do this, David. I simply can't. Please turn it off. Let me out. One or the other, perhaps both. The vibrations are rattling my bones, my insides. I can't breathe and pains are going down my arms."

"Oh my god, you're having a panic attack." David turned the key and the engine fell quiet. He jumped out of the car and ran to Eric's side and opened the door. "Get out. Come on."

Eric clambered from the car and spaced himself from the car about ten feet. "I'm sorry," he gasped. "I don't know what happened. I felt as if I was going to die."

"It's a panic attack," David said. "I should have thought about it. All of this must seem so insane to you, but I can assure you, I know how to drive it and I won't kill you. If there was another way to get us to Kingsport, we'd take it, but there's not. Tell you what. How about you wait here, I'll go turn the car on, and you can just stand here for a bit and listen to it until you get used to the noise, okay? Baby steps."

Eric glanced at the car.

"It'll be okay," Charlotte soothed. "I promise."

He looked at her, his face ashen. "There is no other way to your grandfather's? No horse and cart? No carriage?"

Charlotte shook her head. "Welcome to the 21st century."

Eric glanced back at the car, his expression pinched. "I suppose if there is no other way." He didn't sound convincing.

David hopped back in and started the car only to look over the hood to find Eric in Charlotte's arms, her head sideways on his chest as she spouted consoling words.

Great. How freaking cozy. I leave them alone for two seconds. Two, and he's already got her all wound up in his charms. I bet he's lovin' every minute of this. Agghhh! He pounded the steering wheel. *You're such an idiot! You can't blame them. This is your doing. You were the one who let her go. You all but said right in front of him that she was free. What was he supposed to do? Play tiddlywinks all the way to town, as Lily used to say? Damn it! Damn it, damn it, damn it! There's nothing left to do than grow a pair. Be a man. Take the hit and keep going. Find your happy spot, bud. Come on. Cool it down.*

He ran his fingers through his hair, counted to ten and took some deep breaths. He had to focus. They had to get to Kingsport. It was time to go.

He got out and walked over to the two of them as they untangled themselves from each other's arms.

"I think he's ready to go," Charlotte said. "I gave him some pointers like how to breathe his way through the attacks if he feels them coming on again. He's willing to try." She looked over her shoulder at Eric. "Are you ready?"

Eric sucked in a deep breath. "Ready as I'll ever be." He patted David's shoulder as he passed and murmured, "Thank you for not getting angry."

David groaned to himself. *Can anyone say dickhead?* "No problem," is what fell from his mouth. He really needed to work on his personal skills.

Once they were all back in the car Charlotte reached around the seat and touched Eric's arm. "You've got this," she soothed. "David's a good driver. All you have to do is relax and enjoy the ride, okay?"

Eric pressed the back of his head to the seat and nodded.

"Okay," David said. "As a heads up, you're going to feel a little power when we back up, and when we go. Don't freak out because that's the way this car sounds and feels. It's got a big engine. It's going to rumble and go fast. Ready?"

Eric sucked in a deep breath and clasped Charlotte's hand. "Yes. I'll be fine. Let's go."

David reached over and rolled Eric's window down. "There. That should help. If you start to feel sick, tell me and I'll pull over so you can hurl outside the car. Deal? No puking in the car."

He backed the car out of the barn at a snail's pace. Slow and steady. He shifted into first and shot a sideways glance at Eric. So far so good.

Little by little he accelerated and with each bit of pressure step on the pedal, the black-now-blue beast grew louder and louder. He turned left onto 421, the cool air whipping through the car. They were on their way. In less than an hour, they'd arrive at Charlotte's grandpa's.

As the metal beast flew down the road, Eric wished aloud they could ferry.

It was the first time David ever heard him say that. It would also probably be the last.

Chapter 13

Eric

By the time they reached Kingsport, Eric and the Mustang were friends.

"We should call it Drac," he said, stroking the dash.

"Why is that?" David asked.

"Because of the way it sounds, how fast it is. It reminds me of the silver dragons of Itas."

"What's Itas?" Charlotte asked.

"The Floating Isles." Eric shifted in his seat to look at her. "There are five of them, giant islands that hover in the sky over the kingdom of Banning. Some of the most beautiful scenery I've ever encountered. The lands are lush and green with magnificent waterfalls, and the bluest rivers your mind can imagine."

"That's insane," Charlotte said, sitting forward. "Tell me more."

"Well, a few humans live there, but mostly the realm is the home to the Sona elves and their Seelie king who live in the warm terrain. Up high, though, in the mountains, you'll find the Edryd, the most spectacular silver dragons imaginable. It's like watching slivers of moonlight dart through the sky when they hunt at night."

"Do the elves ride them?" Charlotte asked.

"Oh no. It's frowned upon for anyone to ride an Edryd, probably because they're shapeshifters who take on the form of elves, often times, living among the Sona for many years in their human forms. The only time anyone ever uses them for transport is when the Seelie king or the duke needs to travel. They are then at their disposal."

David stopped at a red light. "I'm still not following. What does any of this have to do with naming my car Drac?"

"Drac is the chieftain of the Edryd and the most breathtaking of the clan. Sleek. Strong. Enchanting. And he has a belly rumble that demands respect and admiration. I thought it fit your beast."

"I think it's perfect," Charlotte said. "Can you take me to Itas someday, Eric?" She clutched his arm and smiled. "Promise me you'll take me when all of this is over."

Eric smiled. He couldn't think of anything more romantic. More wondrous. "I'd be delighted to, my lady."

"Oh God, I think I'm going to vomit," David said, just loud enough for Eric to hear. "I guess it's settled then. Drac it is." The light turned green and David hit the gas, thrusting Eric and Charlotte into their seats.

"Whoa, lead foot," Charlotte laughed. "You wanna take it easy? Are you trying to throw us out of the car?"

David let off the gas and murmured something beneath his breath. He checked his tone and said, "Sorry. The pedal sticks sometimes."

"Yeah. Whatev." Charlotte peered out the window. "Say, is anyone else hungry? I could go for a nice, juicy burger and some fries."

"Me, too," David said. "Eric? You up for trying something new?"

He held a hand to his growling stomach and said, "Right now, I feel like I could eat an ox."

"A side of cow it is, patty style."

Eric's stomach gnarled and knotted with each odiferous establishment they passed. There were signs for things he'd never heard of: tacos, Indian, Italian. One place that sold Chinese almost had him leaping from the car and crawling through its red doors flanked with golden dragons. When he didn't think he could be tortured anymore, David turned into a place called Burger Blaster. The smell was—what was the word Charlotte used a lot? Oh yes. Insane.

They drove around the small brick building into a drive-thru, whatever that was. David reached into his pocket and pulled out the money Lily gave him. Eric had no idea how much was there, but it looked like a lot. He hoped it was enough to purchase the side of cow, patty style.

Eric watched out David's window as he pulled up to a strange box with holes in it. A voice came out of it.

"Welcome to Burger Blasters. Can I take your order?"

Bees swarmed in Eric's belly. What sort of magic was this? He leaned over David and said, "We want a side of cow, please. Braised and pattied."

Charlotte broke out laughing.

So did David. He pushed Eric away.

The deadpan voice from the box responded. "We don't sell sides of cow. Would you like something else? The menu is to your left. Let me know when you're ready."

"What do you mean you don't sell sides of cow?" Eric asked.

"Shush, will you?" David said with a chuckle. He turned back to the box. "Ignore him. He's not from around here. I want six double burger bombs, two with no pickles and no onions. Three large fries and three large strawberry shakes with whipped cream, please."

"You want your buns toasted?"

"Please."

"That'll be twenty-nine fifty-two. Drive up to the second window."

David pulled forward. He counted out the money and gave it to the girl behind the sliding window. Several white bags came Eric's way along with three paper cups filled with something pink, thick, and freezing cold. Eric stuck his nose in one of the bags and took a whiff. His stomach growled. Whatever burger bombs were, he loved them before he ever tasted them.

***

The road twisted and turned, and Drac the Mustang took the uphills and downhills like the roaring dragon it was. Within minutes of leaving Burger Blasters, they were pulling alongside a single-story brick house. David pulled around back and turned the car off.

Eric stepped out of the car and shut the door. He glanced around the gardens and open pasture, his hand shielding his eyes. Two horses grazed in the distance. A few goats meandered in the side yard and a couple of chickens clucked about. It reminded him of home and he was comforted in the common simplicities.

"Eric," David said. "Let's go inside and eat before these shakes melt."

David let Charlotte out on his side and she ran up to the door and knocked. "Grampa? It's me. Charlotte."

No answer.

Knock, knock, knock.

"Grampa?"

David and Eric walked up behind her, their arms loaded with food.

"Weird. I don't think he's home," Charlotte said. "Hang on. I'll get the spare key."

She lifted a statue of a frog in a sea of potted plants, collected the key beneath it, and opened the backdoor. Once inside, Charlotte called out for her grandfather again. A quick search turned up no one. "Hmm, that's odd. His car's in the garage."

"Maybe he's at a neighbor's house," David said. "Why don't we sit down and eat. He'll show up soon enough."

They sat around the kitchen table, unwrapping burger bombs. Eric took one bite and succumbed to sheer pleasure.

He wiped the juices running down his chin, and stared at his drink. He removed the odd membrane lid and tipped it to his lips.

Nothing came out.

Charlotte handed him a straw. "Put it in your drink and suck it up. Like this." Eric watched the way her cheeks suctioned inward. "You might have to do it a couple of times before it comes up because it's so thick. Go ahead. Try it."

"Seems like an awful lot of trouble just to drink something." However, he did as Charlotte instructed and after three tries, cold berry goodness flooded his mouth and slid down his throat. It was heaven. Sweet, cold, delectable heaven. He took a break, sighed, and sucked in some more.

"Be careful, Eric," David said. "You'll end up getting—"

Eric put down his shake and clutched his forehead as hundreds of ice picks hammered away at his brain. Pound. Pound. Pound. The pain spread from behind his nose to the center of his head. It was relentless. Cruel.

And suddenly gone.

He sat back in his chair and stared at his drink as if it were poison.

David looked at Charlotte, chuckled, and completed his thought. "Brain freeze."

Eric flicked a glance at his friend. "You knew this would happen?"

"No, not really," David said, "but then I saw you drinking it really fast and I tried to warn you, but it hit you before I could get the words out. Next time, drink slower."

"Understood," Eric said. His stomach rumbled and he finished off the last of his second burger. When done, he attacked the packets of ketchup by opening a pouch and squeezing it into his mouth.

David shook his head.

Charlotte laughed. "That's ketchup, silly. You're not supposed to eat it plain."

Eric laid the empty packet on the table. "Why not? Are there rules against it? Will it make me ill?"

"Nooo," Charlotte said, her face in a wide grin. "It's what we call a condiment. It enhances food. It's not a food by itself."

Eric sucked another packet dry and set it on the table. "Well, it should be."

Charlotte laughed again, and her melody was comforting to his soul.

"I'll alert the media." David slurped the last of his drink and tossed it in the garbage can.

The kitchen clock tick-tocked the time away. David yawned and got up.

"I don't know about you guys, but there's a couch in the living room that's calling my name. I'm beat."

Charlotte scooted her chair away from the table. "I think that's a good idea. Today sucked on so many levels." She glanced up at him as she stood. "How's your chest, you know, where the necklace burned you?"

"I'm okay." He ran his palms over his face. "Why don't you play something on the piano?"

"I was thinking the same thing," Charlotte said. "Funny you said that."

David shrugged. "Whatever. You always play after you eat. You said it's good for the digestion, remember?"

"I do, and it is. Anything in particular you'd like to hear?"

David moved into the den and stretched out on the couch, a pillow tucked beneath his head. "Moonlight Sonata, please. It's one of your best."

Charlotte smiled. "You always pick that one. How about Humoresque by Dvorak?" She pulled out the bench and sat before an upright instrument that appeared very much like a harpsichord. She patted the seat beside her. "Come here, Eric. Sit beside me."

Eric did as she asked and closed his eyes as the haunting melody lulled him to a place void of dragons, gnomes, and war. A place of ultimate peace. Solitude. Detachment.

Heaven.

Chapter 14

David

The backdoor shut.

The piano fell quiet, the music ending almost as quickly as it began. A stroke of silence passed.

David scrambled to his feet and flicked a glance at Eric who reached for a sword that wasn't there. Not good.

Keys hit a counter. A gravely old voice called out from the kitchen. "David Heiland, is that your piece of junk sitting in my driveway?"

Charlotte squealed and spun around on the bench. "Grampa!"

David grinned. "Yes, sir, that would be mine." But as the words tumbled from his mouth, the grin faded and his brows crowded together. His breathing slowed and he couldn't shake the hollowness in his chest, the sinking feeling he'd been watched and discovered. "I'm surprised you recognized it," he continued.

A stooped old man with eyes as blue as the Caspian Sea and

hazel-colored hair that lay smooth as silk about his shoulders smiled as he stood in the doorway.

"Son, that beaut could be painted pink and covered in cow dung and I'd still know her. Not many of them like her left. Besides, Lily told me what she'd done. I've been expecting you."

Charlotte threw her arms around her grandfather.

"Charlotte, my dear. I'm so happy to see you." He embraced her in a big hug. He glanced over her shoulder at David. "My, my," he said, releasing Charlotte with a kiss to her cheek. He held out a fragile hand to David. "How you have grown, young man. Look at you, all tall and strapping. The girls must be falling all over you."

David took the man's hand, surprised by its softness. It's frailty. "I don't know about that, sir, but thank you."

The man turned to Eric and extended a hand.

"Hello," Eric said, shaking it as David had done. "I'm—"

Grampa squeezed Eric's hand and cupped his other one over it. "You do not need to tell me who you are, squire Eric Hamden, or is that Domnall?" A smile twitched at his lips. He released his hand. "Let's all sit in the living room. There's a bit more room in there. I can't wait to hear all about what you've been up to." He shot David a calculating glance and turned.

David's head swam with confusion, too afraid to consider what dark thoughts went together with the look.

"He knew who I was," Eric whispered to David as the old man and Charlotte left the room.

"Yeah. Weird." Unease rippled through David as they followed the man into the living room. How would he know who Eric was? It's possible Lily would have told him Eric was traveling with them, but how would he know the relationship with Trog? He wouldn't, and Lily wouldn't divulge it. But what if? What if Seyekrad nached the old man?

No. No, no, no. This can't be happening. I have to go to my car. I have to get my bow and Eric's sword. We can't be here, trapped, with no defenses.

He could feel the sweat dripping down his neck. He wiped his sweaty hands on his jeans and somehow found a steady voice.

"Sir, I'll be right back. I need to get something out of the car."

The old man shook his head. "You won't need your sword and bow with me, I can assure you. Please, take a seat. I've been anxious for your arrival."

He can read my mind? Crap! Stop thinking! Stop babbling to yourself.

Charlotte sat on the sofa beneath the window. "Why are you talking so weird, Grampa, and how did you know what he was going to get out of the car?"

Eric and David sat in two cane high-back chairs separated by a low table. David glanced around the room at the bookcases, the wing-backed chair and embroidered footstool in the corner, a book opened in its seat. The dining room just beyond a short-wall partition. There were no paintings. No needless decorations. He didn't remember it being so stark.

The old man grinned, even chuckled a bit. "I have waited a very long time to tell you what I need to tell you. I have been under strict orders by Miss Lily to keep my mouth shut. However, she came to me last night, desperate with disconcerting news. She and I agreed the next time you kids and I saw each other, I would tell you the truth about everything."

Alarms fired all over the place inside David, and judging by Eric's shifting and general unease, they were doing the same in him.

"Can I get you anything to drink?" Grampa asked. He withdrew to the kitchen. "I have water. Tea. What is your pleasure?"

"Nothing for me, thank you," David and Eric said, almost in harmony.

"Nothing for me, either," Charlotte said. She wore a strange expression as if she were trying to figure out a riddle, or the secrets to the universe.

Eric jogged his leg up and down. "I have a bad feeling about this," he whispered. "Charlotte, are you sure this man is your grandfather?"

"Yes," she said, though her voice met with some hesitation. "At least he looks like him, sounds like him, but there's something that's not right, like it's *not* him."

David leaned forward and whispered, "I'm thinking he might be Seyekrad. Be careful what you say."

"I hope you're wrong, David," Eric said, "because if you're not, we're toast."

David sat back, his stomach a knot of nerves. "You've got that right."

The man returned to the living room, a cup of tea in his hand, and sat on the couch beside Charlotte.

"Well, it certainly is good to see you, but I feel like a specimen under a glass," he said, a smile on his face. "Why are the three of you looking at me as if I were a three-headed goat?"

"I think right now, a three-headed goat would be more understandable," Charlotte said. She turned to him. "I'm sorry, Grampa, but you've got us kind of freaked out here. You don't have any idea what kind of stuff is going through our heads, so you gotta help us out."

The man laughed. "Oh, I know what is going on in your heads. I can hear every thought, and let me assure you, I am not Seyekrad, nor has he nached my body." He dipped his chin and glanced at David over the top of his glasses.

David shivered.

"Then who are you?" Eric asked. "Because everything inside of me is telling me you are not Charlotte's grandfather, and I don't know you."

David took a deep breath. There was that brave tone, the one he wanted to summon but didn't have the guts to do. It must be a squire, princely thing.

"I am known by many names, depending on who you ask. To you, my sweet Charlotte, I am Grampa. To your father, I am Arland or Pops. But to Auravalla, or Lily as you call her, I am Aldamar, son of Dorazón and father to Jared of Felindil."

The color drained from Eric's face.

Charlotte sat frozen, her eyes upon him, unmoving.

David gulped, his mouth hung open. "Th-that's not possible."

Charlotte exhaled, and snagged a breath. She shook her head. "I don't understand. Y-you're Slavandria's and Lily's grandfather?"

"I am." Aldamar sipped his tea.

Charlotte drew to her feet. "No. This isn't possible." She turned to face him. "I've known you my entire life. You're Grampa. Period. Not some sorcerer from Felindil. I won't listen to another word."

The man chuckled. "Oh, no, no, dear one. I am not from Felindil. I am from Brac."

She spun around, her eyes glaring. "No. You're from Kingsport, Tennessee."

Aldamar continued, ignoring Charlotte's outburst. "Brac is the fifth star in the House of Lesh, one of six heavenly houses that protect the world of Estaria."

Charlotte shook her head and covered her ears. "No. I'm not listening."

Eric stared at the floor. "I know that word. Where have I heard it before?" Moments later the recollection slid from his lips.

"You're a Numí," he said.

The man nodded and smiled. "You know your mage history."

"Oh my god, no!" Charlotte dropped her hands and whipped around, her cheeks red. "This is such B.S.!"

"Charlotte, please," David said, rubbing his forehead.

"Don't *please* me! This is insane, like literally cuckoo insane."

Eric leaned forward in his chair, his hands clasped. "Your grandfather isn't crazy, my lady. Numí are real. They are soldiers of the heavens."

"What do you mean, *soldiers*?" Charlotte asked.

Aldamar sat his cup on the table. "We like to think of ourselves as guardians of the universe."

"Which universe?" David asked. "Because the last time I looked, the world we're in right now is not in your universe, so why are you here?"

"To protect the paladin, of course."

David groaned. He didn't want to be the paladin. Never did, and he wanted it even less now. He leaned back, running his fingers through his hair.

Eric snorted. "I understand, David. All too well. Don't you wish for once you could escape the truth, the reminders? But you know what, we won't ever be able to because, no matter where we go or what we do, we're always going to be who we are. It's infuriating. It isn't fair, but that's our burden. That's our reality."

Charlotte stared at them. "You guys are pathetic. Are you really buying this story? Tell me, Grampa. Why in God's name would you need to travel universes and pretend to be my grandfather to protect David?"

"I needed to be close to the paladin, and what better way to do that than become part of the *family*. Why, I've known David for as long as I've known you. A few minutes either way and the two of you would share the same birthday."

"Is that true?" Eric asked, his brow lifted.

"Yeah," David said, leaning forward, his hands clasped between his knees. "I was born two minutes before midnight on March 31.

Charlotte was born five minutes after me on April 1. It's one of those fascinating pieces of trivia that people seem to love about us, but I don't want to talk birthdays." He turned his gaze to the man sitting across from him. "How, when did you do it? You know. Become Charlotte's grandfather?"

"Arland Stine became very ill a few days after Charlotte was born. He'd been suffering with a disease, cancer you call it. I saw the opportunity to achieve a goal, so when he passed away, I slipped in."

David shook his head and laughed. "I don't believe it." He glared at the old man, invisible daggers flying from his eyes. "You nached his body. What were you thinking?" He stood. He could feel the fury, the heat rushing to his face. "What gives you the right to take over people's bodies whenever you feel like it?"

Aldamar stood. "I saved Charlotte's father from a terrible heartache and gave her a grandfather she would have never had. I healed this body, slowly so as to not raise suspicion. For all intents and purposes, I *am* Arland Stine, just a bit stronger and much wiser."

"You're a liar," Charlotte said, "and a fraud. I want nothing more to do with you. Come on, guys. Let's go. I've heard enough."

She stormed from the room toward the kitchen and her point of freedom.

"Einar must be stopped." Aldamar's voice quaked through David, splitting reality. "If he is not, he will punch through this world the way he did a century ago. I will not be able to stop it the next time."

David cocked his head. "What are you talking about?"

"David, don't listen to him," Charlotte said. Her voice was tight, strapped with anger, denial, and betrayal.

"I have to listen to this," David replied. "Please. Close the door and come back."

Charlotte slammed the door and returned to the room. She leaned her shoulder against the wall.

David sat back in his chair, his arms crossed. "Talk, Mr. Stine, Aldamar, whoever you are. Tell us about Einar's visit to this world."

"I think it best if I show you."

Chapter 15

Eric

The old man opened his palm upward and blew across it. Over the table an expansive smoky image formed. Inside, people moved about in what looked to be a market. A building with arched, stained-glass windows appeared.

"Hey. That's the church down the street from our school," Charlotte said, sliding past Eric. "Why is everyone dressed funny?"

"Clothing was much different than it is today," Aldamar began. "Modesty was in style, not just for one's own respectfulness, but also for the benefit of wandering eyes as well." He leaned forward and pointed to his temple. "I know I've seen things I wish I could unsee. Haven't you?"

"Not to be rude," David said, "but what's the point of showing us this?"

"Do not be so impatient, my boy. To understand where you're

going, you must understand where you've been. During this time, Havendale was finding its roots upon which to grow. There wasn't much to the town at the time: a church, a school, a bank, and a textile store. Few people had money, but the townspeople were content. Happy."

Eric's pulse set flight in his throat as odd shaped black cars puttered by in the projection. He reached out to touch them, but the image changed to one of a grand three-story building made of stone. On the outside of the building, a waterwheel turned. Inside, workers wiped away sweat as they dumped bags of grain into a hopper. The millstones rotated.

"That's the gristmill!" David said. "The one in the woods behind my house, except it's not destroyed."

A twinge of familiarity tugged at Eric as he peered closer, taking in every wall, every window.

Aldamar nodded. "Yes, it is. Your family was one of the few that had wealth, brought on for the most part by that mill."

Eric's heart pumped faster as he watched, mesmerized, not so much by the process but by knowing he'd stood in that very room mere hours before. Funny how time had a way of changing perspectives.

"What happened to it?" Eric asked. "How did it fall into such disarray?"

"Einar. He destroyed just about everything in Havendale."

David shared a glance with Charlotte. "How did Einar destroy anything in Havendale?"

"It was a tad more than a century ago. Hirth was in its glory.

Trade was plentiful. All the kingdoms flourished, until Avida released the beast from his prison beneath Lake Sturtle. Vengeance was on his mind. He reclaimed Berg, destroyed what was left of Braemar, turning it into the smoldering ruins it is today, and then tried to take Hirth. A great battle broke out between the mages and the dragon, and warriors arrived every moment from Lesh."

Charlotte wedged between Eric and David, her eyes pinned to the warring image in the brume. Her fingers curled around Eric's. Her touch electrified his skin. His breath lodged in his lungs, refusing to leave. He was caught in a swirling vortex of confusion, desperate for her to let go, yet praying she never would.

"Look at all of them." Her voice was soft. So soft. She covered her mouth with her other hand. One, two tears fell as Einar swooped down and plucked people from where they stood, their dead bodies falling from great heights to the ground. "They never had a chance."

Eric squeezed her hand. "It's okay," he whispered. "You're okay."

A flash ripped across the conjured sky.

"Whoa! What was that?" David asked.

"Avida, ripping a hole between worlds." Aldamar got up and moved toward the depiction. "I do not know if it was intentional. She may have been trying to seal the rift to keep more Numí from entering. Whatever the reason, the fabric between our world and yours ripped apart."

All eyes were pinned to the brume. Not a sound hovered in the air. Not a breath could be heard.

The laceration spilled open, a wound spreading wider. Einar

twisted his body around and soared through it, fire billowing from his mouth.

The scene shifted to a forest. A town. Terrified faces.

Fire.

So much fire.

The forest turned to ash. The gristmill hidden by flames. The town a raging inferno.

All except for the church.

A man and a woman emerged from the sanctuary. Eric squinted. "That's you, Aldamar!"

"And Lily!" Charlotte shouted.

Magic—strong, bright, and powerful—shot from their palms, catching Einar in the chest. Each blast, each electrifying tendril from Lily's and Aldamar's hands pushed and shoved the beast. Relentless. Unyielding.

Eric held his breath. He'd heard tales of battles between the Numí and Einar, but he never believed them to be true. He glanced at the old man beside him and a shiver crawled up his spine. Aldamar was Jared's father. Jared's father. The two words sank in.

Powerful. Intense. Godly.

Talk about feeling small. Insignificant. A tiny speck in the universe.

Charlotte gasped and released his hand. "Yes!" she said.

Eric turned back to the brume. Einar tumbled through the rift. Aldamar swept his arms before him. Narrow, sharp beams of light shot from his hands, tracing the gaping wound. The tear stitched.

The image disappeared.

"After Auruvalla and I repaired the damage, we did what we could to heal the town. There was so much devastation. For seven days, tumultuous rains fell, and with it came another ruination: floods. Then came the snow and we fled underground. The blizzard was unforgiving and cruel. Many who survived the fire perished in the aftermath.

"For two weeks, we remained isolated, and it was there we discovered something of great interest." He wiggled his fingers and another projection appeared. Images of tunnels emerged within the fog. Lots and lots of tunnels.

"I knew where we were the instant we stumbled upon them."

"The Opal Caverns," David said, spellbound.

"Not exactly," Aldamar replied, "but they did lead to them."

Charlotte held up her hands. "Wait. Wait. Are you telling us there are mage tunnels beneath Havendale?"

Aldamar nodded.

"Where?" Eric asked. He tucked his hands in his armpits, suddenly aware of how much he'd begun to shake, his body fighting the maelstrom of excitement and emotions swirling within.

A large body of water appeared in the image. Frozen. Deserted. Branches, weighted with icicles, dipped to the ground. Wooden ramps jutted into the ice, their forms barely visible through the heavy snow.

"That's Lake Sturtle," David said. "I'd know it anywhere."

The image shifted to a mammoth cave, its walls smooth from

constant wear. Bones lay strewn over the damp earthen floor. Thin, transparent capes fluttered in ripped chunks from the ceiling and walls. Eric leaned forward.

"That's dragon skin."

Aldamar nodded.

"Einar's lair," David said. He looked at Aldamar, his eyes wide. "Seyekrad's using the tunnels."

The man dismissed the image from the air. "Can you surmise why?"

Another riddle. Eric's brain whirred, the meaning becoming clearer by the second. "The crystals. He's hiding them in the lair." He exhaled a whistle. "Dragon's breath!" He turned to Aldamar, his heart racing. "You've got to get us in there. You have to open us a portal."

Aldamar shook his head. "I cannot do that."

"Why not? You're a Numí."

Aldamar chuckled and shook his head. "If only that were enough. Truth be told, dear boy, my powers have been used to anchor this world, to prohibit the rift from re-opening, even the slightest use of magic elsewhere threatens the stability of the tear."

"Hold on a minute," David said. "Back up the truck. Are you telling us you've been here, in our world, for over a hundred years?"

The old man nodded.

"You haven't been home, you haven't seen your son, your family, in a hundred years?"

"No, I have not."

"What the—that's crazy! Why would you do that? I wasn't even born then. Heck, I wasn't even a thought."

"Auruvalla—Lily—and I decided to stay behind to protect this world. There was something about it that my precious granddaughter fell in love with. She wasn't strong enough to hold the rift together, so I chose to stay with her."

"Knowing you'd never be able to go home," Eric said.

"I couldn't leave my precious Lily. She didn't want to return to Fallhollow. She felt her calling was here. What was I to do?"

Eric shook his head. What was it with people voluntarily giving the ultimate sacrifice? Trog, Charlotte's brother, now Aldamar and Lily. Unselfish deeds, knowing the pain it would cause them if they followed through. Could he do such a thing if needed? He wasn't sure. He liked living too much.

Aldamar continued, breaking Eric's thoughts. "In time, my powers will leave me all together and I will no longer be able to protect this world. The threads will unravel. The rift will open, and nothing will stop Einar from entering. I will die, and he will shed his title of King and become God."

Eric stood and stared the old man in the eye. "Not if I have anything to say about it. We must get the crystals. We must destroy him, and then we can ferry you back to Fallhollow."

"There will be no ferrying for me, young Eric," Aldamar said. "Even Numí die, even if it takes us seven hundred years and a few more."

Eric's stomach left his body. "Seven hundred years! That would mean Jared is—"

"Five hundred plus. Slavandria and Lily, two hundred and a few."

Eric gulped. His mind twisted and knotted. How could someone live that long? It was impossible. Even for a mage.

"Guys," Charlotte said, snapping Eric from his thoughts. "I think we're forgetting what we came here for. We need to find the crystals and take them to Slavandria so she can open the tunnels. Then we can rescue Garret, Gertie, and Twiller's family. That's all. We're not going off on some whacked out dragon-killing quest."

"Slavandria cannot have control of the crystals," Aldamar said. "They must be destroyed."

"What? Why?" Charlotte asked.

"Because if Slavandria uses them to open the tunnels, she will also open them to whatever evil the Dragon King has enlisted. The demons that will enter Fallhollow are far beyond any you can fathom. While she will try to use them for good, all that is malevolent and vile will spread and triumph in its desire. It must not be permitted. Do you hear me?"

Eric kept his face blank, willed his heart to stay calm. He rubbed a hand down his face. "So what are we supposed to do?"

A clock chimed in the house. Aldamar pressed a hand to Eric's shoulder. "Be patient. When the time is right, Einar will get everything he deserves and more, including a few F-22 Raptors." The man winked at him.

Eric's stomach dropped and his limbs grew cold. "Y-you heard me ... us?"

"I am a Numí. I hear all." He turned away. "Even things I would not like to hear."

Eric stood there, numb. He couldn't think. He could barely breathe. He hated the idea of this man, this warrior Numí god, being able to hear his every thought. After all, some were meant to be private. He glanced at Charlotte.

Very private.

"Wait," David shouted. "Where, how are you going to get some F-22 Raptors? Conjure them out of thin air?"

The old man laughed. "Oh, I have no intentions of getting them for you."

"Then how are we supposed to get them?"

Aldamar smiled. "Perhaps you should ask the man behind you."

They followed his gaze and turned toward the front door.

Charlotte stood still as a statue, her face solid as stone.

"Daddy?"

Chapter 16

David

David stood in shock as Mr. Stine swept Charlotte in his arms and held her tight. He kissed the top of her head and tears rolled down his cheeks. She buried her face in his neck and her sobs could be heard across the universe.

"My baby. My sweet baby girl. Where have you been? Your mother and I have been worried sick about you."

Charlotte wiped her tears. She was visibly shaken. "It's a long story. In fact, I don't even think you'd believe me." She looked up at him and wiped her nose with the back of her hand. David handed her a box of tissues from the end table. She plucked a few and tossed the box on the couch.

"Try me," Mr. Stine said, cupping her face in his hands. The joy in his eyes tugged a knot in David's throat.

Is this how his parents would feel seeing him after almost

seventeen years? He couldn't even imagine meeting his parents for the first time. Sometimes he wondered if he ever would.

Charlotte touched her father's face. "Maybe. In time." She avoided his gaze and inched into her seat on the couch. "What are you doing here? What did," she flicked a side glance at Aldamar, "Grampa mean about you getting some planes?"

Mr. Stine sat on the couch. "Pops called me and told me to get here right away. Said it was urgent." His voice quivered. "I thought something was wrong. I never dreamed I'd find you here." He fixed his eyes on her, took her hands in his. "But I don't understand. Why didn't you come home?"

"I couldn't, Daddy," Charlotte said. She pinned her hands beneath her thighs. "There were all those cops, and I didn't want to answer all their questions. Besides, I'm not planning on staying, so I didn't want to get you and Mom all teary and happy only to leave again. That wouldn't be fair to you."

David stiffened, his eyes on her face. Why did she have to be so difficult? She had to stay with her family. Give up the idea of chasing dragons and taking part in harrowing rescues. He had to somehow convince her without her getting all pissed off. Maybe Eric could help. She'd listen to him.

He flicked a glance at Eric, who stood leaning against a wall, his eyes ever watchful of everything going on. His insides fluttered and flipped. Damn. He couldn't get over how much Eric looked like Trog. So much so it scared him.

Mr. Stine raised his voice. "David!"

David startled and faced Charlotte's father. Gah, how he hated that inquisitorial look the man always had in his eyes when he looked at him.

"What is she talking about? Why can't she stay? What have you gotten her into?"

"Daddy, leave David—"

"Quiet, young lady. This is between me and this young man here." He stood, squared his shoulders.

David stiffened. *Don't let him intimidate you.* "I haven't gotten her into anything except maybe a war with a dragon, and a sorcerer who wants to kill me."

Charlotte's dad balled his hands into fists. "Don't get flippant with me, young man."

"Daddy!" Charlotte jumped from the couch. "I love you but I will not stand here and let you pick on him. He's doesn't deserve your anger, and I won't put up with you treating him like he was last week's garbage."

David kicked at the ground, his expression blank, but inside, he was floating to the moon. Charlotte defended him. That was better than vanilla ice cream on top a slice of hot apple pie and that was saying a lot.

Mr. Stine snorted and wagged his finger. "Wait. Wait. I get it now. You're pregnant. You went off somewhere to figure out how to take care of it, and you were too afraid to face me and your mother."

Aldamar shook his head. "Frank."

David snorted. If he'd been drinking milk, it would have come out of his nose.

Charlotte's mouth hung open. "What? Are you crazy? I can't even believe you just said that. No! I'm not pregnant." She threw her hands in the air. "Gaah."

Eric straightened. "Sir, I must object to this interrogation. One, it is of a private nature, and two, I can assure you that your daughter and David have an impeccable relationship, one of mutual respect, appreciation, and distance."

David's chest rose and fell, his thoughts on a time in Chalisdawn where his and Charlotte's *distance* was a bit too close—where the topic at hand might be one that needed discussing. Thank the bejeebie beans he averted that gaffe. Mr. Stine sneered at Eric and snapped back. "Who are you?"

"My name is Eric Hamden, sir." He folded in a bow.

David smirked. "Good grief. Stand up. Geez." He shook his head and caught Mr. Stine's eye. "He's not from around here."

Mr. Stine raised an eyebrow. "And where are you from?"

Charlotte jumped in. "He's from—"

Her father shot her *the look*. "I didn't ask you."

"It's all right, Charlotte." Eric smiled. "I'm from Fallhollow, sir," Eric answered. "It's very far from here. I doubt you have heard of it."

"No, I can't say that I have. How did you hook up with these two runaways who seem to have such little regard for their families and the town that's worried sick about them?"

"Daddy, please."

Eric stepped forward. "You underestimate us, sir, and if you truly believe what you just said, then it is my belief you are the one who lacks regard for your daughter. She loves you and adores you. Just because she is following her heart at the moment does not mean she has lost her respect for you. It merely means she is finding some for herself. Now, if you will excuse me, I am feeling a bit on edge. David, if I might have the keys to your car?"

"We'll go with you," Charlotte said. "Maybe by the time we get back, Grampa can talk some sense into his son."

They walked away, a united front, and retreated through the kitchen and out the back door.

David was the first to reach the car. He unlocked and lifted the trunk.

"Man, he's hot tonight. Why does he hate me so much?"

"I doubt he does," Eric said, collecting his sword and scabbard and strapping them to his side. "He's only trying to intimidate you. Fathers do that sort of nonsense, even where I come from."

"Well, I don't appreciate it." David grabbed his bow and quiver and slammed the trunk. "I've never done anything to deserve that and he's known me almost all my life."

Charlotte walked to the edge of the pasture and folded her arms on the white fence. The sun played low in the sky, casting long shadows upon a landscape splashed in warm shades of sunset orange and gold. Overhead, shades of violet and blue faded into a palate of deep purple and black.

"Penny for your thoughts?" Eric opened his palm, a coin in the middle.

She smiled. "I'm not thinking. I'm wishing. Wishing all of this was over. Wishing I could erase the hurt in my dad's eyes. Wishing I wasn't the one who put it there."

"I know what you mean," Eric said. "Ever since I found out that Trog was—you know—I've been wishing, too. Wishing I'd known my mother. Wishing I could have seen her and my father long before I was born, to see what he was like before the world changed him."

"He loves you, Eric," Charlotte said. "You know that, right?"

"Yes. Deep down I do. And I him. If only he would see me as something more than an object to protect."

Charlotte tilted her chin his way. "What's the one thing you think you could do to, I don't know, be perfect in his eyes? To have him see you as something more?"

Eric looked off in the distance. "Become a knight." He paused. "Yes. That would please him immensely."

"And would that please you?" Charlotte asked.

He smiled. "Yes. It would. It's all I've dreamed of and trained for since I can remember."

David patted Eric's shoulder. "Then let's make a promise now for all of our wishes to come true."

He placed a hand on a fence post. Charlotte looked at him, smiled, and laid her hand on top of his. Eric looked between the two of them and laid his hand on top.

"To prayers and wishes," David said. "May all of them be granted."

"Hooray!" Charlotte yelled.

Three hands rose in the air, followed by laughter, and for a moment, all was right with the world.

If only those moments could last forever.

***

The pizza arrived.

David sat opposite Mr. Stine, the fighter pilot, the seasoned war vet, the former Black Op that could see through and rip apart every bullshit story ever told. The tale was going to be difficult. Somehow, they were going to have to make him believe it.

It took six slices of pizza and two ice-cold beers to get Mr. Stine in the mood to listen.

"It's not what you think," David said. "It's like Charlotte said, it's complicated, crazy, and beyond belief, but I swear to you every bit of it's true."

"Fine. I'm listening." He sat back in a chair, one leg crossed over the other. "Let's start with where you've been for the last two, almost three months."

"Oh, yeah, there's that 'months' thing again," Charlotte said. "I forgot about that."

"Don't play the naïve game with me, young lady. I want to know where you've been."

Charlotte slumped, her face in her hands. "You won't believe me, Daddy."

"Try me."

David rubbed the back of his neck. "Wow, this is going to be hard." He clasped his hands between his knees. "Mr. Stine, I've always thought of you as an open-minded, fair person. You always seemed to be the type of guy to listen to all sides of a story before passing judgment. A lot is at stake here and I don't think your dad would have asked you to meet us here unless he felt you could help us. But, before we go any further, do you know if the FBI or the police followed you?"

"I didn't see a tail, but I can't promise you anything. They are, after all, investigating the disappearance of two teens. Two, honest, trustworthy teens whose worst crimes include sticking bubblegum under a school desk and eating grapes you didn't pay for in a grocery store."

David chuffed. "I wish that was the only thing I was guilty of."

"What is that supposed to mean?"

David leaned forward. His eyes burned. "It means I'm no longer a grape-eating thief, sir. I've grown up. We all have. Charlotte and I aren't the innocent kids that left here in January. We've seen more than we should have ever seen. Death. War. Unimaginable destruction. In fact, I bet our stories could rival yours, maybe even top them."

"Son, I don't know why you're taking that tone with me, but I—"

David sighed. "Mr. Stine, with all due respect, I'm not trying to take a tone with you. I'm exhausted. I'm on edge. There is not one muscle in my body that doesn't ache. Last night was the first time I've had a decent night's sleep in I can't tell you how long. Even then,

Charlotte tells me I was restless."

"You were. I checked on you twice because you were moaning and groaning in your sleep."

"No doubt my nightmares had something to do with that. And you know what? Those same nightmares visit your daughter and Eric every single time they shut their eyes. So, if you really want to know the truth, if you really want to know where we've been and what's happened to us, you need to throw away everything you think you know. You need to trust us, no matter how strange and unbelievable the story gets. If you can't do that, then I'm afraid we're outta here, 'cause there's stuff we need to do and we're running out of time."

David blinked, but never took his gaze away from Mr. Stine's. What a moron he was. What an idiot, talking to Charlotte's father like some punk kid with an attitude. But he had to make the man understand. What better way to do it than with the three people who lived and breathed it?

Mr. Stine stared at David for the longest time, and the more he stared, the more David stared back. Finally, the match ended, and David exhaled. The man got up without a word and walked to the hutch, pulled out a decanter of whiskey, and poured a short glass. He turned back to David, drink in hand, his eyes wary, analyzing, worried.

"You mentioned two things that have me quite distressed. War and death. Hearing those words and knowing my daughter was somehow involved is upsetting. A part of me wishes I could pretend I didn't hear them, but I did, so now I need an explanation." He threw back his drink and returned to his chair. "With that said, I am prepared to listen. It is the very least I can do for my daughter. I can't say the same for you or your friend here." He cast a harsh look at Eric who seemed to take it in stride. David was fairly certain he'd received far worse from Trog. "After all, how do I know he's not a terrorist? A kidnapper?"

"You can start by trusting me," Charlotte said. "He's our friend."

Mr. Stine sat back, his arms folded across his chest. "Fine. Can I assume you used the words death and war as metaphors?"

David shook his head. "No, sir. I wish we were."

The man exhaled a hard breath. "Very well. Tell me how in the hell you got mixed up in a war, and better yet, why you put my daughter in harm's way."

"Daddy, that's not fair."

"And no lies," Mr. Stine said.

David stood. "It started with this." David lifted his shirt, exposing his tattoo, "then it escalated with this." He reached into a pocket, pulled out a folded, wrinkled letter and handed it to Mr. Stine. Somehow, he'd managed to hold on to it even after all the wardrobe changes, the battles. The page was worn, the ink smeared in some places, but for the most part, it was intact and he would do everything he could to keep it that way.

Ten, twenty, thirty silent seconds joined the conversation as the man read the letter that brought down David's world—the words that told him his parents' deaths were a cover up ... that they were actually alive. David counted and focused on his breathing.

"Is this true?" Mr. Stine asked. Disbelief and shock had found a comfortable place on his face and made themselves at home. David imagined he must have looked the same way when the truth sucker-punched him in the heart two months ago.

"Yes, sir."

"Have you seen them? Met them?"

David shook his head. "Not yet. Came close, but we were attacked."

"We weren't," Eric corrected. "The queen was."

"The queen?" Mr. Stine's eyebrow lifted.

"Daddy, you promised to keep an open mind." Charlotte got up and knelt before her father, taking one hand into hers. "It all started for me with a phone call from David."

***

They sat at the dining room table, four empty pizza boxes stacked in the center. The sun had long set, leaving the house dark but for a small incandescent lamp and the light sitting on top of a buffet table. Mr. Stine stood at the window, massaging his temples. He now knew everything his daughter knew, except for Aldamar's and Eric's true identities. Some things were better left unspoken.

He turned to face them.

"I'm at a loss for words, kids. I don't know what to feel. I'm numb. The three of you either have a hell of an imagination or you're telling the truth, both of which terrify me to no end."

"We're not lying," Charlotte said.

Her father held up a hand without looking her way. "You have told me an incredible story, one that no one in their sane mind would believe, and yet I do. I can't imagine what reason you would have to lie to me. That scar on Eric's back, the tattoo, the ring, the horror in my little girl's voice as she told me she was almost murdered. I can't deny what I've seen and heard, but I am having a very difficult time wrapping my mind around dragons and magic and sorcery."

"I have something that might help." David fingered the small orb on the necklace around his neck. "Grampa, what did I call this earlier?"

David hoped Aldamar understood the secret, unspoken conversation and went along.

The old man glanced at it. "I believe you called it a reminiscent vapor, a very powerful memory. Where did you get it?"

"Lily gave it to me."

"Then she must want us to see it," Charlotte said. "How did she say to open it?"

David shrugged. "I don't know. I don't think she did say."

Aldamar said, "If I had to guess, I'd say break it."

"Wait for me," Mr. Stine said. He took off down the hall to the bathroom and shut the door.

"Thanks," David said. "I was hoping you would understand—"

"Of course I understood," Aldamar said. "I can read your

thoughts. As for the vapor, I'm not sure I would advise you to open it. In order to experience a reminiscent vapor, one must be free of all magic. You would need to remove the rutseer, but removing it will leave you vulnerable to Seyekrad's detection. You must decide if the memory is worth the risk."

After a brief huddle, David, Eric, and Charlotte came to a unanimous decision. They wanted to see the memory.

Mr. Stine returned. They filled him in on what they were doing and that it might bring enemies into the open. "Very well," Charlotte's father said. "Let that leper come within a hundred yards of my little girl. There won't be anything left of him when I'm done."

Eric snorted. "I admire your bravery, sir, but you don't stand a chance against Seyekrad. He will put you in your grave with a flick of his finger."

"If you are willing to stand up to him, so am I. I'll die before I let him hurt my little girl."

"All right then," Charlotte said. "Come on, boys. Let's bust up a memory."

Chapter 17

Eric

E ric adjusted the sword pressed against his hip.

Beside him sat David, his quiver and bow on his back. Across from him sat Charlotte, rubbing her arms as if cold. Mr. Stine and Aldamar completed the circle. And the rutseer inside the Eye of Kedge lay on the dining room table inches from the tips of David's fingers.

David held the glass pendant over the table.

"Let it go," Eric said. "Break it."

David shook his head. "I'm trying. I can't open my hand. It's like it's glued shut or something."

"I bet the rutseer's too close to you." Eric wiped it from the table. It hit the carpet with a muffled thump, landing beneath the bookcase in the living room.

The glass pendant slipped from David's hand and shattered on the dining room table.

An image appeared, clear, crisp, clean. A living, breathing visual. Eric swallowed the cotton lump in his throat.

Slavandria lay upon a palatial bed covered by an enormous white coverlet dotted with pink rosebuds. Plush, snow-white pillows pressed all around her. Her hair draped over one shoulder in a single braid, a wide sea-green ribbon woven through the thick lavender strands. Small, wispy tendrils hung loosely about her temples and neck.

A small fire burned in a hearth. A crystal goblet filled to the brim with a misting burgundy liquid sat on the round table beside her, next to a vase of fresh cut flowers.

"Oh my gosh. David, that looks like Lily's room," Charlotte said.

In the corner, Lily sat in an overstuffed chair, her legs tucked beneath her. She wore a forest green nightgown and was humming softly to herself while reading. Slavandria turned her head, her eyes closed, a smile soft on her lips.

She held her sister's hand and looked into her eyes. "I'm so sorry, Valla, for what I've put you through. You have had to deal with so much these past months."

"Shh. Don't be silly. You're my sister and I love you." She leaned forward and kissed Slavandria's forehead. "Get some sleep. Rest. You and the baby need it. I'll be right here if you need me."

Slavandria slipped the blanket down, revealing a very round belly. She rubbed the bump, "Soon, little one. Soon."

She shut her eyes and drifted off to sleep, an angelic smile on her face.

The image shattered into hundreds of pieces only to rearrange to form a new one.

"Wait!" David shouted. "Go back to the baby!"

A leviathan of a ship arrived in a harbor, its fifty sails puffed by the salty breath of the sea.

Eric stared open mouth, his heart racing. He'd seen the ship once before on a trip to Felindil and it sucked his breath away then as it did now. It was the most magnificent ship in all of Felindil, perhaps in the world. Crafted of the finest teak, it measured over three hundred feet long, more than eight times larger than any other ship in the fleet. The tallest of its eight masts was just shy of half the ship's length. Its name—the WindSong.

"Hey, wait," Charlotte said. "Slavandria has a replica of that ship in Chalisdawn!"

"Oh my gosh, you're right!" David said. "And I thought the one in her house was big."

Two young girls about the age of sixteen, ran on the docks and were met with open arms by a tall, over-muscled man with playful, slanted blue eyes that glistened like two sapphires against his bronze skin. He sported a low forehead, a pointed chin and wore his silky, straight black hair neck-length in an attractive, impractical style. He wore a black vest, black trousers, and black boots. Silver rings adorned every finger. Swirling emblems covered his arms.

Eric knew the man before the girls said, "Father!"

Jared.

He glanced at Aldamar in time to see a slight quiver of the man's bottom lip before he bit it away. Eric made a wish—a wish for Aldamar to see his son and granddaughter again before he died. A quick glance at David and Charlotte and he knew they wouldn't mind.

The image fractured again, this one to a terrace and a young Slavandria, her hair up, wearing a gown as lovely and vibrant as emeralds. A man presented a flower. A dance. A kiss on the lips. He turned around.

Eric clicked his tongue, anger boiling up from his feet to his throat. David and Charlotte shouted at the brume ... at the image of Lord Seyekrad Krawl, introduced as the son of the Duke and Duchess of Doursmouth and apprentice to the wizard Sol of Bradenwood.

Eric harrumphed. So Slavandria had an affair with Lord Seyekrad. In all fairness, he appeared kinder, tender. Affectionate. Not the loathsome cretin he was now. He wondered as he watched the two of them together what could have changed him.

As if in answer, the brume shattered once more, the new image arising one of Slavandria in the arms of another man. A tall, dark-haired man with a sword and eyes as gray-blue as the Brindle Sea.

Eric's heart leapt.

Mangus Grythorn, the general of Jared's army. The most lethal mage other than Jared Eric had ever known. He was also cocky, dangerous, powerful, and respectable. And in the new image, he and Slavandria were standing on a seashore, she in a white shimmering gown, him in black leathers. Ribbons were wrapped around their wrists, weaved through their fingers. Bonded.

They were married, and from the looks of it, secretly. Eric smiled, then laughed, his nerves a crazy mess of twinges and tingles.

"She scorned him! She rejected Seyekrad. All of this, all of his hatred is because she didn't return his love?" He glanced at Aldamar. "He wants to destroy everything because she didn't love him?"

Aldamar nodded. "Love does strange things to people, Eric. Apparently, even to mages."

"That's why Seyekrad tortured Slavandria in the woods," David said, "because she chose someone else over him. I had no idea it was *him*. That's the guy that came to see Lily in the library. That's who I thought was going to take me away." David sat back, his hands in his hair. "Wow. Nuts. I guess some people hold grudges forever. In this case, he really needs to let it go."

The room shook with thunder. Black and silver strings of electricity crawled along the ceiling. Aldamar's eyes grew big, his face panicked.

"Forgive me. I must go." He vanished in a flick of bright, white light.

"He left!" Charlotte said. "Why did he leave? We need him!"

The table lifted from the ground and sailed through the air, smashing into pieces in the corner. A man spoke, and the sound of it charged through Eric like a bolt of lightning.

"Is that what you think, Davey boy?"

And there he was, tall, thin, regal, dressed entirely in black, his silver hair glimmering like moonlight upon his shoulders.

"Seyekrad!" David yelled.

Eric leapt from his chair and spun around, his sword drawn.

David jumped to his feet, his bow drawn.

Seyekrad moved closer, his smile twisted in smug satisfaction. "Might I suggest you put your weapons down." His deep tone vibrated along Eric's spine.

A tendril of black mist spiraled down from the ceiling and enveloped David.

Above him, pinned to the ceiling, Mr. Stine struggled against black, sparking constraints, his arms stretched out to his sides, his legs crossed together at the ankles. Angry heat lay in his eyes, not fear. Another human with determination, strength, and a selfless spine.

If only the magic could disappear.

"Daddy!" Charlotte cried out.

Eric whipped his head to his left. His breath hitched. Bainesworth von Stuegler, in all his blond, wretched, healed form, held Charlotte in his clutches, a venomous snake ready to strike and kill.

Energy sparked from her fingertips and danced across his arms, but she might as well be showering him with flower petals for all the good it was doing.

If only she knew how to use her *residual magic*. He'd give every gallion he owned to watch her ignite his body and cast him to the center of Hell in flames.

Anger shook his very core. He raised his sword, the tip pointed at Bainesworth's throat. "Let her go or I'll cut you from navel to nose."

Seyekrad flicked a finger and Eric's blade sailed across the room into a glass cabinet. Shards of glass rained through the air.

"I don't think so, pup." Seyekrad pinned his ice eyes to Eric, a pale hand pressed to his chest. "Your friends' agonizing deaths will bring me great pleasure. Making you watch will bring me even more."

A web of black energy pulsed around Eric, holding him to his spot.

Eric ripped at the cocoon. *Ahhh! Of all that is good in heaven, let me kill him!*

Charlotte struggled and kicked. "Leave him alone, you monster!" Her fingertips fell silent as her nails dug into the constricting arms.

Seyekrad waved his hand.

A silver spark ignited between Bainesworth and Charlotte, the flash almost blinding.

The knight wailed. "Watch it, fool." He shook out one arm at a time while managing to hold onto a struggling Charlotte. "Next time aim for her, not me."

Seyekrad cocked his head in Charlotte's direction. "I did aim it at the girl." He sashayed toward her, his brow furrowed. His gaze traveled over her body from head to toe. "Well, well. This is quite a turn of events." He grasped her jaw. "How did you do it?"

She ground her teeth, the tendons in her neck pulled taut.

He shifted his hand and dug his fingers into her cheeks. "I asked you a question and you will answer me."

She spit in his face. "Drop dead."

Seyekrad laughed. The sound filled the room. "Oh, I like you. What spirit you have." He cupped her chin. "Yes, Bainesworth, I think the Dragon King will be quite pleased with this gift." He turned around and aligned his gaze with David's. "That is, unless you wish to hand over the Eye of Kedge."

"Don't you dare, David," Charlotte shouted.

The Eye! The rutseer! Eric scoured the floor for it. A smile threatened to bloom on his face as he spotted the necklace beneath the bookcase.

"What will you give us in exchange?" David asked, one eye on Charlotte, the other on her father.

Seyekrad laughed again. "Give you? Oh, no, dear boy, I think you misunderstand. There is no exchange involved. See, you're the paladin, and you must die. That is a given. How ludicrous would it be for me to allow you to live while the heir to the throne of Hirth still breathes? Or does he?" He strolled toward David. "I think it's time I found out. Maybe if I rip your brain apart, I'll find him. Then you can die a hero's death."

Moisture evaporated from Eric's lips. His eyes darted from right to left to right again. *Stop him! Roll! Trip him! Do something!*

Seyekrad flicked a finger.

Eric sailed across the room and slammed into the wall. Pain shot like a hot arrow across his chest. His vision skewed. Stars appeared. He struggled to his elbows and knees.

Seyekrad laughed. "Your thoughts give you away, runt. Perhaps I should root around in your brain first."

David lunged, but the mist swirling around him closed in, wrapping tighter to his form.

Seyekrad walked toward Eric. "What will I find inside that gelatinous mess? The identity of the heir? You are, after all, the squire of the most revered knight of Hirth. The great and powerful Trog

236

knows all, which means, his runt would know everything, as well."

Charlotte shouted, "Leave him alone!"

Seyekrad's eyes clouded and turned a milky shade of purple.

Eric's body stiffened. Fingers, hundreds of them, entered his brain, searching, shoving, hurting. He squeezed his eyes tight. One of Magister Timan's lectures sprang alive in his mind. To block a mind sweep, think of one thing. Replicate it. Make a wall of it. Eric thought of a donkey he once had. He repeated the image and put it in every dark space in his head he could find.

Seyekrad's voice grew in frustration. "Why do you not want me inside your head? What are you hiding?"

Eric wailed, his hands pressed to the sides of his head. Tendrils of fire unwound in his mind, searching.

"Stop! Stop it!" Charlotte cried out.

Numbness swept through Eric's body. Memories elongated, thinned so much he couldn't tell one from the next. Only names remained. Connections faded.

Donkey!

Donkey!

Seyekrad's face twisted in fury. "What is this trickery? Open your mind to me!"

More magic burned into Eric. His blood caught fire.

"Leave him be." David shoved the sorcerer in the chest. "It's me you want."

Seyekrad spun around, his face twisted in rage and disbelief, his mouth open. "How did you—"

Charlotte's father crashed to the floor.

"Daddy!"

David guffawed. "What's the matter? Having concentration issues?"

Seyekrad lunged and caught David's head between his palms. "Die, you impertinent pest!"

David's body twitched. His eyes rolled in the back of his head.

Eric groaned. Using a stool for support, he pushed himself up. "No. Get. Away. From him."

"Stop it!" Charlotte screamed.

Green and purple threads of electricity sizzled and cracked across the room, striking Seyekrad in the chest. Air rushed from his lungs and he hunched over, gasping for air.

David fell away with a yell, and careened into the bookshelf, knocking it over. He groaned.

"Seyekrad!" Bainesworth said. "The girl. The strike came from her."

Charlotte kicked and squirmed. "It did not! You did it! You're the one who wants him dead. You want his power, his title, everything that black beast promised him."

"Why, you lying witch! I'll kill you here and now!" Bainesworth's arm wrapped around Charlotte's neck. Her eyes widened. Her feet lifted from the ground.

Eric's gaze flicked to David. His hands moved beneath the books like a leviathan through the sea. Hunting. Searching. He tucked something in his pocket.

Eric expelled a breath of air. He knew what David retrieved. Now to block the observation. Tuck it where Seyekrad couldn't find it. He collected a few more donkeys.

Seyekrad straightened, his hand clutching his heart. "No," he said, wheezing. "Take her to Einar. Let him do with her what he will."

He pointed his finger and circled it in the air. A portal emerged out of nowhere. Its silver fabric pulsed and swirled. Bainesworth and Charlotte fell through.

Eric staggered. "No!"

David yelled her name, but the hole between universes closed.

"Nooooo!" Charlotte's father yelled.

Eric, stumbled, bent over, and retched.

Chapter 18

David

"**B**ring her back, damn you!" Mr. Stine screamed, scrambling to his feet.

Spools of black sizzling magic unraveled from Seyekrad's fingertips and caught Mr. Stine in the chest, lifting him from the floor and slamming him into the china cabinet. With a thrust of his other hand, Eric jettisoned through the air and careened into what was left of the smashed dining room table.

Seyekrad jerked David around and held him by the throat. "Tell me where the heir is! I know you know. Tell me and I'll make sure your friends live."

Faint threads of magic slipped inside David's head, but there was no pull, no fire, just feathers meandering about on a slight breeze. David shook his head and laughed. "Looks like your magic's a little screwed up there."

He didn't know which came first—the smack or the excruciating pain from being backhanded across the face. They both seemed synonymous. Despite the pain, he couldn't help the laughter that bubbled out of him.

Seyekrad hit him again. "You're an insolent bug and I intend to see you squashed once I find the Eye."

David's chest squeezed and his stomach filled with bees as Seyekrad held him by the collar of his shirt and patted him down. The sorcerer snorted. "There it is."

David's nerves scattered.

Seyekrad reached into David's pocket and pulled out …

A jar of caviar?

David laughed until every inch of him hurt.

"What is this!" Seyekrad demanded. "Tell me!"

"Fish eggs. You should try them. Quite good actually."

Seyekrad hurled them across the room.

David laughed as the container hit the wall. He didn't know why. There was something funny about fish eggs flying across a room. "You know, you should really control your temper."

Seyekrad shook him. "Where is it! Where is the Eye of Kedge? Where is the heir?"

"Where are the crystals? Where is Charlotte?"

"Why you … " Seyekrad's fingers closed around David's throat, the sorcerer's nails digging into his flesh like barbed hooks.

David gasped for breath. His body dangled in the air like a caught fish. *Can't die. Save Charlotte.* He reached for Seyekrad's face. *Get. The. Eyes.*

But his airway squeezed shut, and he heard himself whimper.

Air. He needed air.

But there was none. He was falling into space. Time. Darkness. Death.

The end of all things.

His body jolted. He fell to the ground gasping.

Seyekrad landed next to him, writhing.

David wheezed and coughed, his throat raw and tender.

"Get him up, Eric," Mr. Stine shouted.

David took Eric's outstretched arm and grappled to his feet. "Thank you." He rubbed his throat and looked at Charlotte's father who stood over Seyekrad, the back of a dining room chair in his hand.

"Nice," David said.

The sorcerer groaned, moved. Magic sizzled at his fingertips.

Eric stumbled toward the glass cabinet and collected his sword. He found his scabbard a few feet away and strapped them to his hip. "Here," Eric said to David, "I thought you might like to have this back."

David held up his hand and caught the Eye of Kedge. His *caviar*. He slipped it around his neck.

"I don't know how you did it," Eric said, "but I take back everything I said about you being a wannabe magician. That was probably the best trick I've ever seen."

David smiled. "Thanks, but I think that one was all Finn."

Seyekrad clambered to his hands and knees. "I knew you had it.

Give it to me."

His eyes locked onto David's. He lifted a hand and pointed a finger at David's face. Black threads began to unwind.

Mr. Stine kicked him in the gut.

Seyekrad's body flipped in the air once and crashed to the floor. He cradled his arm. "Raise it again and I'll rip it from your body," Mr. Stine shouted. His face and hands were cut. He walked with a limp, but that didn't stop him. He was a fighter and he wasn't going to let Seyekrad get away with what he'd done, even if it meant dying in the process.

David gathered his quiver and bow, collected the arrows pitched about on the floor, and he and Eric took their places on either side of Mr. Stine, who glanced at them, then back at Seyekrad. "Where's my daughter, you sonofabitch?"

Seyekrad lay on his back and laughed. "You humans amuse me so."

Mr. Stine pressed his foot to Seyekrad's chest. "Where is she?"

David's jaw tensed. As much as he wanted to see Seyekrad suffer, he and Eric needed to get to Fallhollow and for reasons unknown to him, he could no longer ferry. He grasped Mr. Stine's arm and whispered, "Sir, can I talk to you for a moment, please?" He motioned to Eric. "Keep an eye on that scum for a minute."

Eric nodded, pulled his sword, and pressed the tip to Seyekrad's throat. "Happy to."

David edged Mr. Stine toward the hallway. "Sir, let me start by saying how much I appreciate you saving my life. I can't thank you

J. Keller Ford

enough. I also agree with this whole interrogation thing you've got going on. Trust me, I want to see him on his knees, begging for forgiveness, but I can't let you hurt him."

"He's got my daughter!"

"I know, and Eric and I will get her back, but we have to get to Fallhollow to do it."

"Then I'll come with you."

David shook his head. "You can't. We need you here."

"What good am I doing here? You can't expect me to sit and wait."

"You're right. I need you to do something else. Something just as important, something Eric and I can't do."

"And what is that?" He wore an irritated, annoyed expression, as if he'd eaten something sour and rotten.

"Prepare for war. We're going to need fighter jets, as many as you can get, Raptors if you can, because I've got a feeling that by the time all of this plays out, Einar will have one foot in Havendale, and we're going to need all the fire-power we can get to make sure the foot is blown off."

"You're asking for the impossible, David. I don't have that kind of authority and in case you don't remember, F-22s are no longer being made. They're caput."

"I know we have stocks of them and don't tell me we don't. The government doesn't destroy the best fighter planes ever made. Find them."

Mr. Stine stammered. "David, I can't just walk into Central

244

Command with this story and expect them to turn over billions of dollars' worth of aircraft to me. I have no proof of a coming war, and if I tell them it will be with a dragon, they'll put me in a straightjacket and put me away where no one will ever find me."

"Mr. Stine, please. You've got to try. You still have friends at the munitions facility here in Kingsport, right? Surely you have someone you can trust, someone that will believe you?"

The man rubbed the back of his neck. "I don't know, David."

"Please, sir. I beg you. This is important. You have to make them believe you. I promise to bring your daughter home, but I need to know that you're on top of this. Can you get it done?"

Charlotte's father rubbed his forehead, his eyes squeezed shut as if the thoughts in his mind hurt. He threw up a hand in defeat and nodded. "I'll see what I can do, but you better bring her home in one piece, hear me?"

David patted him on the shoulder. "Deal." He shifted his bow and quiver. "Work your own magic, sir, and I'll work mine. I have faith in you. Oh, and by the way, your father is a Numí. That's a very good thing." He turned to Eric. "You ready to kick some butt?"

His friend remained stoic, unmoving. David waved a hand in front of his face. Peered in his eyes. Black wriggles swirled in his pupils, snakes writhing, sucking out life.

WTF?

Rage swarmed through David as Seyekrad crawled away, cackling.

"Oh no you don't, you sonofabitch."

He kicked the sorcerer in the face.

Seyekrad gasped.

David unleashed his fury.

"This one's for Charlotte.

Kick.

"This one's for getting inside my brain."

Kick.

This one is for torturing my friends."

Kick.

"This is for every evil act you've ever done."

Blood gushed from Seyekrad's nose. Black and purple colors bloomed on his face. The cracking sound of bones breaking, the splatters of blood on his foot sent a jolt through David. He inhaled. His heart pounded. Never had he felt so much hatred, so much anger. What was wrong with him? Why did he want to keep beating him until there was nothing left? Firm hands gripped David's arms.

"Stop," Mr. Stine said, his voice soothing in the ears. "You're better than this. Besides, you just told me how much you need him."

Tears of anger rolled down David's cheeks. He clenched his fists. "He deserves to die for what he's done."

"I agree, but everything in its time. Right now, we need to find Charlotte."

"And the crystals," Eric said, his voice raspy. He walked as if he'd been spun in a centrifuge.

Seyekrad laughed, the maniacal sound ripping a hole in David's core. "You'll never find them," he wheezed.

David dropped to his knees. "Yes, we will, and you're going to take us to them, right now."

Seyekrad grabbed David by the throat and grinned. "Desire. It's such a fickle thing, don't you think?"

Eric's hand clutched David's leg as darkness snatched him and threaded him through the eye of a needle. His body contorted, twisted, squeezed, and elongated. Eric tumbled past him, his body a blur. They hit the ground, skidding, sliding, tumbling to a stop.

Seyekrad stood and staggered away.

David groaned and scrambled to his feet. "Come on, Eric. He's going to ferry again!"

A portal opened. Seyekrad jumped.

David forced his legs to go faster.

Faster.

Faster.

He stretched out an arm and clutched the hem of Seyekrad's cloak.

David crashed into stone with a tremendous crack. He slumped to the ground.

Seyekrad cackled, opened another portal, and stepped through.

David rolled on his back, his breathing heavy, and expelled a string of expletives that would make a knight blush. How had he failed again? How had he allowed Seyekrad to pull out the darkest part of him that enjoyed inflicting pain? It got him nowhere except alone.

Like Charlotte. Like Eric. He'd lost them both. Some great protector he was.

He rolled on his side and pounded his fist into the ground.

What was he going to do now?

He pressed the heels of his palms to his tired eyes. His head pounded but a sense of calm and determination engulfed him. He was a butterfly in a chrysalis waiting for his transformation.

He was also in the dark. Literally.

He felt around and found his bow and quiver and placed them on his back, keeping the stone wall close by. He reached in his back pocket to remove the hard lump digging into his butt, and pulled out his cell phone. Elation rippled through him as he swiped. A picture of him and Charlotte at Java Joe's lit up the shattered screen. Instant light, but only sixty percent battery power. He sucked his bottom lip. Use it or not? He scrolled through his icons, found the flashlight, and tapped it.

His surroundings came into view.

His breath left his lungs in one exhale.

He was in a cave, a tunnel of some kind. The walls appeared jagged and rough near the bottom, smooth and worn up top. He directed the light upward. Sloughed skin, similar to snake skin but a hundred times thicker, hung in shredded sheets from the ceiling. Pieces clung to the chamber walls. His nose wrinkled at the faint scent of spoiled eggs, the air dank and feral. And then it hit him. He knew where he was. Einar's lair. How long had it been since Einar escaped? Fifty years? Now he stood in a prison meant to hold a dragon beneath a massive lake with no way out.

He leaned against the wall and laughed at the irony of it all.

Until a tingle on his skin beneath the rutseer grabbed his attention.

He pulled the pendant from his shirt. He blinked and bottled his breath. Along the outer rim of the rutseer a green light glowed. Electricity arced within.

"What the hell?"

He shoved off the wall and turned to his left.

Zap!

The bolt from the necklace blasted his chest.

"Ouch! Alright! I get it! Not that way! Sheesh," he shouted at the pendant, as if it cared.

He turned to his right and took a step.

The electricity within the ball danced and sparked.

"Hmm, you like that, huh?" He continued walking, slow, one eye on the cave, the other on the pendant around his neck. With each step, the ball grew brighter, more agitated. David shone the light around the chamber. He pointed the rutseer up at the ceiling.

Sizzling red arcs flew out from the edges.

He jerked his hand back down, the electric tendrils zapping his skin. "Okay, okay, I get it. Whatever you want is not up there."

He kept walking.

And then the rutseer glowed a solid green. The electrical currents converged into one stream, illuminating the center with a bright white dot.

David looked up, to his sides. "What do you see?"

Seeing nothing, he looked down at his feet. There, where the ground was rough and uneven, an elongated gem gleamed white.

He stifled a yell, his heart rat-a-tatting in his chest. Could it be? Had he found a crystal? Was Aldamar right? He collected the crystal and turned it over in his palm. Rainbow colors refracted off the triangular prism. It was an exquisite piece, and Seyekrad would be pissed to discover it was gone.

He pocketed the crystal and continued walking the lair, brushing skins and cobwebs out of the way. Deeper and deeper he went, for how long he didn't know—one, maybe two hours. His feet and back ached, but he kept moving until he could go no more. He was tired, worn out. There was nothing left. He'd been beaten, battered, banged around. His energy was gone. He sat next to a wall that was round and smooth, no doubt from all those year Einar traveled the path. He pressed his head to the wall and thought of Charlotte. Where was she? Was she scared? Was she still alive? He smacked his head. No, he wasn't going there. Of course, she was alive. She had to be. He yawned and closed his eyes. He needed to rest. Clear his mind. Start new.

He was on the edge of a dream when the rutseer grew warm in his hand. He opened his eyes. The rutseer glowed green once more. His heart sped up as two streams of light flared out, each illuminating different stones, one on his left, the other on his right. He followed their points and looked downward. In the dirt below were the last of the crystals. He scrambled to them and plucked them from the ground.

David chuckled and kissed them and the rutseer. "You are one sweet piece of magic."

A drop of water fell on his hand and he glanced up. Another plopped on his forehead. Another on the ground.

Plop, plop. Plop, plop.

David squinted closer at the ceiling. A line of water traversed a crack he hadn't seen before.

Plop, plop, plop, plop.

Faster and faster they came until the droplets turned into a curtain of water.

David couldn't breathe. His skin broke out in a cold sweat. His fingers trembled, his legs shook. No. He couldn't come this far to die like this.

The ceiling above him groaned. More water rained down. Mud swelled at his feet.

He tossed his head back.

"God, if you're there, please get me out of this."

He shut his eyes and muttered, *Accelero Silentium.*

A deluge of water struck him with such a force he dropped to his knees.

"That isn't the kind of help I need!" he shouted. He swept his wet hair back from his eyes and stood.

An explosion sounded behind him followed by a deafening roar.

David ran, his legs pumping as fast as they could go. He twisted and turned around bends. The ceiling creaked and groaned. Water seeped through the walls as his prison collapsed.

He fled around another corner and came to a stop, a wall before him and no other tunnels to be found. He turned toward the rushing water coming at him. If he was going to die, he would look death in the face.

He stood strong, his shoulders back.

The wall of water, as high as the ceiling, barreled toward him.

Come on. Take me. All I ask is that you make it quick.

Images of Charlotte and her first puppy sprang to mind. His first trophy. Lily's apple pie. The day he met Eric. His make-out session with Charlotte. So many memories to take with him. So much to be grateful for.

He tilted back his head and yelled at the top of his lungs, "I love you, Charlotte."

The water crashed down.

A portal opened.

And a hand grabbed him through to the other side.

Chapter 19

Eric

Eric ran uphill until his lungs burned. "David!" He cupped his hands around his mouth and yelled louder. "Daaa-viid!"

Birds twittered and chirped in response. A strong, objectionable odor of rotting grapes assaulted his nose. It was cloying, not sweet, heavy even. There was only one place where such a smell could exist.

Tortello. Wine country.

At the top of the mound he looked around, trying to get his bearings. The landscape stretched wide, but something was wrong. The once green terraces had grown tired and brown. The cypress trees sagged, their roots thirsty for water. He scurried through the wilted sentries and stumbled upon a dry, hard road. A wine merchant approached from the south, his wagon weighted with barrels of his merchandise. Eric waved him down.

"Sir, how far are you traveling today?"

"Windybrook. What's it to ya?"

"My name is Eric. I am a squire at Gyllen. My horse spooked near Bragsworth and I've been walking ever since. I am exhausted and would very much appreciate a ride."

"Where'd ya get them clothes? Never seen nothin' like them and I've seen some strange things in my day."

Eric glanced down at his jeans and sneakers. He'd completely forgotten about his attire. He had to think of something fast.

"I met a merchant from Gramata. He got them from portal jumpers." *Was there even such a thing?* "While in the Port of Lar a band of thieves robbed me of my things and stripped me of my clothes. The merchant felt sorry for me and was kind enough to toss these my way. I know they are odd, but I must say, they are quite comfortable."

The merchant nodded and gestured for Eric to climb aboard.

"Thank you, sir. And my body thanks you, too."

That part wasn't a lie. His entire body ached and he swore in that moment he'd never fight a sorcerer again, but he knew that was a lie as much as the two he'd spoken on the road. Regardless, it got him a ride and he'd be back at Gyllen before nightfall.

The cart bumped and creaked over the pitted road. Eric and the driver rocked and swayed.

"When was the last time it rained?"

"Fallhollow hasn't seen no rain since Einar attacked, just over a month ago. The grapes are fermenting on the vines, rotting long before their pick time. I'm on my way to Windybrook to sell the last of my goods. If it don't rain soon, I'm gonna pick up my family and leave Hirth. A lot of folks have already left for the islands on the far side of the Jade Sea, maybe the Spice Isles of Gramata. I might need to think of gaining passage for my family upon a schooner. Take my chances, ya know?"

Eric nodded. He didn't know, but it was clear the man had given it plenty of thought and was prepared to sacrifice everything he had for the promise of a safer place for his family. Who could find fault with that?

They rode in silence for the most part with Eric napping now and then. He longed for a warm bed. Food. More importantly, news of Charlotte and David. Where were they? How had he and David separated? How would he ever find them?

They arrived at Windybrook mid-day. The driver struck a deal with Eric: he'd provide front door delivery to Gyllen castle in exchange for unloading the full barrels and replacing them with empty ones.

Eric agreed.

Keeping true to his word, the merchant delivered Eric to the main courtyard of Gyllen just as the pinks and purples of sunset feathered the sky. He told the man to wait as he ran into the knights' quarters, found a gallion, and returned with payment. The man thanked him and with a click of his tongue, the horses whinnied and the cart rumbled over the cobblestone and through the ruins of the gatehouse.

The grounds were vacant but for a few laborers hauling debris away. Chickens pecked at the dry soil. The magnificent wisteria tree drooped, its once lush, purple tendrils now brown and brittle. The warm air compressed around him and he suddenly longed for the shower he'd had at David's.

He ran up the steps to the upper courtyard and through the castle's doors. A servant scurried across the Grand Hall, her arms full of drapes.

"Excuse me," Eric said. "Can you tell me where everyone is? The place feels abandoned."

The girl dipped her head and curtsied. "I'm sorry, sir. Everyone has left for war, all except for the queen.

Eric's breath caught in his throat.

"When? When did they leave?"

"Yesterday, sir." She curtsied. "I must go. I do apologize."

She scurried off.

Yesterday. He still had time to catch up to them. With Trog.

Eric hurried up the winding staircase to the royal suites. He'd prepared his words to convince the guards to let him through, but they were gone. Did they go to war, too? A knock on the door presented the queen herself.

"Eric!" She snatched him into her arms. "Where have you been? I've been worried out of my mind. So has Mirith. He's been pining away—"

Eric's jaw tightened. His stomach twisted. "Mirith is here?"

"Yes. He's in David's suite. He refuses to leave."

"Is he all right?"

"He appears to be. Perhaps a bit despondent, but that is to be understood. Why the sudden concern for David's pet, and where did you get those horrid clothes?"

"I'll explain later!"

He fled down two flights of stairs without a word and barged into David's room. Mirith lifted his head and swept his tail to the side. A soft purr emanated from deep within.

"Hey, Mirith. How are you doing?" He sat on the edge of the bed and scratched behind Mirith's ear all the while looking for damage to his scales. "I can't wait to hear how you escaped. Did you eat that gargoyle and some shadowmorths?"

Mirith snorted.

"Yes. I thought so." He slipped from the bed to the floor and got face to face with the dragon, realizing in that instant that his head could fit in the beast's mouth, and that he could lose his head in one bite if Mirith chose to do so. Eric hoped he didn't want to do so.

He looked in Mirith's big eyes that seemed a milky red, and stroked his head.

"Listen. I don't know if you can understand me, but here's the situation. Seyekrad and Bainesworth are trying to take over the realm. Bainesworth kidnapped Charlotte, which really upsets me, and he was taking her to Einar, which means, she's probably in line to become a shadowmorth. I can't let that happen because I have grown quite fond of her. She's unlike anyone I've ever known. She's the only one I have that makes me feel complete, like the world is okay. Like I'm okay and not a complete failure. Do you understand?"

Mirith whimpered and rested his chin on David's bed.

"Ah, you want to know about David. Well, I don't know where

he is. He and I ferried with the cretin, Seyekrad, but David ferried with him a second time, and I don't know where they went. We need to find him, Charlotte and Trog. Are you with me so far?"

Mirith's legs slid forward and he laid his head on the floor. Sadness hung in his eyes. Eric sighed. How did David communicate with him?

He looked around the room and found two bronze warrior statues on the table beside the bed. He grabbed them down and looked at Mirith.

"Okay. I need you to pay attention, you crazy dragon. See this guy?" He held up the statue in his right hand. "This is David. Got it? David." He held up the other one in his left hand. "You see this one? He's Seyekrad. Bad guy." Eric started beating *David* with *Seyekrad* while making gruff fighting noises.

Mirith growled.

"That's right. This bad, bad sorcerer wants to kill David."

Bam! Bam! Bam!

Mirith grunted and growled again and stood. He shook his mane and a couple of orange feathers came loose and floated to the ground. His eyes grew dark red and his stance bulky and angry.

"That's right. We need to kill Seyekrad and Bainesworth so we can find David. Okay?"

Mirith snarled, grumbled, and bellowed. He scraped his foot across the floor.

Eric stroked his head. "Good boy. Let's say we get packed up and get ready to go?"

"That's the most energy I've seen from him since he arrived," Mysterie said, standing in the doorway.

"I had to give him something to fight for." He held up the statutes before tossing them on the bed.

Mysterie entered the room. "I couldn't help but overhear your conversation with Mirith. I'm not surprised to hear of Seyekrad's or Bainesworth's nefarious activities. I've warned Gildore and Trog about it many times. They knew, too, but had no proof."

"I figured as much. Mirith, come on. I have to pack some things before we leave."

Mysterie touched his arm as he brushed by.

He stopped and looked at her, at the living, breathing identical image of his mother. He swallowed. "Ma'am?"

"I want you to know you have never been a failure, Eric. Your father loves you very, very much. He adores you, even envies you in some ways. Right now, he is broken and beside himself, blaming everything that has happened on himself. For him, for you, please find a way to put all this animosity aside. Please find a way to forgive him."

He smiled. "I already have, my queen."

"Will you tell him?"

"Yes, ma'am. I promise to do so as soon as I see him. Do you know where they went?"

Mysterie paused for a moment. Her breath caught in her throat. "The Valley of Tears," she said with pained effort.

That was not the news Eric wanted to hear. The Valley of Tears was a place of murder, where souls were ripped from the dead and rebirthed into shadowmorths. Why in all that is great in heaven would they choose that as their battle site? It baffled his mind.

"How many men did they gather?"

"They are ten thousand strong, but I fear that will not be enough against Einar and his army."

No, it wouldn't be. It would take a paladin, an heir, and a dragon. Before all was said and done, they would have all three.

And Einar would be toast.

***

It was heavy into night when Eric and Mirith set foot across the Haldorian Bridge in their first quest: to save Charlotte from Berg Castle. But a magical membrane pulsed along the border of Hirth and shadowmorths swarmed like black clouds on the other side.

They turned and traveled south along the Cloverleaf River, taking the Hidden Path of the Faeries into the Southern Forest instead. The thick canopy of the Southern Forest, however, offered cover and protection he wouldn't get elsewhere and he and Mirith needed all the protection they could get.

Palindrakes drifted from tree to tree, sometimes dipping so low and flying so close, Eric could feel their dragons' breath on his ears. Their chortles and gurgles and curiosity soon became more of an annoyance than comfort, and Eric shooed them the way he would a fly. Even Mirith snorted at their presence, and at one point, arced his tail, and pointed his crackling, sparking tip at the pests.

"No, Mirith," Eric said. "Not a good idea, though I agree with your thinking. We don't need them telling anyone or anything we're here."

But he was almost certain that they already had. It was in their nature to chatter and gossip. They were, after all, messengers of the forest. It would only be a matter of time before word reached the ears of the wrong sort that a young traveler and his dragon wandered the Southern Forest, alone.

The forest brimmed with the shime, he could sense their gargoylish dragon winged presence now and then, but it only exasperated his fears, not allayed them. He trusted no one, and the sooner he reached Trog and the others, the better off he'd be. After all, the two weapons with the power to kill Einar were trudging side by side on their way to war.

It did make him laugh, though. His thoughts strayed to Sestian, wondering what his friend would think of the whole revelation of Eric being a dragonslayer and Trog's son.

Why, we're practically royalty, Sestian had once said. If they'd only known then what Eric knew now, how different life would be.

It was after mid-day when they arrived on the outskirts of Falcon's Hollow, a hamlet of no more than a dozen stone homes. Eric and Mirith kept off the road, flanking the area. A sinking feeling settled in Eric's gut. The town appeared deserted, cold, and desolate. Mirith nudged him and gestured to their right. In the woods, three grave markers protruded from the ground. Judging by the size of the mounds, the deceased were children. Innocent victims in a game of war. He wondered what happened to them, where their families went, but Mirith shoved him on.

They continued over hills, along riverbanks, the palindrakes taking higher to the sky, their interest in the travelers seeming to wane as they flew away. The journey seemed to take forever and along the way, Eric alternated between overwhelming fear and eternal optimism that he would find David and Charlotte and that everything would turn out for the best.

They rounded a bend in the road and stopped upon a small crest. The view was peaceful, serene. Unusually quiet. Eric's hairs rose on his arms. Mirith's scales fluttered. They continued on, trekking downhill, the late afternoon sun casting dark shadows into the tunnel of trees hugging the road.

Mirith stopped, his body still as stone. A rumble came from his belly that reverberated within Eric.

"What is it, boy?" Eric followed Mirith's gaze, peering through the tree line at the top of the rise. The sunset on the ridge behind them turned the forest ahead into a dark tunnel. The air grew still. Stagnant. Quiet. Too quiet.

Mirith's tail swished the ground. His scales popped open. His feathers flared.

Eric pulled his sword, his eyes peeled to the shadows.

The sound of boots on the forest floor rushed toward them.

A bolt of lightning shot from Mirith's tail in the direction of the attack.

A firebolt streamed toward them.

Fire ignited the trees.

More booted footsteps rapidly approached, this time from their left.

"Run, Mirith! Into the shadows!"

They crashed through the thick underbrush and veered onto a trail taking them downhill.

An arrow whizzed past Eric's head. He ducked and ran, leaping over downed trees, the limbs cutting his face.

Sounds of pursuit grew louder behind them. Eric looked around for a place to hide, but where does one put a dragon the size of a wine cart?

Three men dressed in all black ran from the shadows toward them. One had a crossbow, the other a sword.

Three more emerged from the right, six more from the left.

Mirith slid to a stop only to spin in a circle. Ice formed at his feet and spread outward.

The assassins slipped and fell, sliding toward the little dragon.

Eric swung, slicing two men's throats in one swipe.

More assassins converged, killers hidden by the depths of the forest.

Who were these men? Where are the palindrakes? The shime? Where was the help when he needed it? *Mangus, Slavandria, if you can hear me, help me.*

A bolt lodged in his leg, bringing him to the ground. His leg throbbed, the pain unbearable. Burning.

Mirith opened his mouth and scooped Eric into it as he shot a bolt of lightning into the ice.

The ground sizzled and sparked as Mirith ran.

Eric bounced in Mirith's mouth, his view one of where he'd been, not where he was going.

More arrows sailed past. Another fireball soared down the hillside.

"Mirith! Behind you!" Eric yelled, but the warning came too late.

The dragon wailed a sound that defied nature. Eric covered his ears and spilled to the ground, jamming the bolt deeper into his leg.

He yelled, the pain unbearable.

Mirith tumbled over the top of him and rolled off the mountainside. Trees snapped as the dragon plummeted.

Eric sat up, the smoke burning his eyes. No. He couldn't be gone. He couldn't be. How could he fight these bandits on his own? How could he kill Einar without Einar's heir at his side?

He folded in half, grasped the one inch of bolt protruding from his leg, and yanked. He could feel the warmth of his blood spill over his leg.

From the smokey brume a figure materialized. A tall, lithe man with silver hair and a triumphant expression.

"Well, well. Look at what I found." He knelt at Eric's side. "The last of my nemeses."

"Seyekrad," Eric said.

The sorcerer kicked him, rolling him on his back. Eric yelled, choking back the tears that lingered right on the surface. There was no way he'd let the cretin see his pain.

He opened his eyes to see at least two dozen assassins standing around him, their weapons drawn. His lungs deflated. He wasn't getting out of this alive.

"Go ahead. Kill me," he said.

Seyekrad smiled. "Not yet, pup. I want to make sure your master sees your passing. I want him to see my spell enter your body and wrap around your heart, squeezing your life away. It is Bainesworth's wish." He shoved his thumb into Eric's wound. Slow. Deliberate. His eyes turned dark, and fused with malicious joy.

Eric cried out. He drew in a breath, but his lungs laughed and lied, pretending to expand while collapsing in double time. His limbs tightened and there was pain. His leg was a wildfire, burning from the inside out. He tried to stop them, but the tears came.

He opened his eyes enough to see the stock of a crossbow hammer as it crashed down on his head.

Chapter 20

David

David smacked the ground, the wind knocked out of his lungs.
Breathe. Deep. Breathe! That's it. Calm down. Breathe.

He concentrated on the sweet smells around him, the colors, bringing everything into focus.

Stems of lavender flowers as high as fields of corn towered over him. Wisps of pink clouds stretched and thinned across an indigo sky, revealing a giant moon. A light breeze whispered through the field.

Morning. Not quite sunrise.

A small stout man with unkempt ginger hair and topaz blue eyes appeared above him, his small hand extended, his tufted brows furrowed. "Get up!"

David's lungs won the right to breathe. His eyes blinked. His lips parted.

"Twiller? How? When?"

"No time to explain, Master David. One does not dawdle in Beggars Field. It is the last place you wish to be stranded while night lingers."

"I don't understand." David got to his feet. "How did you find me?"

"You have a rutseer. A very powerful one. I'll teach you how to use it once we leave this place. Tulipakar is just on the other side of this field. We must hurry. The shadows of night will be moving soon."

"Shadows of night?"

"Nothing you need to worry about so long as we reach the other side of the river in time. Now stop your infernal chattering and move."

Panic seized David's heart. A chill crawled up his spine. A strange feeling, as if being watched, settled over him. The hairs on his arms stirred, his skin prickled as if itched from the inside out.

"Twiller, I don't know if you know, but Tulipakar is overrun with shadowmorths and Einar's army."

"I know. Stop jabbering and move." Twiller broke into a jog.

David hurried after him. "If you know then why are we going there? Do you know a way in?"

"Yes. So do you. It's called ferrying. Now please be quiet and take the energy you're using to run your mouth to push your legs."

"Why can't we just ferry from here? Why the marathon? Do you people not ever rest in this place?"

"Not a good time to explain. Run!"

Twiller took off.

Rapid movement rushed from behind. David glanced over his shoulder and froze as a giant, neon blue grasshopper, twice David's height and mottled with numerous green spots, bounded toward him, its bright orange hind wings displayed in full blazing glory.

"Holy crap. What the freak is that thing?"

David spurted into track mode. The creature thundered closer, its mandibles clicking and biting.

"To the river!" Twiller shouted. "Don't look back!"

David zig-zagged through the tall lavender. The grasshopper vaulted toward David.

A hairy leg clipped David's foot. Its wings buzzed.

David tripped and fell. He army crawled along the ground, clawing the dirt, gasping for breath.

Six giant legs stepped on either side. Something wet hit his back. David rolled over, his reflection staring back at him in the insect's humongous orbs. Mandibles clicked closer, chomping, biting.

The forlorn whistle of a train sounded in the distance. Closer and closer it came, growing louder and louder. The ground vibrated. The wind whipped and turned. Debris scraped David's skin. From the corner of his eye, a vortex barreled down upon him.

"Oh God, I'm going to die."

The insect turned its head as the vortex careened into its side, lifting it in the air and jettisoning it on the far side of the field. Seconds later, small footsteps pounded closer. A small hand reached through the stems and flung David to his feet.

"I told you to shut up. Now move! We haven't much time before it returns, and the next time it won't be alone."

David held his hand to his aching chest and ran as fast as he could go. Far away, a grasshopper rubbed its legs. Others answered, their chirps loud and deafening. The eerie sound rippled through David like fingernails on a chalkboard. Faster and faster he ran. A body of water, perhaps thirty, forty feet wide, appeared ahead. Wings buzzed behind them.

"Hurry! To the water!" Twiller plunged into the river and swam.

David dove in. Behind him, two insects landed on the bank, pinching, their alien eyes watching.

Arms and legs on fire, David kicked and kicked. He dragged himself onto the opposite bank and collapsed, his chest heaving, his heart beating wildly.

"What … in the blazing hell … were those things?" David asked between gasps.

Twiller took a deep breath. "Vorgrants. They protect Beggars Field at night from intruders. The roots of the Vila lilies are said to possess a powerful drug, one capable of bringing the dead back to life. All who have attempted to test the validity of the stories have died."

"So why do they attack only at night?"

"It is the only time of day the plant can be harvested without killing the roots. It is also believed the potency of the drug is the strongest the moment when morn begins to wake. But all of that matters not unless you're planning on crossing Beggars Field again, which I'm hoping you're not." Twiller stood and shook the droplets from his hair. "And to answer your next question, it is the only place where the lily grows."

"Thank whatever good luck charms you have here for that." David wiped his face and shivered. "Tell me why we didn't ferry again?"

Sunlight blipped over the horizon. The vorgrants turned and disappeared in the tall flowers.

"Ferrying leaves signatures, Master David. Do you not retain anything I've taught you? If we ferried, we would have alerted the shadowmorths that we are here. Quite frankly, I'd rather take my chance with a vorgrant."

"You've got a point," David said.

"However, you have a rutseer. I do not know where you got it. I do not want to know. But if Slavandria is correct, one word should ferry us without being detected now that we are out of danger."

David's throat constricted. "Wait. You've seen Slavandria?"

"Yes. She told me where to find you."

David laughed and it wasn't happy. "Oh, boy, do I have a few things to say to her. Where is she?"

"The manor, of course. And might I suggest we get there soon before we are discovered."

"Fine. What do I have to do or say?"

"She wrote it down for me." He dug in his pocket and pulled out a piece of parchment the size of David's thumb. "She said to picture the manor in your head and repeat that word once forward and once backward."

David read the word.

Gronclesc.

"You've got to be joking. I don't even know how to pronounce this frontwards, much less backwards. What if I say it wrong? Will we end up somewhere we shouldn't be?"

"I do not know, Master David, but I suggest you do something soon. I sense dark forces seeking, hunting."

David shook his head. "Okay. Hold on. Here goes nothing."

He envisioned the Elthorian Manor in his mind, his room, the fireplace.

"*Gronkless. Selknorg.*"

The rutseer thumped him in the chest then tugged him and Twiller through a hole the size of a peanut and thrust him on a bed. A huge canopied bed. With Twiller on top of him. He shoved the gnome off and got up, his breath still next to the river at Beggar's Field.

"Whoa," he gasped. "That was intense."

Breathe out.

Breathe in.

Mix.

Repeat.

Twiller rolled off the bed and wobbled a bit. He straightened his jacket, smoothed back his hair, and said, "Remind me not to do that again."

David nodded. "You got it, Twills. Whew."

Twiller opened the door. "I will find Slavandria and let her know we have arrived."

"You know what? I think I'm going to go with you. I've got some major questions."

"And you shall get some major answers," Slavandria answered, her form filling the doorway. "Twiller, if you will, please go downstairs to the Peacock room and ask our other guests to come here."

"Guests?" David queried.

"Have you forgotten Gertie and Garret?" Her smile was genuine. Triumphant.

Excitement rippled through David. "They're safe?"

Slavandria nodded. "Very much so."

David shook his head, his brow creased. "I don't understand. How? The last time we spoke you didn't know how to get here without being seen or detected."

She grinned. "It's actually something you did. I was on my father's ship, the WindSong, when I detected you in the lair beneath Lake Sturtle. Your rutseer is quite a masterpiece. Finn is a great forward thinker. He knew what he was doing when he placed his magic in that very useful tool."

David's heart skipped. "Finn? Is he okay? Where is he?"

Slavandria walked into the room and sat on the bed. "I'm sorry, David, but Finn passed away. His injuries from the shadowmorth attack were more than any of the sestras or I could heal."

David's knees trembled as he hung them over the side of the bed. It couldn't be true. Not Finn.

Slavandria continued, "However, he lived long enough to relay some information."

David sat beside her, his heart heavy. He liked Finn. It wasn't fair he should die at the hands of a shadowmorth. He was an amazing creature full of crazy ideas and riddled with bizarre idiosyncrasies. He'd saved David's life. Gave him comfort and shelter. Taught him magic. He was good. Decent. Why did he have to die when jerks like Seyekrad got to live? It didn't make sense.

Slavandria touched his hand. "Are you all right?"

"Yeah." He rubbed the back of his neck. "What sort of information did he give you?"

"Seyekrad discovered your friendship with Finn. I'm not sure how, Finn didn't expand, but I believe he may have been hoodwinked. Seyekrad tortured Finn, mind-weaved with him to discover whatever he could about you, but Finn refused to yield. So Seyekrad placed a spell upon Finn to betray you. He then placed a calling spell upon the rutseer. It summons a person or thing to a certain place, in most cases for unsavory reasons. Finn believed Seyekrad wished to entrap you, kill you. But Finn, through his stupor, managed to counteract the spell with some sestra magic, something to protect you and whomever was attached to you. Because of this, Seyekrad's plan backfired. I can only imagine how angry he became. That's why it makes sense he imprisoned you beneath Lake Sturtle with the intent of sending you to your grave. But he dropped something that made the rutseer light up like a star at night."

David pulled the crystals from his pocket. "These." He held up the three crystals high enough for her to see them while keeping them in his grasp. "But how did you know?"

"Before Finn died he held my hand and entrusted me with a deep secret. Seyekrad placed the spell on the rutseer so that you would follow him. Finn knew you wanted the crystals for me, so he countered Seyekrad's spell with a charm that would not only alert me whenever you found one, but ferry you to me once you spoke the incantation. Quite ingenious, I think. Sadly, he passed before I knew how it all worked, so you can imagine my surprise when a glowing green mark appeared on the back of my hand with an image of an odd shaped crystal in the center."

David nodded, rubbing his tattoo. He completely understood how it felt to wake up with a mark on your body with no idea how it got there or what it was for. So been there. So done that.

David propped a few pillows behind him and sat back, his arms and legs crossed. "Why didn't you come get me yourself?"

"If you must know, my father and I were engaged in a disagreement over my interference in the matter. I explained to him I wasn't going to let you die at the mercy of Einar or his henchmen. Father, in his infinite wisdom, suggested Twiller go, therefore, I wouldn't break my celestial oath. So, he sent Twiller after you while I concocted a non-detection charm that would make my father proud if it weren't used for the purpose to interfere with the destiny of man."

"Yeah, like he so doesn't interfere with the destiny of men." David rolled off the bed, his temper growing. He hated being used. Hated being a pawn.

"You and I know that's a whole other story unto itself, David. Be thankful he breaks his own rules every now and then. If he didn't, you wouldn't be here."

A rocket discharged in his brain and the launch pad was in flames.

"You're right, I wouldn't be here. None of this would be happening if it wasn't for your father!"

"What are you talking about?"

David whipped around. "Your father. He tagged me for this job two hundred years ago. He was the one who preordained my life."

Slavandria shook her head. "No, you're wrong. The Book of Telling ordained the lives of the heir and the paladin. He was merely the vessel responsible for putting it into play."

"Really? And who was the vessel that put you and Seyekrad into play with one another?"

Slavandria's face paled. She closed the bedroom door. "What do you mean? What do you know?"

"We know you had a crush on Lord Seyekrad Krawl. We witnessed your infatuation with that monster in this very house. How could you let him kiss you?"

Slavandria brought a hand to her chest. "Where did you see such a thing?"

"Lily. She gave me a vapor thing."

"David listen to me. Those weren't my memories. I never housed a vapor."

"Are you saying you never had an affair with him?"

"Yes. No." For the first time ever, David had her in an uncomfortable position. "I was young. He wasn't always vicious."

"Oh yeah, that's right, he didn't become evil Seyekrad until you got married to that Mangus dude."

Her face fell into a panic. Her eyes searched his. Desperate. Begging. "Please, David, you must not say that aloud. My father doesn't know.

"I suppose he doesn't know about your child, either."

"What? I do not have a child. Why would you even think something like that?"

She looked at him as if he'd lost his mind. Did she think he was that stupid?

"We saw you. You were pregnant. Very, very pregnant. What happened to your baby, Slavandria?"

"I never had a child, David. I don't know whose memories you saw, but they weren't mine."

He wanted to believe her, but he didn't know what to believe anymore. Why would Lily give him a memory that wasn't true?

David waved her off. "I know what I saw." He scowled, looked away, and clenched his teeth.

A knock sounded at the door. "We'll speak of this later," Slavandria said.

David tucked the crystals back in his pocket.

She turned the knob and admitted Garret and Gertie. Smiles creased their faces.

"David!" Gertie rushed toward him and engulfed him in a hug. "We were told you were dead."

Garret embraced him as well.

David smirked, his eyes on Slavandria. "Somehow that doesn't surprise me." He studied their faces. "How are you doing? Have you been harmed in any way?"

"Not too bad," Gertie said. "We've been alone ever since we were brought here. No one has come to see us. We were forbidden to leave and have had very little to eat. We tried to leave once, but the doors were infused with magic."

Garrett held up his left hand showing the vertical, bubbling wound on his palm.

With his permission, Slavandria placed a healing spell upon it and released his hand.

"Has anyone heard anything from Ravenhawk?" Gertie asked.

"Last I heard," David said, "was that he was in Berg Castle."

"They've been moved," Slavandria said. "Einar has amassed his armies to the north and east along the Valley of Tears. Hirth and its allies have taken up the western ridge. The palindrakes have reported all of Einar's prisoners have been taken to the deepest part of the valley and staked. If this is true, your friends are awaiting a slow and deliberate death."

"We have to stop the massacre," Garrett said.

"We can't," Slavandria said, "not until we locate two important pieces to the puzzle." She glanced at David. "Where is Eric?"

"I don't know. We got separated."

She glanced at the necklace David wore. "Would you mind if I borrowed the rutseer? I might be able to discover when and where the fork occurred and trace where he went."

"Umm, that would be a big no. The last time I took this off, Seyekrad discovered our whereabouts and kidnapped Charlotte."

"I understand your hesitation, David, but I can assure you, you're all safe here. I have wards protecting every inch of this manor. If anything or anyone with ill intent attempts to enter this home, I'm afraid they are going to be in for a shocking disappointment."

Slavandria approached him, her face so close he could see his reflection in her mesmerizing eyes. It took a great deal of effort to force the rattle from his bones, but he managed and held her gaze.

She held out her hand.

He slipped the Eye of Kedge and the rutseer from his neck and handed both to her. "Take them. And here are your crystals, too. They're yours. I want nothing more to do with either of them." He turned his back to her. "I've been told activating the tunnels will allow evil to enter this world, evil so immense it could destroy everything, not just Fallhollow but other worlds as well, including my own. I'd like to suggest you consider that before using them."

She touched his shoulder. He shirked it off. "You've done well, David. We'll talk more when there is time." She turned to Garret and Gertie. "I will try to find out what has happened to all of your friends, especially Ravenhawk, but I fear for their lives if they are sequestered in the Valley of Tears."

A hollow feeling pierced David's gut. "You don't think Seyekrad took Charlotte there, do you?" He met her eyes.

"Let's hope not." She walked out of the room, paused, and looked back once before disappearing from view.

David exhaled. His insides trembled. He folded himself on the bed, his knees drawn to his chest. He'd promised Charlotte's father he'd find her, bring her back in one piece, but had he spoken too soon?

The Valley of Tears.

It sounded so desolate. So hopeless. He was petrified. Petrified of the possibility he would never see her again. Never hear her laugh. Never see the way her jaw clenched when she was mad or feel her hands on his chest, her lips on his.

He looked away, hoping no one would see the tears congregating in the corners of his eyes, waiting for their chance to do the drip drop thing on his cheeks.

Gertie untucked her shift from her trousers and sat on the bed. "You know, it's okay to cry. You don't have to be brave. Not with us. We've all lost people we love. But don't wallow in self-pity too long or you'll fall into the pit. It's a dark place to go and difficult to get out of."

David nodded. He struggled to find words to say but they wouldn't come. For the rest of the day, he listened to Gertie and Garrett tell their stories of everything that had happened since Trog, David, and Charlotte left Gable. Their demise came as assassins dressed in black ambushed them outside the town of Keorne in daylight. Other prisoners had been with them in the beginning, but were sanctioned off like chattel. They never saw the faces of their capturers, but they knew the voices. And they couldn't wait to dislodge them from their owners.

***

It was midnight when Slavandria entered David's room and sat on the edge of his bed. Her drawn face in the candlelight said everything he already knew and feared.

"He's got her, doesn't he? She's in the Valley of Tears."

Slavandria nodded. "It's worse than that, David." She glanced at Garret and Gertie sleeping on the floor. "She's strapped to the Elwood. She is to be the first sacrifice to Einar's shadowmorths."

David's lips trembled. He couldn't believe what he was hearing. He couldn't let her die, especially like that. A single tear fell.

He wiped it away. Anger sank into every pore. The tension and fear in his body morphed and his lips curled into a sneer.

"Then I guess you're going to have to show me how to fight the shadowmorths and save her, right?" David asked.

Slavandria's eyes spoke of sorrow, sadness. "You cannot fight shadowmorths, David. Not all the magic in the world can do that. The only thing that can stop them is to kill Einar."

"Then show me how to do that!"

"You cannot. You are a paladin. Only the youngest heir to Hirth or Einar's offspring can do that, and neither are anywhere to be seen. Pray Eric and Mirith will arrive soon. They are our only hope to end this war and release Charlotte from certain death."

David couldn't believe what he was hearing. How could it come to this? Why were soldiers gathered if there was no way to win? What was the point?

Every nerve in his body trembled. Death kicked back and laughed, his long, boney fingers toying with David's lungs, squeezing and letting go. David clutched his chest and counted. What to do? His thoughts swirled into a thick soup of chopped sentiments, grated emotions, and pinches of crazy ideas.

Slavandria cupped his chin in her hand. "I must go. There is something I need from Chalisdawn. Garret knows what to do if I do not return in time. Listen to him." She kissed his forehead. "We'll get Charlotte back. I promise. Somehow, we will end all of this."

She vanished.

And David set about finding his smidgeon of faith and hope.

Chapter 21

David

David sipped his tea and watched from his window as shadowmorths swarmed over Tulipakar. Black veils, billowing, drifting, turning. They'd been at it for hours. It was as if they could sense the battle, smell the blood that was coming. A feast. New recruits. As the sun began to rise, they banded together, a single great black cloud of hissing terror. As if on a signal, they closed in tighter and headed north.

"They're leaving," David said. "The soldiers took off a few hours ago."

"Are you ready to fight?" Gertie asked. She was decked out in brown leather pants, a matching long–sleeve doublet, and boots to her thighs. She wore two bandoliers stuffed with every sort of hand weapon imaginable.

"Is anyone ever ready to fight when there is no chance of winning?"

Garret sat in a chair to put on his boots. He was dressed in similar garb to Gertie, except he had crossbows, swords, and some small explosive devices Slavandria gave him.

"You're still doubting our resolve?" Garret asked.

David shook his head. "I'm not doubting our willpower or courage, but we cannot defeat that monster out there without Eric or Mirith. That is a fact. If they do not show soon, this battle will be a massacre. All of us will die."

"That may be true," Gertie said, "but I intend to kill as many of those tyrants out there who are responsible for killing my parents, my friends, and my family as I can. If we don't stand up to them, they'll continue to think they can have whatever they want. They will continue to spread their vileness all over this world. It is time to bring peace."

"Through war?" David asked.

Garret stood and faced David, vambraces in hand. "We all have our reasons for being here. Mine are similar to Gertie's. Yours, I believe, is tied to a sacrificial tree. Those knights out there, they fight because they believe in freedom for all, not just for some. They are willing to die for that. What are you willing to die for?"

David stared at the floor. An image of Charlotte formed in his mind. Her smile. Her eyes. The light that would leave this world if she was no longer a part of it. That's what he would die for. A hundred times over.

He held his arms straight out to his sides. "I'm ready. Put the armor on."

Garret and Gertie smiled.

It was time for war.

Chapter 22

Eric

Eric winced as Seyekrad dragged him down a long castle hall, through a field of shattered stone and wood debris. He coughed, his nose and lungs rebelling against the horrid stench of spoiled eggs and rotting fish. Death.

A familiar ceiling painted with grand frescoes passed overhead. He knew them. He'd seen them while searching for the Eye of Kedge and the king's sword.

His stomach lurched.

Berg Castle. The carnage he'd sloughed through was the devastation left by Einar's chase with David. But this time, there was no David. No ferrying to make him vomit.

He wanted to vomit.

Bad.

Up ahead he heard stomping and crunching, the emphatic sounds reverberating clean through to his bones. He lolled his head back and got his first glimpse of his executioner.

He didn't look any different. Still mammoth. Still black as obsidian, molten with liquid amethyst.

Einar stopped his chewing as Seyekrad approached with his trophy. A toss of the sorcerer's arm and Eric slid across the floor. He rolled and groaned and came to a rest at Einar's feet. A talon scraped the ground at his head, the sound shattering the crux of Eric's existence into a million pieces. He knew the danger of that weapon. It had once been lodged in his back.

What he would give to bring his blade down on that offending claw and chop it off. Maybe even rip his heart out. He lay on the floor and chuckled at the thought.

Einar flicked him with the talon.

Eric skipped across the floor, every contact with a fragment of stone a painful reminder of the hole in his leg.

Einar snorted a concoction of putrid derision and smoke. An embodied laughter bubbled from his gut.

Eric stopped breathing. Surely he'd heard wrong.

A door in the distance slammed shut. Booted footsteps thundered across the floor, drawing nearer.

"You summoned me, My Lord?"

Eric gasped for air. *Bainesworth!*

Eric tumbled over shards of rock and bone as Einar drew him near again, his body howling as fragments ripped his clothes and scraped his skin.

Einar chuckled, his voice deep, melodic. Formidable. "I did

indeed. Lord Seyekrad brought you a present."

Eric lay still, his head spinning, his stomach churning as the Dragon King's talon rocked him back and forth. His mind fell numb.

The dragon could speak. He was sentient.

This was not good. He liked it better thinking Einar was nothing more than mindless evil. But that was far from the truth. He understood. He reasoned.

And he was far more dangerous than believed.

Bainesworth folded into a bow. "What sort of present has the great sorcerer bestowed upon me?"

Eric braced for the flick. It came hard, almost knocking the wind from him. He rolled five times before coming to a stop at Bainesworth's feet.

The knight's lips broke into a sneer. "Well, now. Look at what we have here. A puny pup." He knelt beside Eric. "Where are your comrades now?"

Eric spit in his face. "Go crawl in a hole and die."

Bainesworth backhanded him across the face. Blood trickled down his throat.

Seyekrad stepped forward from the shadows, his tone triumphant.

"His friends have been eliminated, My Lord. The paladin, I am pleased to report, has suffered an unfortunate cave-in beneath Lake Sturtle and has drowned."

Eric's heart stopped for a moment. *No. It can't be true.*

Einar laughed again. It embellished the hall. "Good. Good."

"The heir, however, has not yet been found," Seyekrad continued, "but I sense his presence. He is near. As you know, the girl who was traveling with this rat and the paladin has been strapped to the Elwood. The heir will have no choice but to try and save her. He will come. When he does, my detection spells will ensnare him at which time I will deliver him personally to you for your entertainment."

Einar snorted. "And you are certain the paladin has drowned?" His words were drawn out in long syllables, the pace as fast as honey pouring from a jar.

"As you know from experience, there is no way out, except with the help of a bit of magic, which, sad to say, he won't get." He curled his fingers. Looked at his nails.

Einar lowered his neck. "And where is Slavandria?" He spoke her name as if he had tar stretched between his teeth.

"Chalisdawn, my lord," Seyekrad said with a smug smile. "I confirmed it before I used the same spell she used to imprison you beneath Lake Sturtle."

"And has she been extinguished?"

"Yes, my lord. Chalisdawn is burning as we speak."

Eric stared at the ceiling, his hands in fists pressed to his thighs. His insides screamed and panic crept into his throat, strangling him. It couldn't be over. David and Slavandria couldn't be dead.

Einar craned his head in Bainesworth's direction. "What are your plans for this insurgent?"

Fowl air puffed from the dragon's nostrils. The fumes bit and clawed at Eric's lungs. He coughed, his body and head aching with equal ferocity.

Bainesworth said, "I wish to follow you to the Valley of Tears, my liege, where I beg your permission to dispatch the swashbuckling, swelled headed, Sir Trogsdill Domnall."

Einar laughed. "Permission granted, but not until I have killed his prodigy before his eyes. I want him to know what it feels like to lose," he turned his gaze on Eric, "his son."

Eric scuttled backward, his eyes never leaving Einar's face. "You are delusional, that is what you are. Mad."

"Perhaps," Einar said, "but better mad than dead." He careened his neck around toward Seyekrad. "I am ready. Let the battle begin."

Chapter 23

David

David stood on the southern rim of the Valley of Tears, a narrow stretch of land void of life, the earth cracked and dry. Gertie, Garret, and Twiller, along with at least a hundred meadow gnomes, shime, and centaurs gathered round. High on the ridge to the east, thousands of horses and their riders, dressed in black, waited. On the western ridge, another army gathered, sunlight shimmering off their metal armor.

Good to the left. Evil to the right. Which would win?

In the center of the valley, a tree rose tall and strong, its wide, full canopy casting shadows on the ground beneath it.

David's heart splattered.

The Elwood.

And Charlotte was bound to the festering bark, her chin drooped to her chest, her hair in curtains around her face. To her right,

Ravenhawk, in his human form, hung from a tall wooden stake, his body limp.

So this is how Einar played the game. Bait the prey out in the open.

David's muscles tightened and burned. Rage bubbled in his veins, curdling his blood, igniting the fire in his belly.

He ran toward Charlotte, Garret and Gertie at his side, yelling.

Thunder came, but not from the sky.

Hundreds of armored knights and soldiers hurtled over the ledges and charged down the hills. On horses and on foot they charged one another. Arrows flew through the air. The reverberations of the battle surged through David, his heart a pendulum slamming against his ribcage. The ground shook.

Terror coiled his spine. His feet left the ground in a sprint. He ran harder, faster, his arms pumping at his side.

Knights of the west and soldiers of the east collided around him. Weapons clanged. Blood splattered. The wounded slipped and fell amongst snaps and groans.

David leapt, his bow drawn, an arrow knocked.

An arrow pierced his arm before he could shoot. Agony ricocheted through his bones. He fell where he stood.

He glanced around. This was it. The dream he had all those weeks ago. Horses reared around him. Blood splattered. Sounds warped and garbled. A face appeared in front of him.

"You're going to be all right," Garret said. "Bite down on this."

A cloth was shoved in David's mouth.

Garret's hand wrapped around the lodged arrow.

David shook his head and put his hand near the arrow. *No, no, no, don't pull!*

Garret counted, "One, two … "

"Ahhhhhh!" David yelled, spitting aside the cloth and cursing words he didn't realize he knew.

"Breathe," Garret said, wrapping the wound expertly. "This is your chance to make a change. To leave your mark. Go get Charlotte."

Charlotte.

Garret ran off.

A soldier thumped to the ground beside him, his eyes open. Vacant.

Ahh, I can't deal with this! Please end this. Please let it be over.

Another soldier fell.

Breathe.

David blinked. A dream. It was all a dream. A cacophony of shrieks came from the sky.

A black cloud approached, hissing.

Shadowmorths.

Their black wispy forms swarmed down through the Valley of Tears toward Charlotte.

Noooo!

David ran, his hand pressed to his wounded arm. A man wielding a sword shouted his name.

He turned to look. Trog?

Icy, electric jolts burst through the air. The shadowmorths

screeched and fell into black dust only to reform thicker and stronger.

David whipped his head to the left. His heart took flight.

Mirith.

He was alive. Jesus, he was alive.

Threads of magic in blue, green, and gold exploded around him. The ground opened, spitting up dried earth and stone.

Zap.

Sizzle.

Crack.

He caught a glimpse in the corner of his eyes. Lily. Slavandria. Twiller. They were all there. Fighting. Defending.

Where was Eric?

He searched, frantic. There were so many. Thousands come to war. Thousands come to die.

A mass of men dressed in black charged toward him, their swords drawn, their mouths open, yelling.

David shot one, two, three arrows. The men jerked back and fell. More came rushing toward him.

Arrow after arrow left his quiver, each one generating another. Endless supply, just as Slavandria had promised.

His arm trembled, the pain in his arm more than one person could bear. Blood trickled down his arm.

Gertie leapt around him, her crossbow singing.

"Get to Charlotte! I'll cover you!"

His nerves quivered. His legs didn't want to move. So much blood. So many bodies.

Then he saw her face.

David ran before he lost his nerve. Gertie's footfalls pounded behind him. Her crossbow sang. Bolts hissed through the air. Bodies cried out, thudded to the ground.

David swayed, feeling faint. Blood flowed freely inside his tunic, staining his garments a crimson color. He kept on, clinging to the Elwood upon reaching it. She lifted her head and gave him a slight smile.

"What took you so long?" She sounded weak. Tired.

David clawed at the knot binding her wrists. "Oh, you know. Stopped and got a burger. Took in a movie."

A sudden burst of wind hit him from behind. Charlotte's face froze in terror. He followed her gaze. A huge shadow blocked the sun.

Einar.

The monstrous dragon, so plum purple he was almost black, flew over the field, his enormous mouth open, fangs exposed. Flames bellowed inside his throat. He exhaled. Fire flooded the field. Men screamed as their bodies ignited, their souls consumed in flame.

David tugged at the rope holding Charlotte, but the knot refused to budge.

"The dagger," Charlotte said, "the one on your leg."

He reached for it, the pain in his arm intense, and unsnapped the leather frog. "Hurry, David. Cut me loose."

A raven cawed, circled, and flew off. Garret and Gertie fled through the carnage of the Valley of Tears, and melded back into the battle.

David grasped the blade, and sawed Charlotte loose from her bonds.

A downdraft of wind enveloped them. Einar swept around again. Flames shot from his mouth.

A wall of energy—bluish lavender and pulsing—formed a sweeping arc over David and Charlotte and absorbed the blaze.

The beast roared. He soared high in the sky, and dived down again. Tens of smoke-black forms hatched from beneath his wings.

David gulped. They were here. The time had come.

Shadowmorths.

Threads of gold, blue, and green spiraled into the sky.

Bolts of lightning shot from Mirith's tail at Einar.

A hole blasted through his right wing.

An explosive guttural roar spewed from the Einar's throat. He flew high, made another pass, and plummeted toward them.

Mirith volleyed more bolts.

"Come on, Mirith," David said, hoping for a connection. *"Kill him!"*

Einar dodged the spears of light, veering right, then left. He flew low and plucked Mirith from the ground.

"No!" David yelled.

Charlotte gasped and covered her mouth.

Lightning bolts burst into Einar's chest, stomach.

Einar spiraled.

More bolts bombarded the huge body.

Electricity lit up the sky.

Einar wailed.

He soared straight up. Up. Up.

A talon unfurled.

Mirith fell.

Charlotte screamed. "Mirith! No!"

Einar rolled and dove toward the speck in the sky.

He opened his mouth.

Mirith shot a bolt into the mouth of the beast.

And disappeared into a furnace of flames.

"No!" Charlotte screamed. "Oh my God, I'll kill you myself!"

A battalion carrying the royal banner of Hirth charged the battlefield.

Gildore. Trog. Hirth's best, marching to glory. Marching to die.

Feather soft black clouds teemed. Like starlings mumurating, so did the Shadowmorths. Beautiful to watch, but deadly. So deadly.

From their depths emerged Seyekrad, his silver hair a stark contrast to the black leathers he wore. He strode toward them, his pace quick. Determined.

David stared at his dark eyes now swirling as if overtaken by a storm.

"You were supposed to die, both of you," Seyekrad said. "Now I'll make sure you do."

Balls of fiery obsidian shot from his hands. David catapulted backward, and hit the ground, the pain in his chest like a nuclear bomb going off.

Bright lights erupted all around him, the sounds of the war

muffled, as if his ears were full of cotton. Electric bursts surged through his veins.

Charlotte grasped a sword and swung.

Seyekrad flicked his wrist.

She dangled in the air. Her body thrashed. Her fingers grasped at the silver threaded hand gripping her throat.

David threw his hands in the air in surrender.

"Let her go, Seyekrad. It's me you want."

Seyekrad laughed. "What a fool you must take me for." He lowered Charlotte to the ground, but didn't release his grip. Instead he dropped her to the ground and dragged her over the bodies, through their blood as he made his way toward David.

Hatred bubbled in David's gut at the sound of her cries, the kind that made him want to kill.

"Do you not think I know how important this girl is to you?" Seyekrad asked. "Why would I let her go, knowing I can torture your very soul without ever touching you."

"Why?" David asked. "Why are you doing this? What did I ever do to you?"

"You are what stands between me and ultimate power. You see, once you and the heir are dead, I become king of Hirth by royal decree."

"I think Einar will have something to say about that," David said, cradling his arm to his chest.

"Oh, Einar won't be around. You and the heir will kill him today, and then I'll kill you. It's quite simple." He hoisted Charlotte to her feet. Blood and dirt smeared her face, her hands, her hair. Her eyes moved but her essence was gone. It was as if something dark had crept inside and turned off all the lights. "All you have to do is give me the heir and all of this will be over. I'll let your sweet Charlotte go and everything will be as it is supposed to be."

"No. You let her go first."

"Do you think I will negotiate with you?" Silver fibers of magic unraveled from his fingertips and into Charlotte. She jerked and convulsed.

"Okay! Stop! Please. Don't hurt her. I'll tell you what you want to know. The heir is—"

"Me!"

Seyekrad spun around as Trog's sword rained down, barely clipping his forearm.

Trog discarded his helmet. The metal clunked and rolled on the ground. Dark red blotches stained his armor.

Charlotte collapsed in a heap.

Seyekrad snarled. "You. You're the heir?" Laughter bellowed from the sorcerer. "I find that delightfully funny." He snapped his fingers. "Bainesworth, bring me the runt."

The air contorted and pulsed as if a living, breathing thing. A fissure opened in the center. A blond man with broad shoulders stepped through. David gulped. It was the same man who'd taken Charlotte from Kingsport. The same man who'd tortured Eric in the dungeons of Berg castle. Trog's nemesis. And in his grip was …

"Eric!" David yelled.

Trog growled and drew a dagger from his belt.

"Well, well," Bainesworth said. "We finally get to dance, you and I." He tossed Eric aside. A sword hissed from its scabbard. The men circled one another.

Seyekrad weaved about, his face cocked in a grin. "He tells me he's the heir, Bainesworth. What have you to say to that?"

"I'd say I suspected all along, just like I suspected this pup was your son. And now you're going to watch Einar kill the youngest heir to the throne just as he watched you kill his son."

"The hell I will!" Trog swung his sword.

Bainesworth raised his weapon and charged. Metal clanged. The sound echoed across the valley.

Trog kicked Bainesworth and brought his blade down, slicing across Bainesworth's back.

The knight bellowed, spun around, and jabbed a knife into Trog's shoulder.

Trog pulled the weapon from his flesh as if it were nothing more than a splinter. "I have waited far too long for this day, Bainesworth!"

Bainesworth grinned. "Funny. Most men look forward to living, not dying!" He lunged forward, thrusting his knife.

Trog leaped to his right. "Is that all you have?" he coaxed.

The Fauscherian knight charged again. Trog spun to the left and brought his sword down. Bainesworth rolled to the ground then kicked out, knocking Trog off balance.

Eric picked up a sword and swung at nothing. He was weak, off-centered. He stumbled and positioned himself again.

Trog flicked a glance at Eric. "Get out of here, son. Get Charlotte and David to safe ground."

With a great effort, Eric pressed forward, rage in his eyes. His clothing was filthy, covered in holes and blood, his dark hair wet and matted, his face pale and worn, but his resolve didn't waiver. He raised his sword.

"Eric, don't!" David said.

Eric swung.

Bainesworth sucked in his gut, jumped back, and kicked.

Eric's blade flew through the air.

The battle became surreal and time moved in slow motion. David leapt through the air, through a swarm of flying blades, and brought Eric to the ground.

Trog burst forward, grabbed Bainesworth, and struck him with a vicious head-butt.

Bainesworth staggered backward, blood streaming from his broken nose.

A slew of men dressed in black rushed from behind.

A blade sliced Trog's side. He gasped in pain, twisted, and swung his sword.

"Dalvarians!" David shouted.

Eric flung David aside. "Protect Charlotte! Get her to safety." He sprung to his feet.

David stumbled toward Charlotte and grappled her to the ground. Blades and arrows sliced the air over them. Blood splattered the ground, their faces.

David turned to Eric, to motion him to come on. A boot caught Eric in the chin, toppling him backward.

Battles surged all around them. He had to get Charlotte out. He stood and yanked her to her feet. "Come on! Head to the southern ridge!" He thought of home, of the Elthorian Manor.

"*Accelero Silentium*," he breathed, sweat dripping from his brow.

The battlefield remained.

The wailing of human suffering filled the air.

"Oh come on. Don't do this to me. Not now. *Accelero Silentium*!"

A jolt of electricity traveled through his body. His legs gave way. Charlotte slipped from his grasp as he fell.

Seyekrad walked toward him, limping, his features pure and terrible. Red light sparked like fire in his eyes. His clothes hung in tatters. Fragments of blue and green magic still flickered off his shoulders. His own black and silver magic sparked at his fingertips.

"Still trying to use your tiny insignificant spells?" Seyekrad asked. "Do you truly believe they will work?"

"What are you babbling about? What do you mean?" David asked.

"Did you not notice the rutseer is dead? As soon as you used that ball of magic and entered Havendale, all of your mage-given powers kissed the dust. Your magic ring. Your tattoo. All of it. Destroyed by me."

David felt along the ground and gripped a rock twice the size of his hand. Anger, hatred flooded every corner of his body with a low, deep burn. "I had to try," he said. "You understand."

Seyekrad chuckled and knelt at David's side. "Didn't Lily ever teach you to do, not try? Now you'll never know what it feels like to win."

The sorcerer gripped David's throat with both hands.

Charges of electricity sparked through David's skin, his blood on fire. He gasped, his lungs screaming for air. He reached up and grabbed the back of Seyekrad's neck. He pulled the sorcerer toward him and said, "But neither will you."

He summoned all the strength he could and smashed the rock against the side of Seyekrad's head. The sorcerer fell over and all magic blipped from his fingertips.

David clasped his throat and scrambled to his feet.

Trog and Eric continued to dance over the terrain with Bainesworth, their swords glinting in the sun. They parlayed. They jabbed. Fists connected. Bones broke. Blood splattered.

Bainesworth grabbed Eric and caught him in a chokehold. A dagger disappeared in Eric's side.

"No, no, no, no, no," David said, panic crippling his entire being.

Trog punched Bainesworth in the face. Strands of dark hair clung to his face.

Bainesworth grinned like a crazed wolf. Their eyes met. "I'm going to kill you now, Sir Trogsdill Domnall, or rather Sir Trogsdill Brennus, but not before you watch your son, the last and youngest heir to the throne of Hirth, die."

"You're out of your mind," Trog said.

"I don't think so," Bainesworth chuckled. "You, however, will be." He whipped Eric around. "Come get him, Einar! He's all yours."

David stared in horror at the fresh bloodstain spreading across Eric's tunic.

Four soldiers rushed Trog, grappling him, holding him in their clutches while two others punched and kicked him.

David felt the pulsing of his own blood like ice in his veins as he knocked his bow and let the arrows fly.

Eric plunged toward them, his sword swinging at odd angles, the agony on his face clear and present. Bainesworth shoved him to his knees, his blade at Eric's throat.

Trog twisted and turned, ratcheting his body free. He stormed Bainesworth, his sword raised.

A knee caught him in the stomach. Another assailant kicked him in the face, his side, his legs. Over and over.

Trog dropped to the ground, his face a bloody, swollen mess.

David fired another arrow and another, their points finding their marks, but for each one he killed, two more assassins gathered.

This time, a dozen men or more ran at him and Charlotte.

"Time to go!" They stumbled to their feet.

Einar circled overhead and descended onto the battlefield. The ground shook. Everyone ran. Bainesworth laughed demonically, following Trog's gaze. "Silly boy, thinking he can change the outcome of this war or better yet, that his friends, or perhaps even his father, will come to his rescue. Oh, I remember that look well, Trog." He leaned in on Trog so that his face was no more than an inch away. "It is the same look his mother had in her eyes when my dagger slit her throat."

Trog yelled and lunged for Bainesworth.

Two soldiers grabbed him, punched him. Stabbed him.

Two bolts from crossbows whizzed past and into their necks. The men fell.

Gertie and Garret pressed forward, methodical in their every moves as they loaded one bolt after another. They aimed with precision, each launched tip finding its way into Bainesworth's flesh.

He whipped Eric around by the hair. "Come get him, Einar! He's all yours."

Wet strands of hair clung to Trog's face. He appeared wild, deranged as he charged Bainesworth, the blade of his sword a blinding fury of silver light.

Bainesworth yelled out as the blade cut across his arms. He lifted his own sword and …

Trog plunged his sword into Bainesworth's throat.

Bainesworth's eyes opened wide as Trog buried the blade in deeper. The knight fell to his knees, emitting an odd sort of gurgle. Trog grasped the Fauscherian by the hair, lifting his face upward so that their eyes locked.

"I told you one day that your fate would wait for you at the tip of my sword. You should have listened." He pulled the sword from the man's flesh and aimed the tip at Bainesworth's heart. "This is for Gwyndolyn. May your soul rot in Hell."

The blade slid deep into Bainesworth's body. Trog gave a final push then withdrew it. There was a feeble, crippled gasp for breath, and then it was gone.

Bainesworth von Stuegler was dead.

Slavandria yelled from across the battlefield. "David, get Eric and Charlotte out of here. Run!"

A black string of magic threaded around her neck, the stream flowing from Seyekrad. Her eyes flew open. Her voice fell silent.

Panic seized David. Did the sorcerer never die?

Einar stomped closer.

The ground quaked.

Clouds of shadowmorth shrieked and descended on the high ridges. Men scattered, their yells piercing the fabric of time, rattling the core of humanity. Trog shoved his son. "Go. Get out of here." He was out of breath. Bleeding.

Eric clutched his side. "Sir, I ... "

"Now! I gave you an order! He'll kill you if you don't run."

Stomp.

Stomp.

Stomp.

Trog pressed past him, swinging and thrusting his blade at Seyekrad's band of assassins.

David grabbed Charlotte's hand. "Let's go. Now!" He glanced over his shoulder. "Eric! Come on!"

Charlotte broke free and turned around. She ran straight toward Seyekrad.

"Charlotte, what are you doing?" David screamed. He veered off in pursuit.

The world slowed.

The sorcerer shifted his gaze to Charlotte, tossed back his arm and unleashed a spiraling black spell from his fingertips.

David yelled, "Charlotte, look out!"

He reached for her, tried to tackle her, but missed.

Einar roared. Flames scorched the land.

"Charlotte!" David yelled.

A faint blue arc fell from the sky, the bubble sheltering them from the blaze.

David whipped around, his gaze set upon Lily stumbling toward them, sparks of blue magic dancing on her fingertips. He turned back to Charlotte and grabbed her by the waist. "Come on. We have to go!"

"I have to find Eric! We can't leave him here."

From within the fire and smoke, a figure sailed through the air like an arrow, the white steel of his drawn blade flashed against the blackness of the sky.

Eric!

Seyekrad spun around as Eric's blade plunged into his leg. Seyekrad hit the ground with an inhuman wail.

Slavandria staggered and crumpled.

Lily motioned for them to run. "Go. Hurry. Twiller is waiting for you on the ridge."

"We can't leave you," David said.

"We'll be fine. Go, while there is still time. My magic is weak and it won't last long."

Lily helped Slavandria to her feet.

Overhead, a murder of crows appeared, squawking. They landed and shifted.

David's heart thudded.

Ravenhawk and his army.

"Go," Lily said, summoning her spells. "We'll stave them off."

David kissed her on the cheek. "Thank you, Lily. I love you." He took Charlotte's hand. "Come on, Eric." He put an arm around Eric's waist and lumbered across the open emblazoned flatlands, from beneath the wavering shield toward the southern rim where Twiller stood, waiting. Einar pursued, a barrage of weapons lodged in his hide.

Fissures opened in the ground. Cracks and crevices stretched out in every direction.

The dragon lifted from the ground and flapped his massive wings. He swooped down.

David glanced over his shoulder as blue and green sparks bounced off his scales.

Slavandria and Lily bombarded him with spells, but he kept coming. He closed in.

His talons extended. So close. So close.

The nail touched David's back.

David tossed Charlotte to the ground and covered her body with his. Einar bellowed and screeched.

David looked up at the shadow closing in. Ravenhawk and company were relentless, raining the dragon in arrows and bolts, pikes and lances."

"No wonder he's pissed off," Charlotte said. "Eric, when we get to the top of the ridge, you're going to have to kill him. Let us know what we can do to help."

"I won't make it to the top," Eric said, gasping for breath. Blood oozed over his fingers." "Once there, hold him off, let me get in position."

Einar screeched as another weapon impaled his thigh.

They reached the base of the hill.

So steep.

Up.

Up.

Up.

Panting, they climbed.

***

Eric

Eric slipped and slid down the hill, his face contorted, pain screaming through every inch of his body.

"I can't go on. The pain. It won't stop." Blood oozed from his leg, his stomach.

David and Charlotte slid next to him. "We'll help you" David said. "Put your arm around my shoulder. You'll have a better shot the higher up we are."

"I can't," Eric said. "I can't take another step. Go, get out of here while you can. Defend me from up top. I'll have to try from here."

"No. I'm not going to leave you," Charlotte said. She scooted to his side. "Let me take a look. Maybe there is something I can do."

Eric shook his head. "No. There is no time for healing spells."

More axes, spears, and arrows sailed through the air, some not connecting and falling to the ground around them. Einar whipped around and unleashed a wall of fire.

"Eric, please," Charlotte begged. "You're not alone in this." She ran her fingers through his hair. "We can do this together."

Her eyes pinned him in place. Her insistence and tenderness kindled his bones. Her touch sent a tremble through his body all the way to his toes.

"Look at me, milady. I'm broken and no amount of insistence is going to get me up that hill. I'll have to fight from here and you'll have to help me. He's weak. If you get him right over me, get his heart right about there," he held his arm at a slight angle to the north, "I can get him."

Maybe. If he survived long enough. Eric swayed where he lay, faintness overcoming him. He took a deep breath and managed to ward it off, but how long could he keep his unconsciousness at bay? It pecked at him, like a woodpecker knocking on a hollow tree.

Einar roared once again. He whipped and thrashed about, his glowing amber eyes focused on his assailants.

He plummeted to the ground in a thunderous crash and struggled to his feet, his gaze set on Eric. Each step he took rattled the ground and left lake-size prints behind.

"Your friends cannot defeat me," Einar crooned.

An icy hot blue spell from Lily caught him in the neck, shattering a scale or two. His eyes remained focused on Eric.

David stood. "Maybe not, but we can try." He nocked an arrow, and let it fly.

Einar laughed as the arrow bounced off his hide. "You will need something far greater than that to kill me."

Ravenhawk and his band of shapeshifters scrambled up the hill, their weapons drawn. Other warriors shielded in bloody armor appeared with crossbows, axes, halberds, and spears.

"Go, David," Ravenhawk yelled. "Get your friends out of here."

David looked at Eric and shook his head. "No. It ends here." Charlotte cupped Eric's face. "Are you sure this is what you want to do?"

Eric nodded. Dizziness swarmed his brain. "Yes," he replied. "Where is my sword?"

Charlotte shook her head. "There must be another way, Eric. If you stay here like this, you're going to die."

Eric wiped her cheek with his thumb. "I'm going to die anyway, milady. You and I both know this. Go. Stay alive. Let me do what I was meant to do."

Her lips found his, and for a moment the world stopped. Sound disappeared. Nothing mattered. He was at peace.

The ground cracked beneath them.

He leaned back. Stroked her face. Her hair.

"Go. It's okay."

Charlotte held Eric's hand. Tears fell. "Kill him. We'll come back for you."

Eric nodded. "I look forward to it."

Charlotte kissed him once more. "I think I love you, Eric. Please come back to me."

Eric smiled warily. "I would like nothing more, milady. Now go." He glanced up at David. "Take care of her."

David nodded. He clasped Eric's hand. His lips quivered. "Thank you for everything." He placed a broadsword in Eric's hand. Eric squeezed David's forearm, and let go.

Einar stomped toward them and the earth vibrated. He hovered before them, his wings spread, his neck down.

David grabbed Charlotte's hand. "We have to run!"

Einar reared back his head.

Eric closed his eyes. "Of all that is good in heaven, please find my mark." He pitched the sword and watched it sail end over end through the sky, the silver blade glistening in the fiery light before lodging itself in the center of Einar's heart.

The dragon flailed back. Fire shot into the sky. He emitted a raspy, high-pitched unnatural sound and swayed his neck from side to side. Drops of his blood splattered on the ground.

Eric fell back, his eyes to the heavens.

Trog's voice called out to him from a distance. "Eric!"

"Father!" he said, barely above a whisper, his words drowned out by Einar's mutant, pernicious shrieking.

A large thud shook the ground.

Trog yelled. "Eric!"

Einar stamped his foot.

Eric gasped, his breath frozen on the intake as a hard, cold, talon slid into his flesh with an ungodly pop.

"No!" Charlotte wailed. "No!"

The pungent smell of apricots wafted up Eric's nose. He recognized it from his class in poisons. He lay back and stared at the sky.

Rosebay. The beast waxed his talons in rosebay.

The symptoms came right away. Blurred vision. Stomach pain. Confusion.

He dangled in the air like a speared fish. Einar shook his claw. Bones cracked and popped through his skin. Tears fell to the ground, his throat unable to make a sound. Death crept up on him and slowly slipped inside. With a deep guttural growl, Einar shook his claw, and dislodged Eric's shell of a body.

Eric stared at the dragon from the flat of his back, the vision of the beast slipping from clarity to nothing at all. A last puff and roil of smoke and Einar collapsed.

Shadowmorths fell from the sky, many writhing on the ground. A battle cry to retreat sounded, and what physical army of Einar's that remained alive, retreated from the Valley of Tears.

The world collapsed.

Charlotte scurried to Eric's side. "Eric! Talk to me!"

He looked down. Blood, warm and sticky, pooled on his chest. A slight smile touched his lips but faded just as fast. Charlotte. She was here. Till the end. He wouldn't die alone after all.

Trog clambered over the sea of dead bodies, stumbling his way to his son. "Eric." His face came into view.

"Father?" Eric asked, struggling to open his eyes. "Did I kill him?

Did I kill Einar? Is Hirth safe?" His voice fell in a whisper.

Trog nodded. "Yes, son. He's dead."

Eric closed his eyes. Relief washed over him. Charlotte, David, everyone. Safe.

His body twitched and trembled. He was cold. So cold.

A voice spoke above him. The king. He was alive. A tear fell. His uncle was going home to his beloved queen, Mysterie, as he promised her.

Home. Gyllen Castle with its blue turrets cast high in the sky. The Cloverleaf River, where sunlight danced like golden fairies across its surface. The gardens. The mountains.

Gildore whispered something to Trog. They pressed their foreheads together The king looked down at Eric.

"Can you hear me, son?"

Eric stumbled in the gray light enveloping him and nodded once. It was all he could do. He hoped the king understood.

"Then heed my words," King Gildore said, his voice soft and tender. "Eric Rhain Hamden of the house of Brennus, you have performed gallantly this day and as such you have earned your rightful place among those that surround you now on this field of battle. You have proven your skill and demonstrated your virtue in the face of opposition and tyranny. Therefore, by the powers vested in me, I hereby dub thee Sir Eric Brennus, a Knight of Hirth."

Sharp, cold steel pressed to Eric's left shoulder, and then the right.

"In the name of the Heavens, the Numí, and the Saints of Old, I grant you the right to bear arms and the power to meet justice."

A sword laid upon his chest. The king wrapped Eric's fingers around the hilt.

"Take this sword as your badge of noble office, and in your every quest and feat of arms may the glory of all that is good in heaven spring anew." Warm lips on his forehead. "I love you, my boy," the king said, his voice just above a whisper.

Eric shivered. Tears rolled down his cheeks. "Father." A slight smile creased his lips. "I … am a … knight."

"Yes, my son, you are a knight." He kissed Eric's hand.

"Father?"

"Yes, son?" Trog swept a thumb over Eric's brow and wiped the hair from his eyes.

"I am proud … to call you … Father. I … love you."

Eric took in his last breath, and released it on a warm breeze that flitted by.

He would take no more.

***

David

Tears rolled down David's face. He clung to Charlotte, her face buried in his chest. Her sobs could be heard across the universe.

How could this happen? Their friend was gone. Gone. And he was never coming back. It wasn't right. It wasn't fair. David's heart tore and his stomach clenched, the pain unlike anything he'd ever imagined. There were no physical wounds, no blood, no broken bones, yet every part of him felt broken. As if someone had reached inside of him and stolen his heart, his soul, everything that made him human. Everything that made him love. And it hurt. It hurt worse than if someone had punched him in the gut.

He followed the sound of Trog's voice. The knight sat on the ground cradling his son.

"No," Trog said, shaking his head. "No!"

The wail went through David like a hot knife. The pain, the agony he must feel.

"God, you cannot do this!" Trog clutched Eric to him and rocked. "He's just a boy! He's just a boy, damn you!"

Knights shed their helmets and gathered around.

Slavandria and Lily pushed their way through the gathering. Twiller huddled next to David.

Trog's gaze traveled to Eric's wound. His bottom lip trembled. He flexed his hand into a fist and released it.

He glanced between Charlotte, Slavandria, and Lily. "Please tell me there is something you can do. Please," he begged. His voice shook with emotion. He glanced up at Slavandria and Lily. "You are healers, seers. Surely you can heal this."

Tears dripped to the ground.

"I'm sorry," Slavandria said, her voice as parched as the ground she stood on.

Trog cradled Eric to him. "Someone do something," he sobbed.

"Please. Don't let him leave me."

David glanced at the black beast lying on the ground, then glanced off in the distance toward Tulipakar and Beggar's Field where life-giving lilies grew in the thousands. But it wasn't nighttime and he could no longer ferry even if it were. He stooped down beside Twiller and whispered, "You can do it. You can get the lilies tonight. You can bring him back."

Twiller stared straight ahead. "Some things are best left the way they are, Master David. There are lessons to be learned in these moments. Only the selfish would do what you ask." He wrapped his hand around one of David's fingers. "He is at peace." Twiller glanced in Einar's direction. "Let him remain there."

Demonic laughter shattered time.

"You stupid fools!" Seyekrad stood, blood seeping from the wound on the side of his head. You think you killed him? Look! He lives!"

Seyekrad laid his hands upon the dragon. Enchantments sprang from his lips. Seconds later the beast inhaled a deep breath. He stirred and groaned, shattering the somberness. Everyone turned. Swords were drawn. Bows nocked.

Charlotte pushed away from David, her arms stiff at her sides, her lips pursed, and her eyes dark with anger. She strode toward the dragon, her fists clenched.

"You son of a bitch. You think you can take whatever you want, whenever you want."

"Charlotte!" David shouted. "What are you doing?" He ran to

her. Yanked her around. "Are you insane? You can't go out there. He'll kill you."

She flung his touch aside and kept walking.

"Charlotte, stop!"

She glared at him. Her pupils swirled. The irises changed color from blue to purple then back to blue.

David backed up and blinked.

What the hell?

Einar growled and struggled to his feet. Sparks ignited on the tips of Slavandria and Lily's fingers. The ground shook as he regained his footing. He stretched his wings to his sides, the battlefield clothed in their shadow.

Charlotte moved closer.

A stream of fire shot from Einar's mouth in her direction.

What was left of David's heart jumped from his chest and flew away.

She stopped at the warning, her eyes on Seyekrad as he stumbled and clawed his way onto the dragon's neck.

David's breath hitched. Hadn't Eric impaled him? Ahh, how he hated magic.

"Cowards. Both of you," Charlotte yelled.

Einar blinked at her.

"Yes, I'm talking to you, you pathetic waste. Who do you think you are, thinking you're entitled to whatever is here, killing whenever you want?"

Einar snorted. A puff of gray smoke expelled from his nose. His voice rumbled over the land and shook the sky. "My shadow brings night, my footprints make lakes, my fire is brighter than a thousand suns. I am Einar. I am the Dragon King."

"You are nothing," Charlotte yelled. Sparks sizzled from her fingertips. "And I will see you pay for what you've done."

David's breath hitched. What was she doing?

Einar laughed. It tumbled across the sky. "You may try, foolish mortal. I will enjoy picking your bones from my teeth."

He turned around, his weight crushing the ground. A collective gasp filled the air. "'Til we meet again ... witch."

Seyekrad slumped forward, his shape lost within Einar's. The dragon flapped his wings riddled with holes, and slowly rose from the ground.

David clung to a boulder, the downdraft blowing dust in his eyes.

Threads of purple electricity sizzled at Charlotte's fingertips. A plum mist swirled at her feet. She raised her arms and lifted her chin to the sky. Her brown hair changed and morphed into thick lilac strands that cascaded to the ground.

David watched, his mouth open. His breaths left him and he backed away needing to find something, anything to cling to. He glanced to his left at Slavandria. Lily clutched her sister's arm and spoke. Slavandria covered her mouth with one hand, the other rested on her belly. Tears rolled down her cheeks.

David shook his head. No. It wasn't possible.

Swirling wind howled across the valley and whipped his hair. Thunder rolled across the sky.

David dropped to his knees, tremors rocking the length of his entire body. He didn't want to believe what he saw, but there was no denying it. Charlotte was Slavandria's daughter, the baby she never knew she had. How did she not know? How had Lily kept it a secret for so long?

His heart ached for Charlotte, for all she'd believed that was now a lie. Her grandfather was her great-grandfather, and a Numí. A warrior of the universe. Her grandfather was Jared, the most powerful mage ever to grace the heavens.

He turned his gaze to Charlotte, to the girl he loved. The girl he would die for. But she needed no one to die for her. She was strong. She was beautiful.

And she was powerful.

Arcs sparked from her fingertips electrifying the storm clouds gathering above. Thunder boomed and lightning filled the sky.

All around him, bodies lay strewn about the valley, some moving, but most lay dead.

Fires burned.

Worst of all, Einar lived, and the two beings who could destroy him and save the realm were also dead. It was all for nothing. The war. The belief they could make a difference.

Behind him, Trog sobbed, his anguish gut-wrenching. David buried his face in his palms, his heart shattered in pieces.

And as those remaining in the desolation clung to those they'd loved and lost, the heavens felt their sorrow.

The clouds thickened.

And the rains came.

Acknowledgements

The Chronicles of Fallhollow stories have been floating through my imagination since I was a little girl. For too many years, life kept me from following my dream and bringing this story to life. Finally, after much prodding, along with my own relentless determination, I finally set my mind to the task and put the story down. It wasn't until a friend of mine almost twisted my arm to the point of it falling off that I decided to send the first book to Month9Books with the slimmest hope someone else would love the tale as much as I did. Imagine my surprise when it was accepted for publication. That was in 2015. Now, as I hold book two, it's still hard to believe that my dreams have come true and that this story is out in the world. Soon, the final book in the trilogy will find its way to you and it will be a bittersweet end to a story that has been with me for so long. Until then, it is with immense gratitude that I thank the following people for without them, I wouldn't be where I am today.

My husband, Tom—for making dinner, for bragging about me and my books to anyone who would listen. For supplying me with endless cups of coffee and for being my beacon of light when it felt like the world around me was dark and hopeless. I couldn't have done any of this without you.

My kids, Kevin, Bryan, Heather and Clarissa: you've been my inspiration and my biggest fans. I love you more than you know. I'll always remember our own adventure with the miniature 'vorgrants' and the canoes.

Jahlee and Lily: you may be pups, but you've stayed up with me into the wee hours of the morning, keeping my feet warm, keeping me company, giving me kisses when I needed them. My heart swells with your unconditional love. I can't imagine my life without you.

My editor, Cameron Yeager, who never fails to challenge me to be the best writer I can be. You have taught me so much and put a special shine on this book in particular. You're amazing in so many ways.

For the entire team at Month9Books: thank you for your enthusiasm, your support, your patience in answering all my silly, inane questions. Georgia McBride, you get a special thank you for being the amazing publisher you are, for taking a chance on a nobody author with big dreams and a story that dreamed to be told. You have been patient with me and have always been supportive of me and my goals. Thank you from the bottom of my heart.

I also want to thank the following for their undying devotion to this project and my writing in general. I love you guys to the moon and back a gazillion, bazillion times over:

Jennifer Eaton, Sheryl Winters, Valerie Sutton, Jonathan Marx, Kyle Jackson, Shannon Carper: you are the best beta readers a writer could hope for. If I had Einar's wealth, I'd give it all to you and still owe you more. I won't share my coffee or chocolate, though. The line has to be drawn somewhere.

Scott McQueen, my Facebook buddy, my fan, my dragon collector: your enthusiasm, support and unlimited supply of dragon and fantasy pictures have gotten me through some tough writing. Your encouragement when I was floundering, and your love for Trog and my story is appreciated more than you know. I can't thank you enough for connecting with me on Social Media. Keep the pictures coming.

Paula, Marian, Diana, Joan, Dilip and all the old CGI crew: thank you for believing in me and following me on my adventure.

And you, my precious, dear reader: thank you for coming along with me on this journey. I hope you're enjoying the story, and I hope that you'll stick around for the final book to see how the adventure ends. I promise it will be an explosive finale.

J. KELLER FORD

J. Keller Ford (known to all as Jenny) is a scribbler of Young Adult and New Adult speculative fiction. As a young Army brat, she traveled the world and wandered the halls of some of Germany's most extraordinary castles in hopes of finding snarky dragons, chivalrous knights and wondrous magic that permeated her imagination. What she found remains etched in her topsy-turvy mind and oozes out in sweeping tales of courage, sacrifice, honor and everlasting love.

When not torturing her keyboard or trying to silence the voices in her head, Jenny spends time collecting seashells, bowling, swimming, screaming on roller coasters and traveling. Jenny is a mom to four magnificent and noble offspring, and currently lives in paradise on the west coast of Florida with a quirky knight who was silly enough to marry her, and a menagerie of royal pets. Published works include short stories, The Amulet of Ormisez, Dragon Flight, The Passing of Millie Hudson, and her first novel in The Chronicles of Fallhollow series, IN THE SHADOW OF THE DRAGON KING.

You can connect with Jenny at:

http://www.j-keller-ford.com/
Twitter: https://twitter.com/jkellerford
Facebook: https://www.facebook.com/JKellerFord.Author/
Instagram: https://www.instagram.com/jkellerford/
Pinterest: https://www.pinterest.com/jkellerford24/
Newsletter: http://j-keller-ford.us8.list-manage.com/subscribe?u=2
d9c825e0f2107e1885080102&id=495ee5196d

OTHER MONTH9BOOKS TITLES YOU MIGHT LIKE

IN THE SHADOW OF THE DRAGON KING

Find more books like this at http://www.Month9Books.com

Connect with Month9Books online:
Facebook: www.Facebook.com/Month9Books
Twitter: https://twitter.com/Month9Books
You Tube: www.youtube.com/user/Month9Books
Blog: www.month9booksblog.com

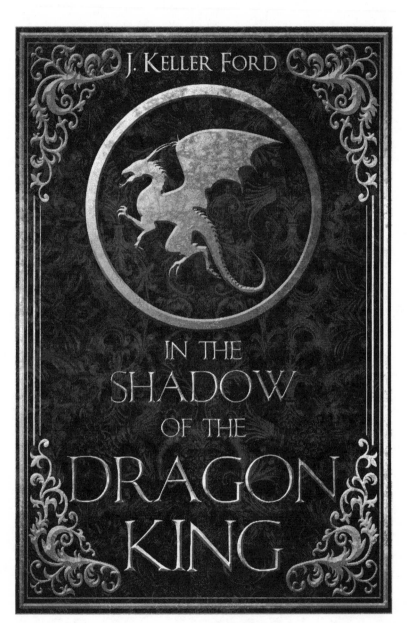

J. KELLER FORD

IN THE
SHADOW
OF THE
DRAGON
KING